1

The flashback came from nowhere.

In the last place that Fiona Gilchrist would have expected it to happen.

Her happy place.

Nearly midnight, so she was alone in the stables with the smell of the horses and the sounds of the big animals shifting in their stalls as they settled to sleep. A soft, welcoming nicker came from a big, warmblood gelding as she lifted her hand to stroke the glossy, dark-chestnut coat that was almost a perfect match for the colour of her own hair.

'How's that poor sore foot of yours?' she asked quietly. 'I've come to give it a wee bath with some Epsom salts.'

The horse swung his enormous head around to watch her put down a stainless-steel bucket and a pile of clean bandages. She could feel the warmth and the huff of his breath on the back of her neck but, as she straightened again to lay the palm of her hand on his neck, she could feel the shiver that rippled across the horse's skin. It was the kind of movement that would be there if the animal had simply been annoyed by the touch of a fly, but she could sense muscles tensing below her hand and she'd been around horses long enough to know that it was the seed of a fight-or-flight response to something deemed dangerous.

It wasn't just this horse, she realised suddenly. It felt like every living creature in these stables was holding its breath. Even the black and white cat who lived in the shadows and the mice who would be sniffing around the bins for any fallen grains or oats.

Everything was on alert. Waiting...

Later, much later, when she could think about it clearly, Fi realised *that* had been the trigger. That feeling like the world had paused because something terrible was about to happen.

The familiar, comforting aromas of clean straw, warm horses and fresh manure morphed into a memory she'd never been able to escape. A sickening, smoky smell of aftershave interrupted by rapid panting of breath laced with whisky. The sounds had become an echo of heavy footsteps on a wooden floor and a key turning in a lock. The soundtrack of being trapped in that room with him.

She could even feel the pain.

Fear was digging sharp claws into her skin now, reaching for something that lay even deeper than her bones.

A horse nearer the main doors to the stables made the kind of snorting sound that suggested it was spooked. Another stamped hard enough for a solid steel horseshoe, which Fi had recently nailed onto its hoof, to thump loudly on the concrete beneath the layer of straw. She could hear – and *feel* – an even louder thump of her heart against her ribs. She edged around the door of the stall and found she had her hands wrapped around the handle of one of the large metal shovels that were used for scooping up soiled straw.

What happened next was a blur. She saw the shape of the man coming out of the shadows of the unlit entrance to the huge

THE MAGIC OF PROVENCE

ALISON ROBERTS

Boldwood

First published in Great Britain in 2025 by Boldwood Books Ltd.

Cover Design by Lizzie Gardiner

Cover Images: Shutterstock and Adobe Stock

A CIP catalogue record for this book is available from the British Library.

Paperback ISBN 978-1-83617-326-7

Large Print ISBN 978-1-83617-325-0

Hardback ISBN 978-1-83617-324-3

Ebook ISBN 978-1-83617-327-4

Kindle ISBN 978-1-83617-328-1

Audio CD ISBN 978-1-83617-319-9

MP3 CD ISBN 978-1-83617-320-5

Digital audio download ISBN 978-1-83617-322-9

This book is printed on certified sustainable paper. Boldwood Books is dedicated to putting sustainability at the heart of our business. For more information please visit https://www.boldwoodbooks.com/about-us/sustainability/

Boldwood Books Ltd, 23 Bowerdean Street, London, SW6 3TN

www.boldwoodbooks.com

For Becky

barn. The horse behind kicked out at the metal bucket in its stall and a high-pitched neigh of alarm from a stablemate joined the clatter of the bucket hitting the wall. The next thing Fi was clearly aware of was that the man was lying on the cobbles of the central walkway. A man she recognised as the stable manager. Her boss.

He wasn't moving. Oh, dear Lord… had she *killed* him?

She stood there, frozen, the horror sinking in. Was this history repeating itself?

Had she finally shown her true colours – as her father's daughter?

But, only seconds later, she heard the man groan. Then he swore vehemently as he pushed himself onto all fours and got, unsteadily, to his feet. Fi stepped back slowly under the glare from his narrowed eyes.

'What the *hell*…?'

'I–I'm so sorry, Ron… I didn't know it was you…'

'Who did you *think* would be wandering around here at this time of night?' He was touching what was probably a large lump on the back of his head. 'You've always been a bit weird, Gilchrist, but this really takes the cake. I should call the police. This is assault. You tried to bloody *kill* me!'

'No… *please*…' Fi backed away even further. The confusion of the flashback was fading. The adrenaline levels in her body were dropping. The absolute panic was gone but the fear was still there. A different sort of fear but still powerful enough to be crippling. A fear of being locked away.

Powerless…

'I'm sorry. I wasn't trying to hurt you.' The words came out in almost a whisper. 'It was… it was… self-defence.'

'From what?' His gaze flicked up to the wild curls on her head and then his lip curled as the blatant stare dropped to rake her entire body. The snort of laughter that followed held no amusement. 'You think anyone would believe that I was that desperate?' He started to shake his head but winced visibly as he spat out his next words. 'Who'd want *you*?'

The thought came from nowhere, but Fi realised that whoever had made up that saying about sticks and stones being able to break you but that words could never harm you couldn't have been more wrong.

This was a physical pain that could only come from injury. It was tearing open old wounds that had never really healed, but at least she'd learned that it was possible to survive. She just needed to think of how she could escape. To get as far away as possible from what she had mistakenly believed was a sanctuary.

It was, ironically, the stable manager who provided exactly what she was looking for.

His eyes were no more than slits as he stared at her. 'You're *finished*,' he snarled. 'You'll never work in this industry again if I have anything to do with it. Get your stuff and get off the property or I *will* be calling the cops.' He turned away. 'I'll be back in fifteen minutes, and you'd better be long gone.'

There was no point in trying to apologise again and there was no way Fi was going to try and offer an explanation. She'd never told anyone. Ever.

She certainly wasn't going to tell someone who embodied the very reason she'd kept it secret. When just three of the words he'd thrown at her were still echoing in the back of her head.

'*Who'd want you...?*'

* * *

The small quarters on the mezzanine floor of these stables had been a bonus when Fi had applied for the job as the in-house farrier and stable hand for this prestigious livery. She'd loved living right in the stables like this but her room offered no comfort when she reached it now.

The clock was ticking.

She had no idea of where she could go. The first place that came to mind was her childhood home in Oban, but that was no more than a fleeting pang of the homesickness she'd never allowed herself to act on. It was not an option. She couldn't do that to her mother. She would be far too ashamed to confess that she'd done something so horribly similar to the crime her father had committed in nearly killing someone before he'd destroyed their world by walking out and never returning.

Besides, there was no time to think of anything other than the most important things she wanted to pack. She had limited time and knew there was no way she would ever be able to come back here.

She sucked in a quick breath. It helped that this felt as if she was trying to run from a fire and could only take what was most precious to her, like the leather tool bag full of her farrier tools. She rolled up her well-worn leather apron and tucked the heavy roll between the sturdy handles of the bag. Then she hurriedly stuffed some clothes into a waxed canvas holdall. She grabbed the personal items from the top of her chest of drawers, including a family photo of herself with her two sisters and their mother.

With no real idea of how many minutes had already gone by, Fi moved towards the door again but then stopped abruptly. Her wallet and her phone were in a top drawer. And her passport. Thank goodness she'd remembered them.

She had also almost forgotten what else was in that drawer, hidden under some underwear that had long since become too tight to be comfortable.

A key.

A large, old-fashioned kind of key that wasn't going to open any door on this side of the English Channel. This key belonged to a little house in the South of France, called La Maisonette, and it had been her sister Ellie who had told her to keep it when Fi had been there last Christmas.

'*You never know,*' she'd said. '*You might need it one day.*'

Right now, she couldn't remember much about the little stone cottage, enveloped by the mist of fear that was pushing her to flee while she still had time.

She could, however, remember the donkeys that lived in the olive grove beside the cottage. She might not be able to catch the thought enough to define it but she knew the memory was significant.

Important.

In this moment, with her world tipped upside down from having been brutally shoved back into a past she'd thought she'd finally put to rest, it felt like it could even be lifesaving.

Fi was clutching the key in her hand as she left the stables behind her, threw the holdall into the back of her little hatchback and drove away without a backward glance.

She was leaving the life she'd been living long enough for it to feel safe. To feel like home.

But it wasn't safe any longer.

It had become part of what she'd run from a long, long time ago.

She knew she had to escape. She hadn't known where to go, but now she did.

She had a direction. Something to aim for. Fi knew where she needed to be.

La Maisonette.

2

'Is she still there?'

Ellie Gilchrist stood up from the comfortable armchair where she'd been sitting to feed her baby and shifted her daughter onto her shoulder so that she could rub her back. From the second storey of her home, she could easily see into the olive grove that lay between this house and the little stone cottage next door.

La Maisonette.

Her whisper felt like she was passing on secret information as she leaned towards where she had left her phone on speaker, perched on the arm of the chair.

'Aye.'

'What's she doing?'

'Nothing. She hasn't moved since I first saw her and that was half an hour before I texted you because I had to feed Bonnie. I didn't go rushing down, because she doesn't look upset and, if she'd wanted to talk to us straight away, she would have texted to let us know she was coming, wouldn't she? She's just sitting there. It almost looks like she's been sitting there all night.'

'With the donkeys?' Laura sounded bewildered.

'Yes... and...'

'And what?'

'Well... it's the strangest thing. I've never seen Marguerite and Coquelicot lying down like that unless they're totally by themselves. It's very cute. They've got their front legs tucked in and Fi's sitting between them, like the meat in a donkey sandwich and... this is going to sound weird, but they've all got exactly the same expression on their faces.'

The huff of sound from Laura – part fondness, but with a good dollop of exasperation – was so familiar from her childhood that it made Ellie smile.

'They're *donkeys*,' her eldest sister said patiently. 'They don't have expressions.'

'Yes, they do. It's that peaceful look. When they're super chilled. Makes me think of Bob Marley and that line about getting together and feeling all right.'

Laura's quiet laughter coincided with a loud burp from the baby in Ellie's arms. Ellie kissed the soft fluff of her daughter's hair. 'There we go. That feels better, doesn't it, *ma poupée*. Now we can get you wrapped up and we can go and see what your Auntie Fi is up to.'

She laid Bonnie down and picked up the long length of soft, stretchy fabric draped over the end of the bassinet. With swift, well-practised movements she wrapped it around her waist, crisscrossed it over her shoulders, wrapped and tied it again.

'She's such a good baby,' Laura said. 'I can't believe she's sleeping through the night at three months old. Lili's only done it a few times and she's about to celebrate her first birthday.'

Bonnie gave her mother a wide smile as Ellie picked her up to hold her securely against her body, poking the baby's legs, in turn, under sections of the wrap.

'Oh...' Laura sounded suddenly relieved. 'Do you think that

might be why Fi's turned up out of the blue? To come to the party? This might be supposed to be a surprise.'

'Hmm...' Ellie pulled up the initial wide belt she'd created with the shawl to cover Bonnie's back and support her head. 'I'm not sure about that. The moment I realised who it was, I felt a shiver run down my spine. And the first thing I thought was, oh my God... what's *happened*?'

'You need to go and talk to her,' Laura said, decisively. 'I'll come, too. Noah will be more than happy to look after Lili's breakfast. Or I can wait a bit and bring her with me? She's due to wake up any minute. I think she knows when I've snuck into the kitchen to try and have a quiet cup of tea before the day gets started.'

'It might be better not to rush over,' Ellie said, slowly. 'You know what Fi's like. If you crowd her, she'll back off. And if you ask too many questions, she'll shut up like a clam.' She was biting her lip. 'This feels... important. I think she's here because she needs us, but it would be too easy to scare her off and it feels like she's only just tiptoed her way back to being part of the family.' She dipped her head so that her lips were brushing Bonnie's head. 'I don't want to mess this up. What I really want to do is go and throw my arms around her and ask a million questions, but something's telling me to just leave her be a wee bit longer.'

'Aye...' Laura broke the silence that fell. 'I remember when I spent Christmas Day by myself at La Maisonette, when I was pregnant and nursing my broken heart, and I went and spent time with the donkeys and... and it *did* make me feel better just being close to them. That maybe everything *was* going to be all right.'

'See? You did know about the donkey reggae vibe. You'll have an earworm now and you'll be hearing that song in the back of your mind all day.'

But Ellie could hear a sound that made her realise Laura had her baby monitor right beside her as she was enjoying her wake-up cup of tea. That made her smile again. Of course she did. 'Is that Lili waking up?'

She heard a soft sigh from Laura and then a cup being replaced on a saucer. She could almost feel her sister dismissing any personal preferences and her smile softened. 'Let me know if you're coming over later,' she said. 'I'll put the kettle on.'

'*If*?' She could hear Laura moving now and the sound of Lili's chirrups was getting louder. 'Don't you mean *when*?'

* * *

The sun had come up enough to be warming the softly scented air around Fi. The scent of the trees laden with olives was nowhere near strong enough to compete with the musty aroma of two shaggy donkeys, but every now and then she caught a whiff of the lemon trees between the olive grove and the little stone cottage.

She hadn't used the key for La Maisonette yet. She'd finally arrived at some ungodly hour in the night after well over thirty hours driving and a channel crossing, spread over four days. She'd slept in the car for a few hours until a faint bird call announced the approach of dawn, and that was when she'd finally finished her long journey to get to where she'd wanted, so much, to be.

With these two gentle, thoughtful creatures she'd fallen in love with the moment she'd met them, months ago now. She was pretty sure they loved her back but, even if they didn't, they weren't going to ask her any questions she didn't want to answer or judge her on what she looked like or what she'd done. They would be happy to simply be with her, and that unconditional acceptance was the only antidote she could imagine to the emotional wound that was still so raw.

Who'd want you...?

Marguerite and Coquelicot, that's who.

A ribbon of light was only beginning to ripple across the horizon as she'd bypassed the cottage and gone through the garden and the lemon orchard to get to the olive grove, but the donkeys weren't the least bit bothered by an unusually early visit. They'd probably woken up as soon as she'd shut the door of her car behind her but they weren't standing up. They were lying beneath a tree, like two huge dogs, with both those big heads – that were so out of proportion to their delicate legs and tiny hooves – raised far enough for them to observe Fi slipping quietly through the gate.

They didn't even get up as she'd slowly approached them. She didn't say anything. She couldn't. It felt like something in her chest – something spiky and heavy – was getting big enough to choke her. It was hard enough to breathe, let alone try and talk, but maybe the donkeys didn't need to hear her voice to remember who she was. Or maybe they could sense her need to be close to them.

She'd knelt down in front of them, extending her hands, palm out so they could sniff her and, after what felt like too long to hold her breath, she felt the velvet tickle of their nostrils and could see the movement of their ears coming forward. Fi had wriggled closer and wrapped her arms around Marguerite's neck and even that wasn't enough to make the donkey scramble to her feet.

It *was* enough to make Fi bury her face against the shaggy coat that felt like an old doormat compared to the glossy horses she was so used to. It also felt like the biggest, and, okay, probably the dirtiest teddy bear ever, but it was enveloping her with the most astonishing sensation of comfort.

Of safety.

Of being home.

And that was when Fi let that comfort seep inside her, deep enough that its warmth could start melting that spiky lump that was filling her chest and crushing her heart. It melted into hot, stinging tears that she had to push out before they had the chance to go solid again, because she'd been living with that lump for too many years already and she had the horrible feeling that, if she couldn't get rid of it now, she never would.

Fi hadn't cried like this in... well, she'd *never* cried quite like this.

She hadn't visibly cried at all since she'd learned that tears were a form of applause for bullies, letting them know that they'd achieved what they'd set out to do in making you feel smaller. Less of a desirable person. Unimportant and unwanted, even. She'd learned to shield herself so that the barbs of the taunts about her body shape or hair or that her daddy was a murderer couldn't penetrate far enough to make her eyes leak and provide proof that they'd found their target.

She cried now until she was drained of all those tears that had been behind a dam for so many years, and then she found that the last of her energy had been washed away as well. The emotional and physical exhaustion of days of travelling that had felt like a fight for survival had finally caught up with Fi and it felt like her bones had melted along with enough of that lump to make breathing easy again.

She couldn't move.

But that was okay. The donkeys didn't seem to be in any hurry to get started on their day, so Fi could just sit here with them.

And wait.

She didn't even have the strength to wonder what it was she might be waiting *for*.

Until she looked up to find that her sister, Ellie, was walking slowly towards her, the look on her face a mix of concern, a plea to be allowed to come closer and an offer of the kind of unconditional acceptance and love that Marguerite and Coquelicot had wrapped her in from the moment they'd whiffled her hands with the feather-soft touch of their nostrils and lips.

Aye... this was what she'd been waiting for. Maybe – finally – she was ready for this. She needed to reach out and see if she could keep a grip on it, even, because it felt like she might not be strong enough to survive without it any longer.

Family.

3

'Come inside?' Ellie's invitation was gentle. 'Let me make you a cup of tea.'

Fi was still sitting on the dry grass. Marguerite and Coquelicot had unfurled their legs and scrambled to their feet to go and greet Ellie and gently inspect the bump of the baby tied to her chest, the dangling legs limp enough to suggest that she was sound asleep. They ignored the small, scruffy white dog who had tucked himself between her feet. Fi cast a sideways glance at the big house on the other side of the olive grove. Ellie's husband, Julien, would be in there.

'I didn't mean our place.' Ellie had always been a little too good at reading her sisters' minds. She turned her head so that the little stone cottage beyond the lemon orchard was directly in her gaze. 'I meant *yours*. Which it is, for as long as you'd like it to be. There's clean sheets on the bed and milk in the fridge because I thought Mam might change her mind about where she wants to sleep—'

'*Mam's* coming?'

'Yes. She's arriving tonight. It's Lili's first birthday the day after tomorrow. She wanted to come a day early so she can help get ready for the party.'

Oh, *no*... How had she completely forgotten that her mother would be in France in the coming days? Fi had swerved her first instinct to run home to the safety of her childhood to try and spare Jeannie Gilchrist the pain of the trouble she'd got herself into, but it suddenly felt like she'd chosen the wrong direction in the maze. She had a dead end right in front of her and she was simply too tired to turn around just yet to find a different way.

Ellie was turning back before Fi could try and hide her dismay.

'But she doesn't want to stay in La Maisonette,' Ellie added quickly. 'She even said she'd like to stay in that little hotel in Vence that we all like so much. Laura wants her to stay with them so she can get full birthday party immersion. I said I'd love to have her in *our* spare room so she can get full Bonnie immersion. Whatever she chooses, I think we all know why she'd rather not be in this wee house, so it really is all yours. Mam doesn't even need to know you're here, unless you want her to?'

Maybe Ellie could sense that it was the last thing Fi wanted. The smile she offered faltered and she looked away, bending her head to brush just the tips of her daughter's hair with her lips. The delicacy of the touch reminded Fi of the way the donkeys had welcomed *her*. She felt her breath escaping in an inaudible sigh. Maybe she hadn't chosen the wrong direction, after all.

The tufty hair was all Fi could see of Bonnie in the wrap, apart from small dangling legs and feet encased in the soft fabric of a sleepsuit.

Baby hair...

She could feel the shape and hardness and weight of that lump in her chest again now. No surprises there, when a part of it was the shape of a tiny baby. This wasn't the first time she'd recognised the irony that something so ethereal could still feel so solid. So heavy...

Her earlier tears had melted enough of the lump for it not to be interfering with her breathing now but the core of it was still there. She knew how to push it into a space where it could be hidden, however. Goodness knows, she'd had enough practice, including her brief visit at Christmastime with the challenge of meeting her sisters' partners and her new niece. But Lili had been well past the newborn stage by then. Spending time with Bonnie was going to be so much harder.

Or maybe not. She was so drained right now that Fi felt a curious kind of numbness that felt soft and squashy, as if she was wrapped in the emotional equivalent of one of those inflatable sumo suits.

She could do this. She had no choice but to try, anyway. And perhaps she had actually reached the centre of the maze rather than a dead end. Maybe she'd reached the place she was meant to be.

It *was* a bit of a struggle to get to her feet, to be fair. Her muscles felt like they'd been left out in the rain long enough to have rusted to breaking point, but she managed to lever herself to her feet and then step towards Ellie.

And the baby.

Close enough to feel the warmth of them, and that was when Fi realised she was shivering. She'd been sitting still for too long and, while it was more than halfway through spring in the South of France, it was still chilly at this time of the day.

'Let's get you inside. I was planning to light the fire in there to air out the wee house today, and you look like you could do with more warming up than a cup of tea is going to provide.' Ellie led the way through the gate, into the lemon orchard, and the question she asked was tentative. 'You've no' been sitting outside all night, have you?'

'No. Just an hour or two, maybe.' Fi's voice felt rusty as well. She hadn't really spoken to anyone for days now. Not that anyone would have ever described her as a chatterbox. 'I tried to sleep in the car for a while when I got here.'

'The *car*?' Ellie sounded astonished. 'You *drove* here?'

'Aye... Is that a problem? Should I not have the car parked on the road?'

'No... It's no problem but... oh, my gosh – how long did it take?'

Fi shrugged. 'Four days. I had to do a few things once I got south of London so that I could take the car across the channel.'

To her surprise she found she *wanted* to talk. If she talked enough about things that didn't really matter, maybe she'd find a way to finally talk about the things that *did* matter. Things that she'd never talked about to anyone. It seemed more than likely that those unspoken words, pushed into any available storage space, had contributed to the solid stuffing of that lump and that whatever her tears had melted had created a weak spot. They wanted to escape. But part of her was fighting back, not yet ready to surrender.

'Luckily I had the insurance paperwork in the glovebox,' she went on. 'But I still needed stickers for the car and the headlights, and I had to buy things like a warning triangle and a high-viz vest in case I broke down or had an accident.' She managed a sound that was almost laughter. 'I'm surprised I didn't need to use them. It was way harder than I thought it would be to use a right-hand-drive car on the right side of the road.'

The grass was longer in the orchard. It had been too dark when Fi had gone in the opposite direction towards the olive grove to notice the splashes of colour amongst the grass – dots of bright red from poppies and the sunny yellow centres of wild white daisies.

Flowers had even seeded themselves in the cracks and joins of the stones walls that had been used to terrace the slope of the property. Mostly poppies, and that made Fi want to smile. On her long drive from Calais to the South of France poppies had become increasingly noticeable. They grew in the inhospitable shingle right beside the motorways and railway lines but they came into their own the further she got into the South of France. Around Luberon, as she neared Marseille, they were illuminating distant landscapes in vibrant swathes of red.

The lemons hanging from the trees around them were all shades of bright green to yellow. Ellie stretched out her hand to pick a ripe lemon and held it to her nose with an appreciative sniff as she kept walking.

'You're so much braver than I was when I first arrived here,' she told Fi. 'Riding a bike was all I could manage. Feel free to use Margot while you're here if you want a left-hand drive. She's in the garage. You conquered the quirks of driving a 2CV when you were here for Christmas and it'll do her good to have some cobwebs blown away.'

They reached the terrace at the back of the cottage, with its flagstone paving, the lovely old Moroccan candleholders and the little wrought-iron table and chairs. Ellie took a key from under the nearest candleholder and unlocked the door.

'Have you still got the spare key I gave you?'

Fi nodded. 'That was when I knew I had to come here,' she said quietly. 'When I grabbed my passport and phone and found the key under some old knickers.'

Ohh... maybe she hadn't used up her lifetime supply of tears. The look on Ellie's face as her sister realised that she had left in a hurry because she was escaping something awful wasn't enough to make them fall. That happened when Ellie gave her a one-armed but surprisingly fierce hug as she protected Bonnie from getting squashed.

'It's okay,' she whispered in Fi's ear. 'Whatever it is, it's going to be okay. You're safe now, hen.'

* * *

Fi had only been in this small house once before, when she'd come to give the donkeys some fresh carrots as a Christmas treat and had gone inside to have a peep at where Ellie had been living after deciding to stay in France and renovate this unexpected inheritance for the three Gilchrist sisters. The impression that had stayed with her was that it had notes of familiarity that reminded her of the wee cottage that had been her childhood home in Oban, Scotland.

At the time, she'd wondered if it was because of Ellie's touch in bringing the house back to life, but maybe it was something inherent in the warm, earthy colours that made it feel so homely. The exposed stone of the walls had a golden hue and the terracotta tiles on the floor had darker notes of amber. The huge old leather sofa was a dark caramel colour that made Fi instantly think of the palomino pony she'd learned to ride on at Dorothy McArthur's riding school in Oban. He'd been called Whisky and he'd been the love of her life for years – her unfailing rock in the turbulence the Gilchrist girls and their mother, Jeannie, had to navigate after being abandoned by their father.

'Sit down,' Ellie suggested as she crouched and reached around baby Bonnie to put a match to a fire that was already set. 'It's an amazingly comfy sofa. I slept on it the first night I was here because I was too scared to sleep upstairs. There were bats in one of the bedrooms.'

Being told what to do was a relief. Fi sank onto one end of the sofa and allowed her mind to deal with nothing more than the colours of this room as Ellie went into the kitchen to make some tea. She stroked the buttery-soft leather beside her and could feel the map of lines and wrinkles that came to any skin of advanced age. She could see the chips and cracks of the tiles on the floor in front of her, too, and wondered if they were as old as the cottage itself. Had people been walking on them hundreds of years ago? Nearer the fireplace, the tiles were reflecting the flicker of flames. The fire was only beginning to exude warmth but Fi noticed she wasn't shivering any longer.

She felt even warmer as she lifted her gaze to the big painting that hung over the fireplace. A smudgy sort of painting that might look clearer if she went a little further away from it, but its colours were perfect for this room and maybe it was better that there was a dreamy kind of blurriness to the image because it was an invitation to give her exhausted emotions a brief reprieve. She could almost feel herself stepping into this painting as she spun back in time to some long-forgotten childhood summer. She was barefoot in that crunchy, golden, sun-dried grass and she was picking wildflowers like daisies and poppies – tiny symbols of love that had stalks, so she could clutch them and present them so proudly to her beloved mammy.

Even when she closed her eyes, Fi could still see herself in that meadow. She could feel the sunshine and the bliss of not having to worry about anything, even if was only for a blink of time. She heard the murmur of Ellie's voice from the kitchen but it was too much effort to respond. She was sinking more deeply into this couch with the sigh of every breath leaving her body.

She felt a soft blanket cover her body like a butterfly's kiss but she didn't even try and open her eyes.

She was safe.

She could rest, at least for a little while.

4

There was a disconcerting moment, just before Fi opened her eyes again, where she had absolutely no idea where she was. She drew in a breath and held it and stayed very, very still.

She could hear voices and it made her think she was still dreaming because she knew those voices as well as her own. Laura, her beautiful, determined, bossy older sister. And Ellie – the baby. The gentle, happy little soul that everybody loved.

Fi could only ever remember being in the middle. Overshadowed enough to feel invisible sometimes. Never able to shine quite brightly enough to be really seen most of the time. But she'd always been loved – all of the time.

'What time is it?' Fi didn't realise she'd spoken aloud until she heard Ellie's response.

'Oh... you're *awake*. We were getting worried about you.'

Laura was beside Ellie. They both looked as though they wanted to hug her but were unsure of whether she would welcome it.

She would welcome it, Fi thought. But she couldn't blame them for being unsure when she'd avoided getting too close for so long. She'd pushed her family away. Or dragged herself away from *them*. The difference was immaterial because the result had been the same. The inheritance of this property, the new connections to France that had been created and the reasons to reconnect with each other had become strong enough to lead Fi to take the first tentative steps to get past a well-established barrier but they hadn't taken her far enough to be safely inside a solid family circle yet.

Maybe, when they knew why she was here, they wouldn't want her to be inside it.

It was hard to swallow because her mouth was so dry. 'How long have I been asleep?'

'Almost all day. It's after three o'clock.'

'*What?*' Fi sat up so fast it made her dizzy. She tried to push her hair back from her face but her fingers caught in the tangle of corkscrew curls and she winced. 'Oh, my God,' she muttered. 'I need to... to...' She couldn't quite catch what seemed so urgent because her head was still spinning.

It was then that she noticed Ellie's little dog was lying on the sofa beside her. She reached out to lay a hand on his back, instinctively seeking the comfort of touching an animal.

'Let me get you a cup of tea,' Ellie said. 'I've got plenty of time. Julien's going to pick Theo up from school and Bonnie's sound asleep upstairs for now.'

'And Noah's taken Lili to the office with him for the afternoon,' Laura added. 'I could run you a bath while you're having that cup of tea. Mam's flight is due to land about 6 p.m. but I'll have to leave in good time because you never know how bad the traffic's going to be.'

Fi's thoughts snapped back into clarity. *This* was what was so urgent.

'I can't stay,' she said. 'I can't be here when Mam arrives.'

'Why not?' Laura asked.

'Where would you go?' Ellie sounded bewildered.

'I don't know...'

Fi's voice wavered and she covered her face with her hands. She felt the little dog move away and the cushions of the sofa dip as Laura sat beside her and put a hand on her arm. Through a gap in her fingers she could see Ellie kneeling on the floor in front of her and then she felt the touch of *her* hands on her knees. The physical connection between the three sisters created a bond that felt like a lifeline.

'What is it, Fi?' Ellie asked, a desperate note in her voice. 'What's happened?'

'I hit someone,' Fi blurted. 'On the head. With a shovel.' She gulped in some more air. 'I tried to kill him... just like Dada did to that man...'

Not that he'd used a shovel. Gordon Gilchrist had used his own forehead and delivered a Glasgow kiss that had been close enough to being fatal to brand him as a murderer in his absence.

There was a moment's silence. Her sisters understood. They'd all tried so hard to protect their mother when they were children even though they didn't understand why their world had been turned inside out. There had been an unspoken agreement that part of that protection was to never talk about it. They could understand why Fi didn't want to be the one to open that can of worms so brutally now, but what they didn't understand was why history was repeating itself. She could feel their fear that she was also going to vanish from their lives forever. They knew how much that would hurt all of them, especially their mother.

'Was he badly hurt?' Laura asked.

'No. He got up very quickly. But he told me if I was still on the property in fifteen minutes he was going to call the police and get me charged with assault.'

'Why?' Ellie asked quietly. 'You must have had a reason to hit him.'

'I thought he was going to... to hurt me...'

Fi knew her sisters could feel that she was shaking. She caught the look that passed between Laura and Ellie.

'Has someone hurt you before, Fi?' Laura asked gently. Her voice sounded calm. Controlled. She'd always been so good at being in charge.

Fi could feel it happening. The breach happening in the dam that had been so solid until now. She could almost see the hairline crack appearing in the huge wall of emotional concrete she'd used to bury things that could have so easily destroyed her. She could feel the weight of what was behind that dam – the countless tears that had never been allowed to fall – until this morning. But those tears had been spilling over the top of the dam. This crack, if it got any bigger, could release so much more it might be enough to drown her.

She didn't want it to happen.

It felt like failure.

But there was a part of her that did want it to happen. Because she was so tired. And that dam hadn't been simply to protect herself. It had been supposed to protect her family – not to become so wide it felt like her family was in a place she had no passport to visit.

As she found herself nodding slowly, it felt like she was doing more than responding to Laura's careful question. It felt like a kind of surrender. The crack was getting bigger – and maybe it was supposed to be happening.

There was a slightly harsher note in Laura's voice now.

'A man?'

Fi swallowed past the sudden constriction in her throat and nodded again.

The silence was shocked this time.

'Dear Lord, Fi...' Ellie whispered. 'Did he *rape* you?'

Fi didn't need to nod. She knew they could see the truth all too clearly in her face. They could probably sense it in the wave of shame and fear that was rolling out from somewhere very deep inside her.

'Was it the same man?' Laura sounded fierce now. As if she was ready to find a shovel and go after him herself.

Fi shook her head. 'No... it happened a long time ago. A very long time.'

Ellie's indrawn breath was a gasp. 'Was it why you left home? And went so far away?'

Again, Fi shook her head. 'No. It was in my second year at uni.'

Another meaningful look passed between Ellie and Laura. Fi could actually *feel* them sharing memories. Joining the dots.

'Does this have something to do with why you dropped out of vet school?' Laura asked quietly.

'Yes.' The word was no more than a whisper.

'And why you avoided coming home for so long?' Ellie's words were thick with tears. 'Oh, *Fi*... why didn't you tell us then?'

'I couldn't. I wanted to but...' She shook her head. 'I just... couldn't.'

'Why *not*?'

Fi ducked her head. 'I was too ashamed.'

Laura's breath escaped in an outraged huff. 'What the hell did *you* have to be ashamed of?'

Too many things, Fi thought.

But she couldn't keep the truth hidden any longer. Too much of it had already escaped, so they might as well know the worst of it. Or at least *part* of the worst of it.

'Because it was *my* fault that it happened.'

There was a beat of... what was it... disbelief? Outrage, even?

'I *wanted* him to be attracted to me,' Fi confessed. 'I wanted to be like everybody else and to get over how stupidly shy I'd always been. I wanted... *him*.' Her inward breath became a gulp. 'I thought I was in love with him.'

'You wanted a lover,' Ellie said quietly. 'Not a *rapist*.'

'Fiona?' Laura's quiet voice broke a short silence.

'Aye?' Fi's response to Laura was wary. She knew this was serious if her full name was being used. She also knew she had no choice but to make eye contact with her sister.

'Listen to me. It was...' Laura pulled in a quick breath and her next words came out slowly and deliberately. Quietly vehement. '...Not. Your. Fault.'

Ellie was nodding, tears streaming down her face.

And then they were both hugging Fi. Until she felt she couldn't breathe and it was too much. Any physical touch from a human was an intrusion into her personal space that made her hover close to that fight-or-flight button that would release all the adrenaline she might need. These were her sisters and she knew perfectly well that she was safe, but she still needed the buffer zone of at least a little physical space. She had to wriggle free.

They understood. Instantly.

Ellie sat back, rubbing her nose and sniffing. Laura got to her feet.

'I'm going to make us all a cup of tea,' she said. 'And then you're going to tell us the whole story, Fi, because there's no way we're going to let you believe, ever, ever again, that it was, in any way, *your* fault.'

* * *

Fi didn't tell them quite the *whole* story.

She left out the bits that would have hurt them. Like the freedom she'd felt when she'd gone far enough away from home that she was no longer just one of the 'Gilchrist lassies'.

The middle one.

The pony-mad one.

The chubby one – with the hair like a wire pot scourer, poor bairn.

She'd been the first of them to leave home and she'd gone all the way to the University of Surrey, where she'd earned a place on a five-year course for veterinary medicine and science. The confidence gained by doing so well in her first-year subjects of anatomy and physiology had given her the courage to try and be more like her sisters. To fit in. To be seen.

She did tell them how special she'd felt when one of the professors, Murray McKay, noticed her, praised her work and took the time to encourage her. How, over more than a year, she'd developed such a crush on the charismatic, good-looking man who had to be in his early fifties. She confessed that she'd begun to take note of advice the other girls who lived in the residential halls gave each other and had started to experiment with make-up and clothes that revealed more of her generous cleavage.

She told them how he'd offered to help her, one evening, with an important essay and had worked with her for so long they were the only people left in the building. She admitted that she'd been thrilled when he'd kissed her. But that everything had changed after he locked the office door. That it went too far and he just wouldn't stop even when she'd begged him to.

She didn't tell them that he'd put his hand over her mouth to stop her talking any more. Or screaming. Because Ellie was already crying.

Laura was as white as a ghost and her voice was shaky. 'How could we not have known that something that terrible had happened to you?'

She didn't tell them how she'd tried so hard to pretend to herself that nothing terrible *had* happened to her. That she'd put her head down and focussed on her studies, but that hadn't stopped her grades from plummeting when she discovered that she was never, ever going to be able to get past what had happened because she had a reminder, inside her body, that was going to be part of her life forever. But she couldn't even go to what had happened after that in her own head, let alone confess what she had done. That she really *was* the murderer that everyone had said their father was. Maybe it was selfish to protect herself from anyone else ever knowing what the real ending had been, but this wasn't negotiable. Fi could feel that mental door slamming shut hard enough to make her whole body shudder.

'I didn't want you to know,' Fi said, her voice shaking, but that only made the truth of her words more genuine. 'So I didn't come home. It was easy to say that it was too expensive to travel that far and that I had to study for my exams and that I needed my holiday work at the riding school to help pay for next year's fees. I didn't go back the next year, but it was months before I told you all that I'd dropped out.'

'You said you'd changed your mind about being a vet and you wanted to be a farrier and you'd been offered an apprenticeship.'

'I *had* been offered the apprenticeship. That bit was true. But it was even harder to come home after I'd dropped out,' she added. 'Because I couldn't face Mam. Not after all that money she'd put into helping me go to vet school. I knew how disappointed she would be in me, giving up on my dreams like that. Our family had had enough to be ashamed of. If people at home found out what I'd done, it would have started all over again.' Her voice dropped to being barely audible. 'They'd have said I was no better than my father...'

'Mam wouldn't have been bothered by any gossip. Nobody

would have found out, anyway. She was worried about you. We all were.'

'Did you tell *any*one?' Ellie asked.

Fi was silent. She hadn't even told *them* everything, but her own words were failing her now – because she could hear echoes of words she'd never been able to bury completely. Words she could never say aloud herself because that might bring them back to life and make them real enough to destroy her all over again.

'You wanted this, you can't deny it. And don't bother telling anyone, because no one would believe that you weren't begging for it. Every-body's seen the way you've been throwing yourself at me. I finally took pity on you, that's all. I mean... look at yourself in the mirror, Fiona Gilchrist. Who'd want you...?'

The look on her face must have said more than enough because Fi found herself wrapped in the arms of both her sisters.

And they were all in tears.

'You can't go back and be on your own,' Ellie said finally. 'Stay here, with us, at least for a while. Until you're ready for a new start.'

Laura nodded but her face was still creased with pain. 'Mam has to know,' she said softly. 'She would never forgive us for keeping it a secret from her.'

'I can't tell her.' Fi shook her head sharply. 'I can't do that to her. I just can't...'

'It's been hidden for too long already,' Laura said gently. 'Nobody else has to know, but it's not fair to keep it from Mam. She needs to know so that *she* can tell you there's nothing to be ashamed of. That none of this is your fault. That she loves you as much as we do.' She took an audibly deep breath. 'Is it okay with you if *I* tell her? When I pick her up at the airport?'

Fi looked from Laura to Ellie and back again. It felt like she hadn't made genuine eye contact with either of her sisters in more than ten years but she'd shut herself so far away she hadn't even realised how much she'd missed them.

Until now.

And her heart ached as she acknowledged that she'd missed her mother even more.

'Aye...' Her agreement was no more than a sigh of sound. 'I think I'd like that.'

It was a step into unchartered territory.

A new beginning, perhaps?

It felt huge.

But fragile enough to need careful handling. Like a nervous horse, perhaps.

Maybe that was why Ellie was trying to lighten the atmosphere with her smile and cheerful tone.

'I'll tell you something else you might like. I made a daube de boeuf in my slow cooker yesterday. It's full of carrots and garlic and it's got bacon as well as the beef brisket, and I tipped in a *whole* bottle of red wine.'

When had she last eaten any real food? 'That sounds *so* good.'

'It should taste even better today. I'll bring some over for your dinner.'

The sudden cry from upstairs startled them all.

'That's my wee Bonnie awake,' Ellie said.

Fi watched her heading for the stairs.

Laura was watching Fi. 'There's a wonderful old bath up there,' she said. 'And there's some gorgeous soap and shampoo and conditioner that I put in there for Mam. Help yourself to anything.'

'I will. Thank you.'

'I'd better go, too. I'll need to find somewhere to park at the airport so I can go inside to wait for Mam to get through customs.' Laura wrapped her arms around Fi to hug her tightly. 'I'm so glad you're here,' she said softly.

'Me too.'

It was an automatic, polite response. It was only after the words had left her mouth that Fi realised how heartfelt they were.

5

Jeannie Gilchrist sat in silence, her heart breaking as Laura quietly told her that Fiona was in Tourrettes-sur-Loup and why she had fled from Scotland.

And the real reason she'd distanced herself from her family.

She stayed silent as Laura drove from the airport in Nice towards the mountains, absorbing the shocking revelations, and then fished in her handbag to find the neat rectangle of fine folded cotton she knew was in there. People shook their heads at her using old-fashioned handkerchiefs instead of tissues these days, but she loved the embroidery and the pretty, scalloped edges of the soft fabric.

She wiped her eyes and then drew in a new breath, steeling herself to face whatever needed to be faced. To do whatever needed to be done and, above all, to protect her precious daughters. As she always had, since the perfect life she had been lucky enough to find had managed to shift from a dream into a nightmare.

Laura was slowing the car and Jeannie recognised the stone wall and the wrought-iron gate of the wee French house that represented another unexpected corner she had turned in her life.

La Maisonette.

The house her daughters had inherited from an uncle they'd never met. The brother-in-law that Jeannie had never met because he'd been an adventurer who could never find the time to get back home. She'd only set foot in the cottage once, on Ellie's wedding day, well over a year ago now, and the disquiet she'd felt within those ancient stone walls had led to her choosing to stay with Laura in Vence last Christmas. Any reluctance to go inside now was completely overridden, however, by the need to comfort Fiona. To hold the baby that needed her the most right now.

'Is Ellie still with her?'

'No. She rang me while I was waiting for you at the airport to say that she'd taken some dinner over, but she's gone back to her house. She thinks it might be better if you both have some time together – just the two of you. She wanted me to wait this morning, before I came to see her, and I knew she was right. Fi hates being crowded and she might never have told us what was really going on if we'd cornered her.' A small smile tugged at one corner of her mouth. 'And, you know, sometimes you just *need* your mammy.'

There was a catch in Laura's voice that brought new tears to Jeannie's eyes. Motherhood had softened her eldest daughter, hadn't it? Or maybe it was the love she'd found with that gorgeous Frenchman of hers. Whatever the reason, the bossy, slightly sharp but capable child she'd probably relied on too much in those early, dark days had become a woman she was more than simply proud of. Someone who was developing a compassion that hadn't always been one of her strongest traits.

Not that she'd tell Laura that, of course. She knew that the soft brush of her fingers across Laura's cheek with even a hint of her own smile would convey her appreciation of who she had become, the care she was taking of her sister and of the space she was giving her to be alone with her middle daughter.

The front door was unlocked and Jeannie let herself into La Maisonette.

'It's just me,' she called quietly.

Fi jumped up from the sofa and came straight into her mother's arms.

'Oh, Mam... I'm so sorry...' Her voice broke. 'I've messed everything up, haven't I?'

'*Och... mo leanna*,' Jeannie murmured. 'Dinnae fret now... It's okay...' She was holding Fi so tightly it was a wonder that she wasn't struggling to escape, but it felt as if she needed to try making up for all these recent years of not being able to hug, or even touch, this beloved child of hers.

Tears were fair streaming down her face again. She'd thought she'd lost Fiona so long ago.

And she thought it was somehow *her* fault. Had she treated her differently to Laura and Eleanor? Because she was the one who reminded her most of her father? The way he had been before the troubles started. The gentle giant of a Scotsman that she'd met by chance when he'd come into the emergency department of a hospital in Glasgow needing a wound stitched. The man with the shock of curly auburn hair and the darkest brown eyes who'd looked as if he couldn't believe his luck when she'd agreed to meet him for a drink after work.

Had she not looked as carefully as she should have because, even if she denied that it could make any difference, she could see too many echoes of the man she'd loved so much? The man who'd simply walked out of her life.

It was true, that saying, that a mother could only be as happy as her least happy child.

She'd known, in her heart, that her least happy child had always been Fiona no matter how well she'd managed to hide it even as a young bairn. It was no defence that she was denying her own pain because caring for the physical needs of her daughters to have a roof over their heads and food on the table had to be what mattered the most. But that was so long ago. There was no excuse for having let it become just the way things were.

No excuses now. Jeannie wasn't going to let this opportunity slip through her fingers.

'It's going to be okay,' she whispered again. 'You're where you need to be, hinny. With your family.' She finally relinquished her hold on Fi to fish inside the sleeve of her cardigan. '*Och*... where's my hanky got to?'

'Oh, Mam... I've made you cry. I'm sorry... this is all my fault.'

'More like my fault, I'd say.' The hanky was a bit damp but it still worked. She could feel Fi staring at her as she wiped her eyes.

'You were never one to make a fuss,' she said. 'Eleanor would cry and Laura would get cross but you learned to bottle things up and keep them to yourself.' With a sigh, she sank onto the couch and shook her head. 'I helped you do that and I shouldn't have. I encouraged you to go and spend so much time with those ponies at the riding school. I helped you find the money to chase your dream of being a vet, and look how far that took you away from your family.'

Fi sat down on the sofa beside her. 'You were doing what you knew made me happy, Mam. Like you did for all of us. You were the best mother we could have wished for and... and I've let you down. Don't ever say it was your fault. Please...'

Jeannie knew how the protection had gone in both directions.

They were all bullied, but they couldn't have gone anywhere else, could they?

What if Gordon had come back as unexpectedly as he'd left, and they were no longer there?

There were some friends who stayed loyal but Jeannie knew the girls had been taunted at school and she'd been subjected to the kind of put-downs that women could be so good at. The way a conversation would stop the instant she walked into the post office. The flick of a glance down her body and back up, to meet her gaze so fleetingly it was a blatant dismissal of any worth she might have. She ignored it, to try and protect her girls, and maybe they did the same, to protect her. Never talking about it was the easiest way to try and move on. To let their lives heal.

To hope that hearts could also heal.

Was it possible that this was actually the real beginning of that happening?

'On one condition,' Jeannie said. She took another breath to emphasise how important her next words were. 'Don't you ever say it was *your* fault, either. None of it. Your daddy leaving us made life hard and we all did the best we could. That another man could have hurt you even more makes me sick to my stomach...' Jeannie had to stop speaking and press her fingers to her mouth. 'I don't know how to help you, *leanna*... I wish I did.'

'It helps that you're here.' Fi said softly. 'That it's not a secret any longer.'

'It should never have had to be a secret. He should never have got away with it. I'd like to tell that Professor McKay exactly what I think of him. It's not too late to report him. For him to get what *he* deserves.'

'It is too late,' Fi told her. 'I heard he died last year. Cancer.'

'Karma, more like,' Jeannie muttered. 'Mebbe he *did* get what he deserved, then.'

She reached to hug Fi again and, in the silence of that embrace, the gurgle of an empty stomach was loud enough to make them both smile.

'Was that you or me?'

'Me,' Fi admitted. 'I haven't eaten much of anything for a long time. I've had such a knot inside of me.'

Jeannie had a sudden, overwhelming urge to feed her daughter. To nurture her. 'Do you think you could eat something now, pet?'

Fi nodded. 'It does smell good in here, doesn't it? It's something Ellie made yesterday and she put the leftovers in a pot to heat up slowly.'

It smelled like meat that had already been slowly simmering in a rich sauce for many hours.

'I think it's beef. Something French with a whole lot of wine in it.'

'A boeuf bourguignon? Or a daube de boeuf?'

'Aye, that second one, I think. She's left a baguette to slice up to go with it. Would you like some?'

'I'd love some. Shall I get it?'

'No, you stay there.' Fi's smile was almost shy. 'I want to look after you for once.'

Jeannie let her, because she knew so well that looking after someone else was often the best way to get past things that were threatening to come crashing down around you. She'd done it for years, looking after her girls. Ignoring the people who wanted to punish her for what her husband had done. Going to work every day – or night, sometimes – as a nurse in the local hospital so that she could pay the bills and buy the food to cook for them and to keep the house clean and the garden looking like someone cared about it.

She watched Fi moving around the tiny kitchen, slicing up

the long roll of crusty bread and stirring the pot of stew that was heating.

No. It was a *daube de boeuf*. And a *baguette*.

Because she was in France now.

And, oh... the sound of the language always took her back in time. How long was it now? Coming up to almost forty years, for goodness' sake. It had been on their first date that she discovered the good-looking Scotsman whose hand she'd stitched could speak fluent French. It had already been love at first sight for Jeannie but listening to Gordon's deep voice murmuring in her ear in the language of love when he'd kissed her for the first time had taken everything to a completely new level. She could never love another man as much as she'd loved him.

Fi opened a cupboard to take out two bowls. Then she opened a drawer and Jeannie could hear the clatter of cutlery being chosen, but she was still thinking about the past.

Despite everything, that love had never quite died, had it? Her life might have healed but her heart never had. Not completely. How did anybody ever get over losing the love of their life?

She still loved Gordon Gilchrist.

She still missed him.

No wonder it had been so disquieting to come back to this country. To step into a house that Gordon's brother, Jeremy, had owned and presumably used as a holiday home in later years. It had fair given her the shivers when she'd walked in the day of Ellie's wedding and had seen that painting hanging over the fireplace.

She deliberately avoided looking at it now. That Fiona was here and needed her family was quite enough for them all to be dealing with. There was wee Lili's first birthday party the day after tomorrow too. This wasn't the time to even think about what

Jeannie had known she'd have to face during this, her third visit to this part of the world.

There were wisps of steam rising from the bowls Fi was putting on the table and the aroma made Jeannie realise that she was hungrier than she had expected after such an emotional upset. Even if she wasn't, sharing a meal, just herself and Fiona, was exactly what she wanted to do.

'Come and eat,' Fi invited. 'I feel like I might fall asleep again otherwise.'

'Good food and sleep,' Jeannie nodded. 'It's exactly what you need. I'll sleep here too,' she added. 'So you're not alone.'

'You don't need to do that, Mam,' Fi said. 'I'll be fine.' She put a larger bowl filled with slices of the crusty baguette on the table. 'I don't think I've shared your bed since I was three years old and I was jealous of the new bairn you'd brought home from the hospital. I'm no' jealous of Ellie any longer, I promise.'

It was so good to hear her huff of laughter that it brought tears to Jeannie's eyes.

'I can sleep on the sofa,' she said. 'Or the little bed upstairs. And it's for my benefit as much as yours, hinny.' The need to be close to her child squeezed her heart hard enough to bring the threat of more tears closer, but she blinked and managed to find a smile. 'It's a new day tomorrow,' she added. 'And we've got Lili's party to look forward to.'

Jeannie stood up to move to the table but she couldn't help her gaze straying sideways for a fleeting moment to look at that painting of the ruined building in the meadow of wildflowers. She knew she was going to feel that ripple of sensation down her spine again – a mix of trepidation and conflict that added up to real fear. But there was something else there as well. Something that hadn't been there the first time she'd seen this artwork.

Something that felt like... hope?

She glanced at where she'd left her handbag. The urge to open it and retrieve what she knew was in there was strong but she pushed it aside.

This was Fiona's time.

And then it would also be Lili's time.

Maybe after that it would be time for Jeannie to admit to an even bigger reason that had drawn her back here to France.

6

There was a surprising amount to do to throw a fairy party for a baby girl's first birthday celebration.

Fi was dreading the actual party. Julien and Noah would be there and she had no idea how much her sisters might have told these men they were so in love with. They were both still virtually strangers to Fi but they were also officially a part of her family now, which kind of gave them permission to ask questions she might not want to answer. The busyness of preparing for the party was exactly what she needed to prevent the reappearance of what had been a crippling shyness when she was a teenager.

Ellie collected them straight after breakfast the next morning and took Jeannie to Laura's house where she was going to babysit both her granddaughters while the three sisters went shopping in the biggest supermarket in Vence. With it being a public holiday the next day they needed to collect a cake that had been ordered from the patisserie and ensure they had everything they needed, like the ingredients for a charcuterie board for the adults and supplies to make cupcakes, fairy bread and a fruit platter for the children.

'I've got a flower cutter for making the fairy bread so they'll look like daisies,' Laura said. 'Don't let me forget to get the butter.'

'Don't tell me you've come without a list?' Ellie was grinning. 'Who *are* you and what have you done with my big sister?'

'I've got a list. I might have forgotten to put butter on it, that's all.'

The banter made Fi smile. There was a new lightness in her step this morning. The colours, on food packaging she wasn't familiar with, looked astonishingly bright – like the bags of mustard-flavoured crisps, cans of cassoulet and even the red-and-white gingham lids on jam jars. The snatches of French she could hear being spoken around her were musical drifts of sound, and the smell of an astonishing array of cheese and charcuterie in the delicatessen aisle tickled her nose and made her mouth water.

Her whole body felt like the curl of an embryonic smile. Some of the credit for feeling so much better had to be due to the deep, dreamless sleep of her first night at La Maisonette, despite having already been asleep for a good part of the day. Fi knew that far more of this new feeling was due to the level of reconnection she'd found with her family, however.

To feeling as if she was back where she belonged.

Feeling loved.

It was only now that it was lifting that she realised how heavy the burden of her secret had been and how far away it had pushed her from the people she loved the most. How had she managed to ignore the pain that it was causing on both sides? She had missed out on the support she could have had herself, but she hadn't been there in any meaningful way when her sisters had been facing life challenges, had she? Fi had a lot to make up for, and making herself go to a party despite dreading it felt like a good first step in the right direction.

'What are hundreds and thousands called in French?' Ellie

asked as she reached for a golden-foil-wrapped block of butter. 'And do they even have sandwich sliced white bread?'

Laura consulted her phone. '*Nonpareils* are sprinkles. Or possibly *vermicelles multicolores*. They should be in the baking supplies aisle. I have seen the kind of commercial white bread we need.' She made a face. 'I've never bought it, though. I get all our bread fresh at the boulangerie.'

'There are toys in here,' Fi exclaimed, looking around as she followed the trolley. 'And clothes. I need to get a birthday present for Lili.'

'There are better places to shop,' Ellie said. 'There's a lovely bookshop in the Grand Jardin that has toys as well.'

'I could drop you both off in the square on the way home,' Laura said. 'You can go shopping, and if you can collect the cake from the patisserie near the bus stop, I can go straight home and make sure Mam's coping.'

* * *

Ellie and Fi scrambled out of Laura's car near a charming, antique carousel at one corner of the central square in the small city of Vence. They walked beneath the delicate green of spring foliage on the majestic plane trees that enclosed the Grand Jardin, heading for a shop on the other side of the square.

Fi was drawn straight to the shelves of stuffed animals. She picked up a panda bear and then a fluffy green frog but put them both down quickly.

'Oh... it has to be this.'

A soft toy donkey. Grey and white with fabulously long ears and a tail with a black tuft on the end. She chose a pink gift bag with fairies on it and they made their way to the cashier, but her attention was caught by a small display of children's picture books near the counter and she paused.

'That was my favourite book when I was little.' The cover of the classic story of Madeline was so familiar with the Eiffel Tower and the two straight lines of little girls walking in front of the blue-gowned nun. 'And look – it's in English!'

'There must be lots of children here being brought up to be bilingual in French and English. It's a perfect gift.' Ellie was smiling. 'Do you remember Laura reading it to us?'

Fi nodded.

'You could be the first person to read it to Lili. I think Laura would love that as well.'

Fi found herself swallowing hard. This was going to be another difficult step back into her family but, if she could find the courage to let her adorable nieces into her heart, it could add something she had come to believe she would never have in her life.

Whether or not she deserved to have the joy of even other people's children in her life was another matter. One that could stay safely locked away, for as long as possible. She'd already given her family more than enough to process, and perhaps they all needed the time out that focussing on Lili's birthday was giving them.

They collected the birthday cake from the patisserie and admired the beautifully crafted, white-spotted red mushrooms on the top with a tiny fairy doll sitting amongst them.

'C'est génial,' Ellie told them. 'Merci infiniment.'

'I need to learn some French,' Fi said when they were back out on the street. 'What's génial?'

'Awesome. C'est génial is "this is awesome".'

'I'll remember that.'

It was an easy walk to Laura's house from there, back past the

Grand Jardin. Outside the boulangerie an old woman was sitting on the footpath, her back against the wall, a battered hat on the ground with coins in it. She had a cane basket beside her, filled with tiny bouquets of white flowers and green leaves.

'Oh!' Ellie paused. 'I'd almost forgotten. It's the first of May tomorrow.'

Fi lifted her eyebrows. 'Of course it is. That's Lili's birthday. Don't you remember Laura joking about having been in labour on Labour Day?'

'Yes, but it has another significance here as well.' Ellie was opening her wallet. 'It's why they gave Lili her name, in fact. It's not only Labour Day here but *la Fête du Muguet*.' She handed a note to the woman. '*Six, s'il vous plaît.*'

'*Merci.*' The woman counted out the posies – each made up of three stems of blooms and one leaf, tied with a piece of rustic brown string in a bow.

'*Merci à vous.*' Ellie's response sounded automatic. She held the posies up to Fi to sniff as they walked on.

'Mmm... Lily of the valley.'

'It's a tradition to give these flowers to all your friends and family on May Day,' Ellie told her. 'It dates back to some medieval king. You'll be able to ask Julien about it at the party. I think he paid more attention to his history lessons at school than Noah did.'

Maybe she noticed that Fi had suddenly gone silent.

'You will come to the party, won't you?' Her tone was anxious. 'It's just family,' she added, reassuringly. 'Like it was at Christmas.' She caught Fi's gaze and her face softened. '*Your* family.'

Fi took a deep breath. 'I'm looking forward to it,' she said.

* * *

Fi took her own car to Laura's house the next afternoon, because it felt like an insurance policy that made it so much easier to gather the courage she needed. If it all became too much, at least she had the means to escape back to the little house. And the donkeys.

Surprisingly, she really *was* looking forward to the party. She could hear a burst of laughter as she followed the trail of pink and silver balloons they'd tied onto tree branches that led to the terrace at the back of the house.

Male laughter.

She was ready for this. Ready to meet her brothers-in-law and accept the kisses on both her cheeks because... well... this was France and that's how people greeted their friends and family.

What Fi wasn't ready for and what stopped her dead in her tracks was that it wasn't only Julien and Noah out here on the terrace. There was another man with them. A total stranger.

And... he had to be *the* most beautiful man Fi had ever seen in her entire life.

He looked like a film star. Or a model that could have been used for some famous statue – like Michelangelo's David – that needed someone with a perfect face and a body to match. He was tall and slim, with black, wavy hair and dark eyes...

Dear Lord... dark eyes that were looking straight back. At *her*...

Fi couldn't move.

She couldn't even take a breath.

A heartbeat longer and this could have been excruciatingly embarrassing, but she was saved by a small human shape that appeared with a huge smile on his face.

'*Tatie* Fi...'

It was five-year-old Theo, Julien's son and Ellie's stepson, and he was closely followed by the rest of her family. Bonnie was in her mother's arms, dressed in a pale pink sleepsuit dotted with red hearts.

'She's so *cute*.' The urge to reach out and touch one of Bonnie's tiny hands was irresistible. Her hand was actually starting to move towards her niece as Ellie smiled proudly.

'Would you like a cuddle?'

Fi's hand stilled. The urge now was to make it into a fist. Instead, she held it up in a universal 'Stop' signal. She was smiling, too, but shaking her head at the same time.

'No,' she said, in mock horror. 'I don't do babies. I'll cuddle a foal any day of the week but human babies are too scary.'

Ellie laughed. 'You'll get used to them.'

Lili was also being carried by her mother and she had a fairy dress on – a mossy green froth of tulle that was embroidered with bright flowers and had butterfly wings attached to the back. Both baby girls had soft headbands on that looked like daisy chains. Jeannie looked like the proudest grandmother on earth as she kissed Fi and beamed at Lili.

'Isn't our Lili a wee poppet? She's the dead spit of Laura at that age. I should have brought photos.'

Any lingering awkwardness at Fi's reluctance to hold Bonnie went unnoticed as more greetings were exchanged.

'You look *gorgeous*,' Ellie told her.

'It's the same dress I wore for Christmas. The only dress I own, in fact. I bought it for your wedding.'

Ellie's wedding to Julien that Fi had found an excuse not to attend in the end because, despite loving that her sister had found such a happy ending to a heartbreaking time in her life, it had been too daunting to be a part of the celebration.

Thank goodness the black tiered dress, tights and ballet flats had been amongst the clothes she had hastily stuffed into her holdall before she escaped her room above the stables. Fi was also grateful that she'd always worn her favourite necklace – a silver horseshoe on a long chain. It was the only accessory she possessed now but it was all she needed with what was a remarkably flattering dress.

She knew she looked as good as it was possible for her *to* look.

And that gave her an odd frisson of something that felt like relief. Because, although she didn't shift her gaze from her sisters and their babies, she knew that *he* was still looking in her direction.

Even the thought of looking back was sending enough colour into her cheeks to feel noticeably warm. How ridiculous was that? Fi knew perfectly well how invisible she was to men in general and to attractive men in particular. With a firm shove, she sent her thoughts in a different direction, reaching into the pink gift bag.

'This is for you, Lili,' she said, lifting out the soft toy. 'Happy birthday, sweetheart.'

Lili's face lit up and she reached for the toy.

Theo gazed up, his eyes wide with admiration. *'C'est un âne!'* he exclaimed.

'A donkey,' Ellie nodded.

But Theo was too excited for an English lesson. *'Tout comme Marguerite et Coquelicot. Papa,'* he called to his father, *'regarde!'*

Julien was coming towards them.

So was Noah. And the beautiful stranger.

'There's a book for you too,' Fi told her niece.

But Lili wasn't listening. She was watching her father coming towards her. Her face lit up in a huge smile and she held both arms out towards Noah, dropping the toy donkey. 'Pa-pa,' she crowed.

Theo swooped to pick up the toy and Noah took Lili from

Laura's arms, but he was smiling warmly at Fi. 'We're so glad you could come,' he said. 'It's good to see you again, Fiona.'

'You too. I'm very happy to be here.'

Holding his daughter prevented Noah getting close enough to kiss her but Julien stepped in to fill the gap, leaning to brush a kiss onto one of her cheeks and then the other. 'Welcome,' he said. 'Can I get you a glass of champagne?'

'Yes, please.'

As Julien turned away, Fi could see that Theo was showing the toy donkey to the stranger, who had crouched to be at the little boy's level as he admired Lili's gift. Theo's face was the picture of a child's joy at being the centre of attention to someone important. Someone who was looking as though every word Theo was uttering was of great interest.

Julien gave his head a shake. 'How rude of me,' he said. 'You two haven't met, have you? Christophe, this is Fiona Gilchrist – Ellie's sister and *ma belle-sœur*. Fi, this is Christophe Brabant – my oldest and dearest friend.'

'Which makes him part of our family,' Ellie added.

Yes, he certainly looked as if he was a part of the family. He straightened from his crouch, but not without ruffling Theo's hair by way of apology at the interruption, before he stepped closer to Julien.

And Fi...

She could actually feel the distance shrinking between them, as if her own body was aware of him moving through the air towards her, even though she was keeping her gaze on Ellie.

'We saw him out walking his dog just down the road as we arrived,' Ellie said. 'And he's friends with Noah and Laura as well, so we had to invite him to the party.'

There was a note of something like an apology in her explanation, clearly intended for Fi. Had she just realised it would have been a good idea to have provided a warning of the presence of a man she didn't know? Was she trying to assess how much reassurance, or possibly protection, her sister might need in this situation?

Fi lifted her chin a little. She didn't need to be wrapped in cotton wool. She wasn't automatically afraid of every man she met. She could handle talking to men in social situations. She had male friends, for heaven's sake, like Gavin – who'd taught her everything she knew about being a farrier. Men were fine. As long as they didn't try and cross her boundaries. Or startle her.

It was sweet that her family wanted to protect her but she was more than capable of protecting herself. She knew the first signs of danger all too well and she could instantly douse any flicker that suggested a physical attraction, the start of a crush or worse, a signpost to the path of actually falling in love with someone.

Just over Ellie's shoulder, Fi caught a glimpse of Laura laughing as she watched Noah lift Lili above his head, making their daughter shriek with glee. Jeannie was raising her phone to capture a photo or perhaps a video of this happy family scene. With the sun catching her golden-red curls and the sparkles on the wings of her pretty dress, Lili really did look like a fairy child.

It was easy to smile at the magic moment. Fi even managed to let her gaze touch that of Christophe – just for a heartbeat.

'Hi,' she said.

Oh, help... she could almost see the coating of shyness on the word as it hung in the air between them, but Christophe was smiling.

And what a smile it was. A heart-melting curve that was soft enough to suggest he was aware of her discomfort and to offer a reassurance that she had nothing to worry about.

Of course she didn't. He was simply polite enough to be charming.

'*Enchanté*,' he said.

'Christophe's a vet,' Ellie said into the slightly awkward silence that followed. 'I met him the day I ran over Pascal with my bicycle.'

Fi went very still, hoping against hope that Ellie would pick up on her silent plea not to divulge the information that she'd once dreamed of the same career. It wasn't something she wanted to talk about, especially when the rawness of why that dream had been destroyed had only just been exposed.

She seemed to. 'You'll love his dog,' she added. 'She's nearly as big as a horse. She's over there under the tree with Pascal, who fell totally in love with her when she was a puppy even though she was already twice his size.'

Fi followed the direction of Ellie's gaze. The enormous black, tan and white dog was lying in the shade of one of the old olive trees.

'Oh...' Fi could feel swirls of anxiety evaporating into nothing around her like wisps of steam. 'She's a Bernese Mountain Dog, isn't she?'

'She is. Her name is Heidi.'

'She's gorgeous.'

'She is...' Christophe seemed to be searching for the right words. 'The love of my life.'

Julien had returned with the glass of champagne for Fi.

'I think the feeling is mutual,' he said. 'Heidi drools all over him. But' – his shrug was expressive – 'maybe it's not so mutual... *Cette chienne* drools on everyone.'

Christophe clapped his hand over his heart as if he was wounded to the core, but he was laughing.

A ripple of sound that made Fi catch her breath and turn away.

She walked towards the table set up on the terrace and laden with food. Theo, with some fairy bread in one hand and a handful of potato crisps in the other, was ducking under the tablecloth that reached the paving stones. The magic mushroom birthday cake with its single candle took centre stage, along with the pretty butterfly cupcakes they'd baked yesterday and the colourful plate of flower-shaped fairy bread. Some of the little posies of lily of the valley were in small vases to decorate the table, but the charcuterie board Laura had put together this morning had to take the prize for being the most spectacular offering.

There were several different cheeses, with slices of baguette to accompany them. There were folds of salami and paper-thin prosciutto and small bowls of olives and the baby French gherkins called cornichons. She could see bunches of grapes and tiny heritage tomatoes in shades of green and a red that was dark enough to be almost black, pâté with a crust of ground black pepper, and those crispy Italian breadsticks – what were they called?

Fi bit her lip, lifting her gaze as she tried to remember. Her glance caught Ellie walking back to the house without Bonnie in her arms, but the baby wasn't in her father's arms either.

Christophe was holding her. Looking down at the baby's face and rocking her gently while he was nodding at something being said around him. Did he have a family of his own? He certainly looked as if he was more than comfortable with an infant in his arms. The shaft of longing that came from nowhere was sharp enough to be painful. Because she wished that things could be different? That *she* could hold Bonnie like that...? Or was it more to do with the person who was holding the baby?

She dropped her gaze back to the table.

Ah... *grissini*... that's what they were called.

The relief of remembering was out of all proportion to the

importance of the snippet of information. Why did it even matter?

And why was Fi so fascinated by this collection of food when she didn't feel remotely hungry?

The answer to more than one of those questions came as she heard another rumble of laughter from the men nearby.

Three men, but it was so easy to distinguish one voice from the rest, even though no words were being spoken.

Christophe's voice.

His laughter.

How could nothing more than a sound feel so much like a physical touch?

What was more puzzling, however, was why, instinctively, she felt like stepping closer, instead of running away.

7

'What a grand party it was... Well done, Laura. I don't think I ever gave any of you girls a birthday party like that. You were lucky if I found the time to make a cake.'

'That's not true, Mam.' Laura was sitting on the floor of La Maisonette's living room playing with Lili. 'You always made us a wonderful cake. And top hat treats. Oh...' She tapped her forehead. 'Why didn't I think of making them? All you need are some marshmallows, chocolate and Smarties. They used to be my favourite party food.'

'I'll make them for you at our next party.' Ellie was on the other end of the sofa to Jeannie, breastfeeding Bonnie. 'Even if it's mine.' But then she sighed. 'I'd better start planning for Bonnie's first birthday though. The bar has been set far too high. What am *I* going to do? Find a unicorn to do pony rides?'

Fi came out of the kitchen to put a basket of bread on the table, beside plates loaded with ham and cheese. 'You could put a sparkly horn on Marguerite or Coquelicot. I'm sure they'd be delighted to join in the fun and give rides to everyone.'

'Do you know, we've never thought of letting Theo ride them? He'd *love* that.'

'I could get a wee saddle and do some lead training with them while I'm here, if you like.'

'Where would you go to find a saddle?' Jeannie asked.

Fi shrugged. 'I could ask Christophe. He'd know where the nearest saddlery or tack shop was.'

It was impossible to miss the glance that flicked between Laura and Ellie.

'What did you find to talk about with him for so long yesterday?' It sounded like Laura was deliberately keeping her tone casual. She wasn't even looking at Fi as she reached to pick up Lili's new stuffie. 'Look, sweetheart. Donkey. Can you say "donkey"?'

'Pa-pa,' Lili said.

Fi joined in the laughter but she wasn't thinking about the only word Lili knew so far as she turned to fetch the pepper grinder and jar of mustard.

No... she was remembering that long conversation. When she'd tried to slip quietly out of the group to go and pat Heidi but Christophe had followed her moments later.

'He was easy to talk to,' she said as she put the condiments on the table. 'He speaks English extremely well.'

'He does,' Ellie said. 'I had no idea how well because he only spoke French the first time I met him. He's just as fluent in Italian because his mother's Italian and his father was French. He was born in Menton, which is the closest French town to the Italian border, but moved to Vence as a child. That's how he became friends with Julien. He's lovely, isn't he? And Heidi is just gorgeous. They adore each other.'

'They do,' Fi agreed. 'I don't think I've ever heard anyone call their dog the love of their life.'

Laura laughed. 'I wonder what his wife thinks of that? Or his girlfriend.'

'No wife,' Ellie said. 'I've never heard the full story, but Julien said he had his heart so badly broken with his first love that he joined the "why buy a book when you can have a whole library" gang. And, yes, I believe he's had many girlfriends but I expect it's only one at a time. Nobody who loves children and animals as much as Christophe does could be a heartless playboy. Julien doesn't agree with me but I think he'll settle down one of these days. He's like a second dad to Theo, Lili adores him and he was over the moon when Bonnie was born. He might not even realise it himself, but he needs a family of his own.' She reached down to scratch the ear of the little white dog who was curled up beside her feet as if she was looking for a way to change the subject. 'I'm glad it wasn't Heidi I ran over,' she added lightly. 'You couldn't put her in a bicycle basket and go shopping like I used to do with my wee Pascal. She's nearly the size of one of the donkeys.'

'She's not even fully grown yet,' Fi told them. 'But that was something else we talked about. How, when Christophe found he'd bought a house with two abandoned donkeys next door, he'd been happy to help look after them.' She glanced at Ellie. 'He said they were very important for them both in such a difficult time in their lives, after Theo's mother died.'

'That's true,' Ellie said quietly. 'Julien and Theo named them after the poppies and daisies that grow everywhere around here. Theo still loves them, so we'll always look after them but... Fi's idea of training them is brilliant. They might like having something more to do than stand around looking cute.'

'Did you know that there are herds of donkeys kept in the forests around here?' Fi asked. 'They get moved around and are kept in one area with electric fences, to eat all the undergrowth. It helps to reduce the risk of fires.'

'How do you know that?'

'Christophe looks after them. Along with his friend, Didier, who's the farrier who looks after our donkeys' feet.'

Our donkeys?

Aye... it felt like the creatures who'd given her such a welcome when she'd arrived back here *were* part of her own family. She'd told Christophe that she was a farrier herself and that she had her own tools in her car, so she could do the next trimming of Marguerite's and Coquelicot's hooves.

It felt as if Laura and Ellie were being careful not to exchange another glance that might suggest there was something significant in that snippet of information that revealed they'd found more than Christophe's dog to talk about.

There wasn't, of course. He'd been easy to talk to. Like any veterinary surgeon would be when he was talking about animals, including his own beloved pet. As far as Fi had been aware, any significant glances during that conversation had been entirely between Christophe and Heidi. He'd been being kind, that was all, taking the time to talk to her.

Maybe that was why she had lain awake for so long last night, remembering every minute of that conversation. That kindness could be what had made Christophe Brabant even more attractive than his ridiculously good looks did.

And Ellie was right. He had to be a genuinely kind man to have a dog who made no secret of how much she adored her owner. Dogs – and horses – knew when someone could be trusted. She was undoubtedly also right about the many girlfriends in his past, and present, life. What man who looked like Christophe would have the slightest problem attracting feminine attention?

'I think I did know that,' Ellie said. 'Didier was telling Theo about the forest donkeys the last time he was here and we were watching the girls get their pedicure.' She was smiling as she eased her nipple out of the slack mouth of a now sound-asleep baby. 'I love it when she gets completely stoned on milk. I'll tuck her into her car seat and then I can have my lunch. I'm so hungry and it never gets old, having the French version of a ham and cheese sarnie.'

'I'm a wee bit peckish myself.' The click of Jeannie's knitting needles stopped as she reached the end of a row. She poked the needles into the ball of lemon-coloured wool and left her knitting on the arm of the sofa as she got to her feet. 'I'll put the kettle on for a pot of tea, shall I?'

'I'm onto it,' Fi told her. 'Just come and sit yourself down.'

Laura reached for her baby bag and extracted a jar of baby food and a plastic spoon. 'What's on the menu today, Lili? Ah... *risotto aux champignons. Miam, miam...* Let's warm it up. Are you going to come and sit on *Maman's* knee to have your lunch?'

Lili held out her arms to be picked up.

'She doesn't say much,' Fi said, putting the teapot onto a trivet. 'But she knows what she wants.'

'Mushroom risotto? For a wee bairn?' Jeannie shook her head. 'You would have been having something boring like mashed carrots at that age.'

'Or neeps and tatties.' Ellie was smiling. 'But look at us, Mam. We've all grown up just fine.'

'Aye, that you have.'

'Remind me to show you the menu that comes home from Theo's school every week,' Ellie said. 'They have a four-course lunch. Salad, main, cheese, and fresh fruit for dessert. I think today's meal is roast duck with cauliflower béchamel.'

Lili opened her mouth like a baby bird to accept each spoonful of her risotto during lunch and Laura managed to eat some bread and cheese herself at the same time. Fi ate a ham sandwich but she was only half listening to the chatter around her.

She was wondering what sort of saddle would be suitable for a donkey. Something treeless would be easier to fit, she decided: small and light with a handle on the front for a child to hang onto.

She tuned back into the conversation as Jeannie was deciding which of her daughters' homes she would spend her afternoon in today.

'I think I'll go back with you, Laura,' she said. 'Lili's due for her big sleep and I can get some more knitting done. I need to finish Bonnie's cardigan before I leave or it'll be no use at all. It's already feeling like a Scottish summer here.'

'Cardies are always useful,' Ellie assured her. 'How long are you staying?'

The sudden silence only lasted a heartbeat but it sent something like a tiny shiver through the air.

'I haven't quite decided,' Jeannie said. She hesitated, then added, 'There *is* something I want to do while I'm here, if I can.'

'Oh?' Laura was wiping Lili's face. 'What's that?'

'I want to find out more about the artist who did that painting over the fireplace.'

It was just a tiny tremor in her voice that gave away the depth of what was hidden under those words. Or maybe it was the feeling that something very fragile and irreplaceable had been picked up, without permission, and was in danger of being dropped.

Whatever it was, it made them all turn slowly to look at the painting.

The silence was longer this time.

It was Ellie who took a deep breath and spoke carefully. 'I'm not sure that would be possible,' she said.

'Why not?'

'I saw that painting in one of the summer markets in Vence when I first came here,' she said. 'It was... well, it was on my first date with Julien. And then, quite by chance, we saw it again. In a gallery in a little village up in the mountains. We asked about the artist and we got told that nobody knows his real name. He's called the "hermit" because nobody even sees him during the winter. The woman in the gallery told us that he used to be homeless but he lives in a stable on a farm now and that's where he does all his painting. He only comes to the markets in summer.'

Fi had no idea why Ellie was sounding so guarded but, if there were sides to be taken here, she would be on Team Jeannie. She wanted to know more about this artist, too. She could even feel the tenuous strings of a bond forming. Because she'd felt safe living in a stable? Because it had been a place to hide away from the world when she'd needed to? Or was it because she'd felt herself drawn into that painting within minutes of entering this little house? When she'd felt as if she was finding something as precious as Jeannie had apparently picked up.

Was it too far-fetched to think it could be the same thing?

The... what was it... the glue, perhaps, that held people together as a family, whether or not they shared a genetic link?

There was something else going on here, however. Ellie was looking more than uncomfortable. And Laura was staring at their mother.

'You were upset when you first saw that painting, weren't you? It almost made you cry.'

Ellie bit her lip. 'You thought you'd seen it before, but you couldn't have.'

Jeannie got to her feet. She went to where she'd left her old-fashioned handbag that was big enough to accommodate her knitting. She opened the clasp and drew out a thin cylinder of rolled-up papers.

'Laura's seen these before,' she told Ellie. 'But you and Fi haven't.' She removed the rubber band that was securing the roll and flattened the papers.

'That's art paper,' Ellie exclaimed. 'The kind I use for sketching.'

Fi touched the corner of the textured paper. 'Are these old ones that Ellie did?'

'No. They're a lot older than that. I found them in the attic at home.'

She lifted the first sheet of paper and they all stared at the pencil lines that were smudged as they flowed over a hilly landscape but sharpened into focus to feature the ruins of a stone cottage in the foreground.

Jeannie cleared her throat. 'These were done by your father.'

In what felt like a suffocating silence they all looked from the cottage in the sketch to the remains of a small, stone building in the painting over the fireplace.

'Oh... *God*...' Ellie breathed. The words were a soft groan.

Fi turned, with everyone else, to stare at her.

'You know something.' Jeannie's tone was shocked.

Laura looked pale. Pinched, almost – as if she was shrinking back into herself. Or the past?

Fi had a sudden flash of memory. Ellie was about four years old and she was crying, resisting being pulled up the stairs by the grip Laura had on her hand.

'Take her other hand, Fi. We've got to get upstairs...'

'Why?'

'Dada's home. I heard the gate slam...'

Even now, after so many years, Fi could feel the fear that it was one of the bad days. Maybe one of the worst days, when someone, probably Mammy, might get hurt. She had to deliberately take a slow, deep breath. To remind herself that she was safe. That they were all safe.

But it didn't *feel* as safe as it had just a minute or two ago.

'Watch Bonnie for me,' Ellie's movements were wooden as she got to her feet and went to the front door to go outside. 'I need to get something out of the garage.'

When she came back a minute or two later, she had an old book in her hand. She made a space on the table and put it down. Fi could see the title of the story.

'*Swallows and Amazons*,' she murmured. 'Isn't that an old movie?'

'It's not the book that's important,' Ellie said. 'It's these.'

Beneath the cover was a slightly tattered looking envelope, the flap open enough to reveal that it contained faded, black-and-white photographs that looked as old as the book. One by one, she laid them flat on the table.

Jeannie had gone very pale. She picked up an image of two young boys sitting on a stone wall, holding ice creams and beaming at the camera. Her tone was hollow as she turned the photograph to read the scribble on the back.

Jeremy and Gordon. Cornwall.

She sounded shocked, but why was it so unexpected to find an old family photo in the house that had belonged to her brother-in-law?

'I put this book back in the garage and tried to forget about it,' Ellie said. 'I didn't want to bring up bad memories for you, Mam, but it was for my sake too. If it wasn't for this book and this photograph, Julien would never have taken me to this village and we wouldn't have been in that terrible accident that nearly killed Theo.'

Ellie touched another photograph. Two little boys were crouched beside a channel of water in a cobbled street, playing with a toy boat.

'The village is called Saint-Martin-Vésubie.' It sounded like Ellie was about to cry. 'And it's where we saw the painting in the gallery. I think it's close to where this artist lives. I *saw* the artist – in the market when I saw the painting for the first time. It was...' Her voice trailed away, as if she didn't want to try and describe the moment.

'Oh, *my*...' Jeannie whispered. 'I knew there was a connection. Deep down I could feel it but I wasn't sure I *wanted* to know for sure. This village is where Gordon was born. He took me there on our honeymoon... I remember that little stream in the middle of the main street...' Her voice broke.

Fi looked at her sisters. Ellie was reaching to touch Jeannie. To offer comfort. Laura looked...

...angry. Furious, even.

'*I* don't want to know,' Laura said, her voice icy. 'If it *is* him, why would any of us care? He didn't care about us, did he, when he walked out and never came back? I don't understand why you're doing this, Mam. I don't...' Her chair scraped on the tiles as she pushed it back. 'I don't want any part of it. I need to take Lili home for her nap, anyway.'

It was typical of Laura to take a decisive action to control both a distressing situation and her own emotions. Fi could feel the same pull back to ingrained behaviours. She wanted to do something to calm the raw emotions that were swirling around the room. To be the peacemaker. But the only thing she could think of doing was to help Laura as she frantically gathered Lili's toys to stuff them into the baby bag. She wanted to reassure her that everything would be okay, but how could she do that? A door to the past was about to be opened and it could be a disaster, but it was too late to stop this happening.

That fragile thing had already shattered. She could feel the shards all around them. One careless move and someone was going to get hurt.

Maybe they all were.

8

When tension was enough to make it feel like you could cut the air with the proverbial knife, Fi had long ago learned that the best place to be was outside.

Preferably with horses.

Or, perhaps even better, she had now decided, with donkeys.

Having a reason to spend quite a lot of time with them was a bonus, which was why Fi was carrying her leather tool bag and farrier's apron as she headed for the olive grove in La Maisonette's garden.

If she had gone to simply sit near Marguerite and Coquelicot – as she'd done when she'd first arrived here – she would undoubtedly have felt a lot better for bathing in the peaceful vibes the donkeys exuded, but she didn't have the cushion of exhaustion as a buffer against disturbing thoughts or emotions today. It would be too easy to go over everything that had happened in the last couple of days and get sucked deeper into an evolving family drama. Fi couldn't afford to do that. It already felt like she was walking through a minefield of potential triggers for flashbacks she desperately needed to avoid.

Had she jumped from a frying pan into the fire by coming to France?

Was she, in some way, responsible for what was happening?

She'd stayed away from her family for so long to avoid causing unhappiness for herself and for them, but within days of them all being together there was a rift developing that was threatening to tear the Gilchrist women apart.

'Hey, hinny...' Fi left her tools near the trough and went to Marguerite first, offering her hand to be whiffled and then stepping close to stroke her neck and rub the base of her ears. Coquelicot waited patiently for her turn.

'I might give you both a brush before I do your toenails,' Fi told them. 'Would you like that?'

Marguerite's eyes were half-closed. If they both stayed this relaxed she might not even need to tie them up at the fence to trim their hooves. The rubber hairy pony brush she'd found in the back of her car was ideal for shaggy coats, and the donkeys clearly enjoyed the effort she put into the grooming. They helped occasionally by shaking out some loose hair and small clouds of dust. Fi stepped back after a more vigorous shake, rubbed her nose and then sneezed.

The sound had the effect of jolting her out of the pleasant distraction of her task and Fi found herself glancing over her shoulder. Towards the far side of the olive grove and the silent, solid shape of Julien and Ellie's house. She knew her mother was in there, having moved from Laura's house yesterday after a family meeting that had ended in tears. She knew plans were being made for Julien to take Jeannie to visit the village where the painting had been found because he was due to take his grandmother, who lived not far away, to a hospital appointment. Jeannie could go with them on the return trip and Julien could act as interpreter for her when they went to Saint-Martin-Vésubie on their way home. Ellie wasn't going to go. She said there wasn't room for her and Bonnie in the car, which was true but Fi suspected she was trying not to antagonise Laura any further by supporting their mother's quest.

Echoes of things that had been said were fighting for room in her head but Fi tried harder to push them away. The donkeys had been perfectly happy for her to handle their legs and lift their feet while being groomed, so she fastened her leather farrier's apron around her waist and tightened the straps around her legs to hold the padded chaps in place. She put her hoof knife and nippers in the pockets and picked up a rasp.

Marguerite obligingly lifted her foot when Fi ran her hand down her leg. For some time she was able to focus completely on cleaning out and then carefully trimming both the frog and sole of what felt like a toy hoof after the width and weight of the horses' feet she was more used to. It wasn't the first time she'd looked after a donkey's feet, however, and she remembered what Gavin had taught her about making sure the interior shape was concave enough to keep any pressure on the wall of the hoof and not the sole. She used her nippers to clip off the excess horn and then the rasp to smooth any rough edges.

By the time she'd finished Marguerite's feet and stretched her back before starting Coquelicot's, the level of focus needed was slipping and snatches of what had become a confrontation yesterday were sneaking into the gaps.

Ellie had started the defence of Jeannie's desire to investigate the connection she was so sure of.

'*Why are you so against this, Laura? Was he really so awful? I remember the way he'd tuck me under his arm and read me things from the newspaper.*'

'*He was never a monster.*' Jeannie had been adamant.

Ellie wanted to agree with her. '*I missed him so much.*'

Fi had missed him too. So much. Was that why she'd been irresistibly drawn to a man easily old enough to be her father? A man she'd desperately wanted to notice her.

To love her.

'*He was never a violent man,*' Jeannie had added.

'*So why couldn't he control his temper, then?*' Laura had been struggling to keep her voice calm. '*He couldn't control a lot of things, could he? I remember the day he wet his pants and I cried and cried. I knew nothing was going to be the same ever again. People pointed at him when he was too drunk to walk a straight line or speak a coherent sentence.*'

'*There was something wrong.*' Jeannie's statement was more like a plea. '*But he wouldn't listen to me and go to the doctor and then it was too late to help him because he'd disappeared...*'

'*Aye... because he'd lost his job and then he tried to kill someone in the pub.*'

'*That might have been an accident.*' It had been Fi's only contribution to the tense discussion. The thought had come from the same place as that of feeling a bond with an unknown artist who lived in a stable. That people could behave in an unacceptable manner, like hitting someone over the head with a shovel, because of something they had no control over, so it wasn't fair to blame them, was it?

'*So why did he run away?*' Laura had shaken her head sharply. '*He was as ashamed as we were. You and Ellie were too young to know how bad it was, but it broke Mam's heart and that's why we never, ever talked about it. The only way to make it go away was to pretend it never happened.*'

Fi had been too stunned to say anything more. It was so clear suddenly, but she'd never put two and two together. She'd been brought up to believe that the solution to dealing with something so traumatic was to pretend it had never happened? No wonder she hadn't gone home to her family when she'd most needed them. And now Laura wanted to reinstate the unspoken pact?

How many times did history have to repeat itself before it was blindingly obvious that something wasn't going to work?

Her mother had lived with unanswered questions about why her life had fallen apart. Why she'd lost the father of her children and the man she must have loved so much because, even now, she was defending him. Protecting him, even? Surely she deserved whatever peace she might find by searching for those answers?

She let the thought go with a sigh and turned to Coquelicot. 'Let's have a wee look at your tootsies, Poppy.'

Half an hour later, she straightened again and rubbed at the ache in the small of her back, but she took a moment to admire the neat shape of both the donkeys' pedicures.

'*Bravo!*'

Fi's head snapped around at the sound of the male voice but, surprisingly, what she felt was curiosity rather than fear.

Because she'd recognised the voice?

'*Christophe!* What on earth are you doing here?'

'I was with Julien and I saw you from the window so I came to say *bonjour.*' He waved his hand in the direction of the house and Fi followed the movement. She could see Heidi sitting on the other side of the fence, watching Christophe's every movement.

She looked back to find him smiling. There were crinkles at the corners of his eyes but Fi could feel the focus of his gaze right down to her bones.

Oh, help... The last time she'd seen him, she'd been confident she looked perfectly presentable. The best she could look, in fact. The pendulum had swung a long way to the other end of that spectrum right now, however. She'd tied her wild hair up with a scrunchy to keep it out of her face while she was working, and she knew it would look like an exploding firework. She was wearing dungarees and a workman's apron that could only be described as masculine and she was streaked with dirt and dust and probably smelled like a donkey.

Not that it seemed to make any difference for Christophe. He walked closer, bypassed Fi and went to pet Marguerite. He clearly knew exactly the right place to scratch her because she flattened her ears and let her eyes drift half shut with the pleasure of it. Then Christophe ran his hand down the donkey's neck, over her shoulder and then right down her leg. She obligingly lifted her foot.

Christophe made an approving sound and sent another smile in Fi's direction. 'You are very good at what you do. I am impressed.'

Fi had to drop her gaze so that he couldn't detect the level of pleasure the compliment had bestowed.

'It's been a while since I worked with donkeys but perhaps it's easier. Simpler, anyway, when you don't have to put any shoes on.' Fi busied herself with taking off her apron and putting her tools back in the bag. She pulled the scrunchy from her hair and the curls fell around her face and neck to give her the comfort of feeling slightly less exposed.

'*En fait...*' Christophe cleared his throat. 'I wasn't being completely truthful.'

Fi's eyebrows rose sharply. Was he actually *un*impressed with her farrier skills?

'I did not come to simply say *bonjour*,' he said. 'I came to ask for your help.'

Fi stared at him. From the corner of her eye she could see that Coquelicot had moved closer. It was automatic to seek the reassurance of reaching to touch the warmth of another living creature but she didn't break the eye contact with Christophe.

His gaze was steady.

Warm.

But he wasn't smiling now. He was looking very serious.

'I told you about my friend Didier, who helps me with the forest donkeys.'

Fi nodded. 'You did. He's a farrier, like me.'

'Like you,' Christophe agreed. 'But he's had an accident. Yesterday, he was putting shoes on a horse who was not impressed with his work. He kicked Didier on his knee and broke his leg. Rather badly. He needs surgery and he will not be able to work for some time.'

'Oh, no... I'm sorry to hear that.'

'We are supposed to be working with the donkeys in La Sine this week. It's a big forest, very close to here. I can look after any problems with their health but I cannot do their hooves, so...' His lips curved into a meltingly persuasive smile. 'I am hoping you might like to help me? Just for a day or two?'

Oh, my... what woman could resist a plea that came with a smile like that?

'It's a very beautiful forest,' Christophe added. His smile held a hint of mischief now. 'Do you like trees, Fiona?'

The way he said her name was unlike anything she'd ever heard before, as if one syllable had been absorbed by the others but somehow elongated at the same time. It sounded... Italian, that's what it was.

Musical. Dramatic, even. She could imagine him throwing his hands into the air as he said it.

It was different.

She liked that.

She liked that he was impressed with her work too. It made her visible in a way that wasn't the least bit threatening because it was about something that wasn't personal. Or physical.

Okay... there *was* a warning bell sounding in the back of her mind that this feeling of being visible, being noticed, could be the first phase of developing a crush. But recognising that was a good thing. She could control it. She could walk away from it if she needed to. Or she could even get closer to it, if she was brave enough. Going close enough to a fire to warm yourself was a very different thing to going close enough to get burned.

'Yes,' she said, slowly. 'I do like trees. But...'

But could she go into a forest with a man who was virtually a stranger. Alone? Without the safety net of having a single member of her family nearby?

Away from the current tension that was giving her that emotional minefield to step through so carefully and into the peaceful environment of an ancient forest? Into a place where she didn't have to get dragged back into the past or take sides or watch all shades of distress wash over the faces of the people she loved?

Fi wanted to support her family. She would support whatever decisions were made and, if necessary, she would do whatever she could to make sure any rift was healed. But she wasn't sure if she was quite strong enough to take on that role just yet. She was still recovering from her own recent trauma. She needed...

...a little time out? Just for a day or two?

This was a new beginning. Maybe it was time to make herself a little more important?

Fi took a deep breath. She shifted her gaze and saw that Heidi hadn't moved a muscle. She was still sitting in exactly the same spot. On guard.

'Does Heidi go into the forest with you?'

'*Bien sûr*,' Christophe said. 'She is the love of my life. She goes everywhere with me.'

A dog, a forest, a man who was easy to talk to, who thought she was good at what she did and could say her name as if it was something beautiful but would never, in a million years, be attracted to her. And there were donkeys.

What more could a woman ask for?

She let her breath out and it almost sounded like a sigh of relief. She was deliberately stepping out of the minefield, albeit temporarily.

'Aye... I'd be happy to come and help you.'

9

The soft drape of greenery from the forests that cloaked the hills and valleys of so much of the land in this part of France had, so far, been simply a part of the view – to be admired as a backdrop, along with the baby mountains guarding the medieval villages and the wash of blue that both the sky and the Mediterranean Sea contributed.

That changed forever shortly after Fi climbed out of Christophe's Jeep SUV that he'd parked by a cemetery that seemed to be about halfway between Tourrettes-sur-Loup and Vence. He let Heidi out of the back seat and then opened the tailgate, where they'd stowed equipment in the cargo hatch. Fi carried her farrier's apron and tool bag and Christophe put a pack on his back and picked up a cooler bag.

'I have drugs I might need, like antibiotics or a sedative,' he told her. And then he smiled. 'And our lunch, of course.'

Ohh...

That *smile...*

Fi couldn't hold his gaze for more than a heartbeat. She had waited by the gate to be picked up this morning wondering what on earth had made her think it was a good idea to go somewhere she had never been before, in the company of a man she barely knew.

This was crazy, wasn't it?

She had hoped to get away from the tension in her family and dodge the triggers lurking in memories of the violence in her childhood, but could this really be a reprieve? Was it too late to change her mind?

Yes. She would be letting Christophe down if she took back her offer to help. She *wanted* to help. Okay... maybe what she really wanted was to use her skills to earn more praise from someone who could appreciate how good she was at her job.

Someone who was so outrageously charming and attractive that being good at what she did was the only way she could make an impression?

Not that she wanted him to notice her in any other way, of course. It was just nice to feel as if her company was wanted. Needed.

Feeling as if *she* was wanted was like a hug for her soul. What did it matter if it was for something she was good at doing rather than her personality traits or how she looked? This was vastly preferable, in fact, because it wasn't threatening. What was wanted was something she could provide.

And it could, for just a blink of time, silence that toxic mantra that could slither out of nowhere in her head.

Who'd want you...?

She'd taken a deep breath and reminded herself of her confidence that she was safe with this man. His dog adored him. Ellie and Julien considered him to be one of the family. They knew where she was and who she was with.

And this couldn't be anything other than purely professional.

Good grief, Fi was wearing her shapeless dungarees that still smelled of donkey from her grooming and pedicure session with Marguerite and Coquelicot. The practical garment made her look even chunkier than she actually was and, in case that wasn't enough to put anyone off, she had tortured her hair into two braids to keep it out of her face and the tight pigtails stuck out enough to make her look like Pippi Longstocking.

She could still feel her heart rate increase, however, as they walked away from the vehicle and onto a track that led into the forest. A small bus that had been parked closer to the cemetery gates drove past behind them and it felt as if the possibility of other people being in the vicinity was also vanishing. Heidi seemed to know exactly where she was going and Christophe increased his pace a little to keep up with his dog. Their distance from Fi was increasing and the light was changing as she walked under the canopy of oak trees that looked as if they could be hundreds of years old. It took only a very short time, with twigs, acorns and dry leaves crunching under her boots, and looking up to see streaks of sunlight dancing amongst green leaves and lighting up patches of bark on the trunks and branches, to feel as if the rest of the world had been left behind.

That she was walking into a magical space.

A soft whistle from Christophe stopped Heidi disappearing around a bend ahead, and he slowed, waiting for Fi to catch up.

'Ça va?'

It had only taken a couple of days of being amongst French people to learn the ubiquitous query of whether someone or something was okay and how to respond.

'Oui, merci,' she said. 'Ça va bien.' Then she needed to switch back to English. 'It's so beautiful in here.'

'We love it. We walk here for an hour or two every day that we don't go up into the mountains. It's one of the reasons I love to live here. I could never count the number of beautiful places there are to walk, but it's special to be able to spend a whole day in this part of the forest.'

'It's so peaceful.'

'It will be more peaceful if I stop talking,' Christophe said. The way he wrinkled his nose to suggest that he wasn't happy with himself was...

...cute? Fi could have reassured him that he was not spoiling the ambience. That she liked the sound of his voice and that unique accent he had. She even opened her mouth to say something but the words evaporated before they could reach any air.

'It will be like...' Christophe waved a hand in the air. 'What do they call it in Japan? A bath in the forest?'

'Forest bathing.' Fi nodded. 'I've heard of that.'

But she had always been aware of the physical and emotional benefits of getting close to nature. As a typical middle child, she'd been content with her own company, especially after Laura had become so infatuated with Ellie she almost took over the role of a second mother. Trees, meadows and animals had been Fi's refuge as she'd negotiated the turbulence of tween and teenage years, and her best days had been a combination of all those things.

As she walked in Christophe's company with nothing more than the sound of their footfalls and the call of birds to break the silence it brought back a treasured memory. She'd finished the after-school chores at the riding school, which was how she earned her lessons and time with the ponies, and she'd ridden Whisky into the nearby woods on a sunny, spring afternoon when the bluebells were in flower. She couldn't remember what sort of trees they were under, but maybe they had been oaks as well, because it had looked exactly like this when she'd tipped her head back. So many trees, growing so close to each other that the ends of their branches were entangled, as if they were holding hands. Dark trunks and then branches and then twigs were like visible arteries and veins of an enormous living entity, and the sparkles of sunlight shifting in and out of the leaves made it come to life as if it was wearing a ballgown covered with shiny gold sequins.

Fi could almost smell the woodsy, floral perfume of a carpet of bluebells. She could definitely feel the touch of the happiness she remembered of knowing that nothing else could be quite as perfect as her world was in that moment. It was enough to make her sink into simply enjoying this walk, and that, in turn, dissolved any tendrils of awkwardness that could have sprouted from walking with someone else in complete silence. By the time they reached their destination, being in Christophe's company had, in fact, earned the familiarity of something that she wouldn't hesitate to choose to do again.

The delight of finding more than a dozen donkeys standing between the trunks of the huge trees was the icing on an unexpectedly delicious cake. Like Marguerite and Coquelicot, these donkeys were small – no more than about ten hands high – and they were shaggy. They were all shades of grey and brown with the distinctive black cross of Jerusalem donkeys that ran down the length of the spine and tapered to a point as it draped over both shoulders. Their muzzles were white and those extraordinary ears were filled with soft, pale hair but outlined as darkly as the cross on their backs. As dark as all those eyes that were staring at them, some half-hidden by heavy fringes.

'*Fermo,*' Christophe said to Heidi, pointing at the base of one of the trees outside the electric fence enclosure for the donkeys. The huge dog immediately lay down, kicking one back leg out and putting her nose on her front paws.

'We'll put a halter on two donkeys to start with,' he told Fi. 'And tie them up beside each other. If you can help with the first examination, you can do the hooves while I check the next one. It's what works for me and Didier. Is that okay with you?'

'Perfect. That way they'll get used to me being here instead of Didier.' Fi scanned the group and noted one donkey standing at some distance from the rest. 'Are they all okay with being handled?'

Christophe could see where she was looking. 'I'll check the photographs I have but I think that donkey is new to the herd, so I don't know him. Or her. Some are a little...' Christophe was searching for a word. '*Ansioso*? *Anxieux* in French.'

'Anxious?'

'Ah... *c'est ça. Merci.*' There was a twinkle in his eyes. 'Sometimes there are too many languages in my head and they bump into each other.'

Fi ducked her head. He was seriously charming, this man.

'That's okay... I have treats that might help me make friends with them.'

'Treats?'

'Ginger biscuits. My mother loves them with a cup of tea, so she always brings a couple of packets with her. And I have Polos.'

'I remember Polos from being in England. They are peppermints, yes?'

Fi nodded. She reached into her pocket and brought out a tube of the mints. 'I'd heard that donkeys love peppermints and ginger biscuits and I tested the theory when I came over at Christmas and went to meet Marguerite and Coquelicot.'

She put them back into her pocket and watched Christophe as he set down and opened his backpack and then used a stick to push the electric wire of the enclosure down far enough to step over it easily, a couple of halters and lead ropes in his hands. He offered the back of a hand for the closest donkey to sniff and Fi could see the way the other donkeys edged closer, curious and friendly. She liked the way Christophe showed the first donkey, a little grey jenny, the halter before he slowly put it on her.

'You know me, don't you *cara*?' he said softly. 'We are *amici, oui*?'

What would it be like, Fi wondered, for it to be normal to have so many words to choose from?

'How many languages *do* you speak?' she asked.

'I grew up speaking both French and Italian. My mother speaks English very well and I learned more at school and singing pop music. I missed Julien when he went to boarding school in England, so I did my first year of university there with him before I started to become a vet. I also speak some Spanish and Portuguese.'

'Wow... that's amazing.'

'Not so much.' He shrugged off the compliment, leading the donkey towards a young tree that had a trunk thin enough to loop the rope around. 'If you learn more than one language when you first start to speak, it becomes easier to learn more. And mine are all part of the family of Romance languages that come from Latin. Apart from English.'

'Hmm... English is not a very romantic language,' Fi agreed. 'French is the official language of love, isn't it?'

Christophe laughed and the sound made her own lips curve into something close to a grin. What could have become an embarrassing thing to have said was simply amusing.

'It's about the grammar, not the words of love,' he said. 'But yes, both French and Italian can be very romantic. Now...' He picked up the stick that he'd used to lower the electric wire and pushed it down even further this time. 'Do come in,' he invited.

Fi put her apron on and set out her tools near the tree as Christophe caught and tied up a second donkey to a tree near the water trough. Then they both went to the little grey jenny.

'How do you say donkey in French?' Fi asked. 'I heard the word at Lili's party but I've forgotten.'

'*C'est un âne.*' Christophe was running his hands over the donkey, feeling for any abnormalities and looking for any obvious injuries.

'*Âne,*' Fi repeated. She'd remember that this time. Anne would make a rather nice name for a girl donkey. Like Jenny did in English. Or were they called something different here? 'What if it's a jenny?' she asked. 'Female?'

'*Une ânesse.*'

'Are they all *ânesses* here?'

'Most of them. The others are... how do you say... fixed?'

'Gelded.'

'*Si.* Some of *les ânesses* are *enceinte* – pregnant. Like this little one.' Christophe leaned over the donkey's back and had his hands on either side of a swollen abdomen. 'I can't tell how far along she is and *une ânesse* can be *enceinte* for more than a year, but I will try and find out when the conception happened. We'll need her out of the forest before she has her baby. It could be in danger from the *sangliers.*'

'*Sangliers?*'

'Wild pigs.' Christophe picked up a stethoscope and placed it on the donkey's chest. He held the disc with one hand, his other hand on her neck, and Fi was sure that he wasn't even aware that he was reassuring her with the rub of his thumb, because he was focussing on what he was listening to and what it was telling him about the function of the heart and lungs. He took her temperature after that, used a small torch to check her eyes and wiped out her ears with a gauze pad, presumably to check for mites or excess wax.

Fi was holding the halter as Christophe worked through a thorough checklist and recorded his findings in a notebook. She tickled the jenny's ears and muzzle gently and spoke quietly to her, earning her trust before it was time to start working on her hooves, but that didn't distract her from watching the examination. Or, rather, watching Christophe's hands. They were as beautiful as his face, large enough to be in proportion to his height but with the delicate long fingers of a musician and the deft, precise movements of a surgeon. His touch was gentle but sure and Fi could sense both his confidence and the wealth of experience and intelligence that underpinned it.

It was mesmerising to watch.

Until Fi realised that she was so caught up in the moment, she could actually imagine what the donkey was feeling. Tiny goosebumps prickled on her arms as she could have sworn she felt the brush of Christophe's fingers on her skin. It was just as well that Christophe chose that moment to declare the first donkey to be in good health, gave her a dose of worming paste and moved on to the second donkey. It was time for Fi to start her part of this work, and those goosebumps were long gone by the time she began trimming the first set of a rather daunting number of donkey pedicures.

* * *

Christophe Brabant had been captivated by Fiona Gilchrist from the first moment he'd seen her at Lili's birthday party, but that had been, to start with, only because of how incredibly beautiful this woman was.

She could have stepped straight from a Titian canvas with that porcelain skin, the softness of those enticing curves and... *Dio mio!...* that *hair*. All the Gilchrist girls were stunning, with their fiery hair, but Fiona's was by far the most mesmerising – the shade of the polished skin of a sweet *marron* – dark enough to

hide the flicker of flames until it was touched by light, especially
from the sun. He had felt the heat from that colour kindle a spark
somewhere very deep in his own body, and the urge to touch one
of those curls – to stretch it out and watch it bounce back into the
shape it was determined to be – had been surprisingly powerful.

Until he got close enough to make eye contact, that was.
When he'd sensed something that was, to be honest, a little
shocking.

Because it felt remarkably like fear.

His response had been instinctive. He knew about fear, on
both personal and professional levels, and he'd worked with
enough frightened animals in his time to know how to soften his
body language and step back physically and metaphorically, far
enough to be reassuring. He'd also seen the way the tension
around Fiona seemed to fade to being imperceptible when she'd
been distracted by catching sight of Heidi, and he could actually
feel the pull she had to go and be close enough to touch his
beloved dog. He'd recognised that, too. How many people had he
already seen in his time as a vet who, for whatever reason,
preferred the company of animals to that of people?

He got that.

He trusted his dog far more than most people, especially
when it came to loyalty. Or love.

Why Fiona might be one of those people was a little sad but it
was also... intriguing.

Different.

So was her career. He had never met a woman who had
chosen such a physically demanding and potentially dangerous
way to earn a living. She was good at it, too. Very good. It was easy
to take frequent glances at what Fi was doing without her realising that he was watching her – when he was slowly running his
hands down a donkey's legs, for instance, checking for inflamma-

tion in joints that might suggest arthritis, or standing still with the disc of his stethoscope between the last rib and a back leg so that he could listen for normal sounds of digestion.

He liked the way she treated the animals and he could see the trust she was earning with her gentle but confident manner. Heidi had liked her instantly, as well, and that said a lot about what Fi was like as a person. Animals could sense far more than most humans. He really liked the care she was taking to get each hoof shaped as perfectly as possible, too, and he knew that wasn't always easy. Some of these forest donkeys had been rescued from unfortunate situations to join the herds, and in some cases the lack of attention to their feet had left their hooves in very poor condition, but he'd never seen anything as bad as he did when he got close enough to the new arrival in the herd, a halter in his hand, and could see the gelding's feet. Those hooves curled up like an exaggerated pair of Aladdin's slippers. Was this why the little donkey was standing so still away from the group? Was it too hard for him to walk at all? Where would you even start to try and fix them?

'Fiona?' he called softly. 'Could you come here, please?'

She was just as horrified as he was when she saw the state of this donkey's feet.

'Oh, my God,' she whispered. 'You poor wee thing...' She reached out to touch the donkey but it shied and then stumbled to try and avoid her hand.

The donkey tried to avoid Christophe as well, but the stony ground made it lose balance and it was Christophe's body that prevented a possible fall. He wrapped his arms around the neck to support the animal.

'*Piano... piano...*' he murmured. '*Doucement...* we are not going to hurt you, *caro...*'

He kept talking, just holding the frightened animal, his heart breaking a little to think of what might have happened in the past to create fear like this. When he looked up, he wasn't surprised to see Fi blinking as if she was trying not to shed tears. Just a heartbeat of eye contact was enough for that connection to feel very real. She had a big heart, this woman. She was capable of caring – *loving* – without limits.

Too much? Had she – like he had himself – given far too much, to the wrong person, perhaps, and been badly hurt?

Some things, once they were broken, could never be the same again, could they?

Like trust.

And hearts.

Was that why she was afraid? Hiding?

He could feel the donkey leaning harder against him now. As if it was letting out a sigh of relief because it knew that it didn't need to be scared.

Christophe caught Fi's gaze again. 'Can you help him?' he asked softly.

'Aye,' she said. 'If he'll let me.'

She came closer. Slowly. They took their time reassuring the donkey, who calmed down enough to stay still as Christophe put the halter on. He didn't tie him to a tree. He would hold the lead rope himself, he decided. That way, perhaps the donkey would be able to feel the reassurance that they were both here to help him.

For more than an hour he watched a masterclass in hoof shaping. With the donkey standing on the ground, the first tool Fi used was a pair of large nippers to cut off the bulk of the curled, excess hoof.

'How long do you think it's been since someone looked after him?' Christophe asked.

'Too long.' Fi's tone was grim. She was out of breath and stood up only to stretch her back and wipe perspiration from her face. 'I would guess more than two years. How old do you think he is?'

'I'll look at his teeth later but he seems quite old. And he knows you're helping him, so he must have been cared for at some point in his life. He would never be this calm, otherwise.'

Fi picked up each leg and used a knife to peel and shape the underside of the hoof and then she studied the way it sat on the ground.

'It will take a long time to look normal,' she told Christophe. 'Months and months. They might never be perfect but I want to get the pressure of the weight in the right place so it will start to grow properly – down and not straight out.'

She used the nippers again to adjust the shape and then finished with a rasp.

By the time all four hooves were done, he could see that Fi was hot and tired. He suspected her back was aching badly as well.

'We are going to take a break now,' he announced. 'It's time for lunch.'

He led Fi away from the donkey enclosure because he knew that nearby there was a clearing with a rustic wooden picnic table with benches attached.

'It's a place for the hunters,' he told her. 'They come together to share food and wine.' He shook his head. 'And then they go hunting again.'

'With *guns*? In this forest?'

'*Oui*. Not now – the hunting season is finished until September, but they hunt the *sangliers*. Look... you can see the damage the pigs can do. They've been here, looking for acorns and tree roots to eat.' He pointed out a large section of the forest floor, just off the wide track, that was ploughed up into a mess of soil, rocks and broken branches.

'It looks like someone's been digging with a pickaxe.'

'They use their sharp horns. And they're big.'

Oh... the way Fi's eyes widened made something tighten deep in his chest. 'Don't worry,' he added swiftly. 'They stay away from people if they can, and Heidi is here. She'll let me know if a *sanglier* is close. We will keep you safe.'

He opened the zip on the insulated bag as soon as they reached the table.

'Are you hungry?'

Fi nodded. 'And thirsty. Have you got some water in there?'

'I do. And something else.' Christophe lifted out some small pear-shaped bottles of dark orangey-red soft drink and flipped off the lids. '*Aranciata rossa*. My guilty pleasure.' He gave her the ghost of a wink.

'It looks like Irn Bru,' Fi said. 'That's our national drink in Scotland.' She took a sip. 'It tastes a bit like it, too. Yum yum.' She was smiling at him. 'How do you say "yum yum" in French?'

'*Miam miam.*'

She laughed. 'Of course. It's the same sound. And in Italian?'

'*Gnam gnam.*'

She only caught his gaze for a moment but he could see the way her smile had made her eyes light up. Or maybe it was a sliver of sunshine through the treetops that had reached far enough to reveal the sparkle that softened the brown of her eyes and sprinkled bright flecks of gold and red in her hair.

She was... *bellissima*. So beautiful. He knew he couldn't let the thought show in his face, however, so he focussed on the contents of the bag again.

'I hope you like this.' He handed her a wrapped parcel of food.

Fi opened it and took a bite. And then she closed her eyes as she chewed, an expression of sheer pleasure on her face. It was just as well she couldn't see him, Christophe thought, because there was no way he couldn't watch her eating the food he had prepared. He could feel her enjoyment so clearly, he could taste the sandwich himself before he even took a bite.

'Ooh...' Fi opened her eyes and stared at what she was holding, the tip of her tongue appearing to catch a reminder of the taste. 'What *is* this?'

'A stromboli. It's pizza dough baked with things inside it. Like a sandwich. There's ham and salami and olives and cheese – mozzarella and provolone – and some sun-dried tomatoes and—'

'And it's the most delicious thing I've ever eaten,' Fi interrupted. She took another bite.

'*Grazie mille,*' he responded.

She swallowed hurriedly. '*You* made this?'

'I did.' He shrugged. 'I love to cook. My nonna taught me, the way she taught my mamma. We all love to cook. And to eat. And we all know that the best thing is to make other people happy with our food.'

'I'm happy.' Fi was looking at her food rather than him and she sounded enchantingly shy. '*Miam miam...*'

She peeped up at him for just a fraction of a second from beneath a thick tangle of eyelashes that were the same, rich red-brown colour as her hair.

Ohh...

He could fall in love with this woman in a heartbeat if he let himself.

Maybe he couldn't stop that happening.

What he could do, however, was to ensure that he kept it hidden well enough that nobody would be able to guess. Especially Fiona.

It wasn't simply that she deserved more than he could ever

offer her. Or that, no matter how much pain someone had been through in the past, it was still possible to be hurt again.

No... this had a selfish motive as well. There was something so enchanting about this third Gilchrist sister that meant he didn't want to lose sight of her and, if she got even a glimpse of what he was thinking, or feeling, he knew she would run – so far and so fast that it was more than likely he would never see her again.

10

'This is so kind of you.' Jeannie Gilchrist climbed out of Julien Rousseau's car when they arrived in the village of Saint-Martin-Vésubie, close to the Italian border and just another fifteen minutes' drive into the mountains from where they'd dropped his grandmother and mother at their home in Roquebillière after the hospital appointment.

'It's my pleasure,' Julien said. 'My *mère* and my *grand-mère* were delighted to see you again. You are all Bonnie and Theo's grandmothers, which means you are very much a part of our family.' He led the way from the parking area to the main street of the village. 'This is the Rue Docteur Cagnoli. The *rue principale*. You call it the high street?'

'Aye. I remember this.'

'Everybody does, if they've been here before. It's the only village that has a *gargouille* like this. A little canal.'

The ripple of the fast-moving water in the channel that divided the cobbled street felt like it was sweeping Jeannie back in time. So much so, she could imagine she was holding the hand of the man she was so much in love with, her other hand resting on her rounded belly. She'd been so incredibly happy that day. Enjoying a dream honeymoon, with so much to look forward to when she and Gordon returned to Scotland to prepare for the birth of their first child.

The pain of what had been lost was enough to bring the threat of tears to her eyes. Hastily, Jeannie distracted herself from sinking any further into the past.

'Why did they build it?' she asked. 'Do you know? And where does the water come from so fast?'

'I believe it comes from a mountain spring and I've heard that it was built about the fifteenth century, in case of fires in the town.'

That made sense. And perhaps it had been a success, because some of those medieval houses still existed on this narrow, sloping street that was crowded with various shops, restaurants and businesses. At a fork in the road, a curious house filled the middle of the Y shape. It had a big front door, with an alcove above it that contained a small religious statue. An arrow was painted on the wall as a direction to an *église* – possibly the church whose bells Jeannie had heard chiming the hour a little while ago. It took her a moment to realise what was odd about the house was that the second storey, with its green-shuttered windows, was bigger than the ground floor.

'It's called *La Maison du Coiffeur*,' Julien told her. 'The hairdresser's house. It's a famous example of how a tax could be avoided because it was counted by how much ground the house stood on.' He shook his head. 'Times haven't changed so much, no? People still hate paying a tax.'

Jeannie made a sound of agreement. There were definitely things that didn't change over time. Including people? Why did she feel the need to try and find the truth of why her husband, her children's father, had left them? Perhaps Laura was right in not wanting any part of this search. What if she discovered that Gordon had never been the man she thought he'd been? That he'd become so unhappy he'd simply moved on? That he had another family here in France... And another wife?

It was enough to make her look over her shoulder at the street she'd just come down. She could simply turn around and go back, couldn't she?

Or maybe not.

'The gallery is just down here, on the right,' Julien said. 'We discovered it when we were walking back from visiting the church...' His glance at Jeannie was a little wary. '...where Ellie's grandparents got married? Her father's parents?'

Jeannie gave a single nod. She knew. She'd been to see it herself nearly forty years ago. Her breath came out in a sigh as she remembered wishing that they had got married in the pretty church in Gordon's childhood village instead of a registry office in Scotland.

'It was important for her to come here,' Julien added quietly. 'It connected her to the French heritage she hadn't known she had.'

No. She couldn't change her mind now. Coming here today was important for herself. If this was a dead end, she needed to know, or it would haunt her for the rest of her life.

'It's an odd thing, that kind of connection.' It was Julien who spoke first. 'It seems like something unconscious. Like the way a bird knows how to build a nest?'

Jeannie nodded again. It *was* something at a cellular level. She'd felt that strange, deep touch when she'd first seen the painting hanging in La Maisonette.

Maybe Julien was reading her thoughts.

'I know Ellie is worried about what you might find out here but... I can't help wondering if the reason she felt so strongly about that painting is because of a connection she had no way of knowing was there. That it *was* painted by her father.'

They were outside the gallery now. There were several paintings in the window but none of them were done in that choppy, three-dimensional technique. Were there any like the mountain chapel in the summer meadow inside? Jeannie's mouth felt very dry but she straightened her spine. She had to do this.

'*Ah... Docteur Rousseau! Quel plaisir de vous revoir.*' The woman in the gallery was clearly happy to see Julien again. '*Bienvenue... Comment puis-je vous aider aujourd'hui?*'

A rapid conversation in French followed that Jeannie couldn't understand. There was quite a lot of the kind of Gallic shrugging and facial expressions that suggested the answer to a question was not known or, perhaps, shouldn't be divulged but, finally, the woman found a scrap of paper and began drawing what looked like a map.

'She hasn't seen him for months and she can't tell me much more than she did when I first came here. Except that, while everyone calls him *l'ermite* – the 'ermit – his real name is Gideon.'

Jeannie could feel the blood draining from her face as the shiver ran the entire length of her spine.

'And this' – Julien showed her the map – 'is where he lives.' He lifted his eyebrows. 'It's not too far away. Do you want to go there?'

Finding words was impossible. It was obviously more than a coincidence that the name Gideon was almost the same as Gordon. Her heart was hammering against her ribs but Jeannie pressed her lips together and nodded decisively.

* * *

Brown-and-white cows, wearing collars and bells, looked up with only mild curiosity as Julien drove past the signage on the main entrance to a farm that advertised itself as a *vacherie*.

'It is also a *fromagerie*,' Julien told Jeannie. 'They supply milk from their cows but they also make their own cheeses. We need to find the next road, which will take us to the old stables.'

The turn-off was onto no more than a rutted track. The overgrown branches of spruce trees brushed the sides of the car and it was long enough to feel like the destination was completely isolated. At first glance the long, stone-built structure looked derelict with a broken window roughly covered with wooden planks and a door half open, hanging on an angle off its top hinge.

Julien was frowning. 'Stay here,' he instructed Jeannie. 'I will go and see if anyone is home. If they are, they may not be happy to see us.'

Jeannie watched him walk to the door. He lifted his hand and knocked and then she heard him calling.

'Bonjour! *Êtes-vous là, monsieur*?'

She was holding her breath as she waited but there seemed to be no response. Then Julien took a step forward. He looked a little hesitant as he peered around the partially open door, but then he took another step and vanished from view.

Jeannie waited again. The seconds ticked past and tipped into being long enough to make her anxious about what was going on. Was Julien in danger? Ellie would never forgive her if something had happened to her beloved husband, the father of her tiny baby. She would never forgive herself. Getting out of the car she almost ran to the door, hesitated only long enough to take a deep breath and slipped inside.

She'd expected darkness in an ancient building with almost no windows, but she couldn't have been more wrong. Most of the end of this old stables that couldn't be seen from the driveway had been replaced with glass and light flooded a large open area with terracotta tiles visible above bleached, hand-hewn beams. The floor was packed earth, a dark ochre shade of wet clay as hard as concrete, and the space was full of totally unexpected colour from dozens of canvases – sitting on easels or propped against the walls. The same kind of colours that were in Ellie's painting. Gold and yellow, blood-red and a glistening white. The colours of summer. Of warmth and sunlight with a background of earthy, homely colours.

The impression only lasted a blink of time, however, as Jeannie's eyes were adjusting to the dim light at the other end of the building. There was a bed in one corner. A small table, a sagging armchair and a potbelly stove. Julien was standing halfway between the door Jeannie had entered and what had to be the artist's living space.

Standing in front of the stove was a tall man with unkempt hair, bushy eyebrows and a beard, all of the same mix of grey and white.

Surely this man was too old to be Gordon? He would only be in his mid-sixties if he was still alive.

But Jeannie was walking forward, one slow step at a time – as if, she thought, she was a bride walking to meet her groom, down an aisle that divided a crowded church. Julien was the only other person here, of course, but Jeannie wasn't looking at her son-in-law as she kept walking towards the stranger. Because something was pulling her forward and it felt as if the entire world had gone completely still. It was holding its breath until she knew.

And she did know, as soon as she was close enough to look into this man's eyes.

'*Gordon*...?' The word came out halfway between a question and an exclamation. A shaky word. A plea, even?

He was staring at her.

'*Non*,' he said. '*Non, non, non*...'

He sounded desperate. His distress was as raw as the fear that Jeannie could see in his face.

Fear that was tipping into terror. And then, as if a switch had been flicked, his expression became completely blank. His body stiffened and he simply fell backwards, making no attempt to break the fall. There was a horrible thud as his head hit the floor and Jeannie could only stare in horror as his body started to jerk uncontrollably.

Julien moved past her so swiftly she felt the air move around her. Jeannie was a nurse. She knew exactly what to do to care for someone having a seizure but she couldn't move.

This was *Gordon*. He'd recognised her. And he'd been terrified of her?

Maybe she'd never know why. Had she found him only to be watching him die?

Julien shoved the armchair back to clear space. 'Find something soft,' he told Jeannie. 'To put under his head.'

She ran to the bed and stripped off the blanket. Julien folded it to make a protective covering on the hard floor but a pool of blood told them it was too late to prevent injury. He must have bitten his tongue as well, because there was a trickle of blood on his chin. His eyes were open, his hands in fists as his arms and legs continued convulsing.

His breathing was ragged and his lips were going a worrying shade of blue, but Jeannie knew not to try and put anything in his mouth or restrain his limbs. There was nothing more they could do now except wait for the seizure to finish and then put him into the recovery position and make sure his airway was open.

They had to wait.

But Julien looked at his watch again. 'It's going on too long,' he said quietly. 'And he's injured himself. I'm going to call for an ambulance.'

11

'Are you sure you don't mind doing this?'

'Are you kidding?' Fi climbed into Christophe's big, black vehicle. 'Another day in the forest is exactly what I need.' She reached into the back seat to offer Heidi her hand and wiped the sloppy lick off on her dungarees before putting her safety belt on. 'Besides, I want to check on the little gelding whose feet were so bad last time. I've been thinking about him. Does he have a name?'

Christophe shook his head. 'I keep photographs of all the donkeys in my notebook, with a record of problems with their health and what treatment they've had. That's their only identification.'

A thought occurred to Fi. 'Do you get paid for looking after them?'

'No.' He shrugged. 'The owner of the donkeys is Alain, who is the brother of Didier. He pays for things like the *médicaments* but we do the work to help. In our... what's the word for it? Time that is not at work? Time to do things that you enjoy?'

'Leisure time? Spare time?' Fi slid a sideways look at

Christophe. He worked full time in a busy veterinary clinic but he loved his work so much he chose to do it for free in his spare time? It didn't matter whether it was more for the benefit of Didier's brother or the donkeys, it was still something only a very nice person would do.

But she'd known he was special, hadn't she? From the first moment she'd seen him. If there was ever a competition for a perfect human, then Christophe Brabant would have no trouble making the shortlist. He was clearly as beautiful inside as he was outside. He was intelligent, passionate and kind enough to have simply wrapped his arms around a frightened, sad donkey and not only hold him long enough to make him feel safer, but he'd stopped doing his own work to provide reassurance during the long process to start treating those badly neglected feet. That was probably why he needed to devote more of his own free time to finish what needed to be done for the rest of the herd. It was definitely why a noticeable part of Fi's heart melted every time she remembered him hugging the little donkey.

Sometimes, but only when it was completely safe, like when she was alone in her own bed in the middle of the night, she would let herself think about how that donkey must have felt. What it would be like to be held in Christophe's arms like that. It was increasingly easy to imagine the feel of his fingers brushing her skin too. To get those goosebumps again and to feel parts of her body melting that were quite some distance from her heart.

'Leisure is good,' Christophe decided. '*Comme les loisirs*, in French. For *les passe-temps*.'

'Things to pass the time.' Fi nodded. '*Exactement*.' She was happy to throw in the new word she'd picked up in the couple of days since she'd seen him. 'Do you know, I think I could enjoy learning French.'

'*C'est une très bonne idée.*' Christophe's tone was casual but approving. 'A very good idea.'

'I also think the donkeys need names. At least the special ones. I'm going to call the one with the bad feet... erm...' She searched for a name. 'Joseph. Because, you know, they're Jerusalem donkeys with that cross on their backs.'

Christophe laughed. 'So should we call the pregnant one... Mary?'

They shared a flick of a glance as they both laughed and, for the first time, Fi felt that melting sensation deep in her belly when she was in Christophe's company and not safely alone, but it was gone too fast to worry about. And, besides, there couldn't be anything remotely threatening about something that was cushioned by laughter.

'*C'est une très bonne idée.*' Fi used the same tone he'd used only seconds earlier and, for some reason, that was also amusing to them both.

She couldn't quite make herself catch his gaze again, so she looked out of the window as they took the winding road from Tourrettes-sur-Loup towards Vence. There were houses on either side but they were so well screened by trees it felt like this road was part of the forest they were catching glimpses of to their right – a sea of green that seemed to be stretching all the way to the bright blue streak of the Mediterranean glimmering in the distance.

Her breath left her lungs in an audible sigh. Aye... this was *exactement* what she needed today. Did Christophe – given that he was Julien's closest friend – know anything about the drama that was currently unfolding in the lives of the Gilchrist women? If he did, he clearly wasn't about to broach the subject. Fi liked that he was respecting her privacy, but how good would it be to tell somebody whose reactions wouldn't be based on their own emotional involvement or the need to protect somebody they loved?

'Have you seen Julien recently?' she ventured.

'*Non.*' Christophe indicated to make a turn that would take them in the direction of the coast rather than into the centre of Vence. 'We were to have an evening of wine tasting yesterday evening with Noah, *comme d'hab*, but...' He was choosing his words carefully. 'It was not... convenient.'

'He would have been at the hospital, with my mother,' Fi said. 'And... and my father.'

How strange was it to hear those words pass her lips? She still wasn't at all sure how she felt about this bombshell of a development in her life. The glance from Christophe told her that he did know what was going on. That he understood how difficult it was but he wasn't going to pry. And that, curiously, made her want to tell him everything.

'My father disappeared when I was seven,' she told him. 'I'm thirty-four now. It's more than a quarter of a century ago. So long I don't really remember him.'

Another look from Christophe came with an empathetic tilt to his lips. 'My papa died when I was eight,' he said. 'I don't remember much, either, except in here...' He took one hand off the steering wheel to pat his chest, over his heart. 'I still remember him. I still miss him, every day.'

'We weren't supposed to miss our daddy,' Fi said quietly. 'Everybody said it was the best thing he could have done to run away like he did. That he wasn't a good man. That he drank too much and couldn't do his job any longer and that he'd made us all unhappy and... and he'd hurt someone. Very badly.'

'What was his job, *amore*?'

Just a few words, but the tone and the choice to ignore every negative thing she had revealed about her father made it clear that Christophe was not interested in gossip. What had to be an endearment on the end of his query made it even clearer that it was *her* opinion that mattered.

That *she* mattered...

'He was an engineer,' she told him. 'He was born in France but his father was Glaswegian, so they moved back to Scotland when he was very young. He worked building boats in Glasgow but then he met my mother and they got married and moved to Oban and he worked on fishing boats after that. He used to call me *chérie* but I never knew I had a French grandmother. Or an uncle, until my sisters and I inherited the house here.'

'He called you *chérie*,' Christophe echoed. 'He loved you.'

Again, he'd only taken a tiny piece of information. The detail that had made her heart squeeze hard enough to break off a piece as she'd remembered it when the sisters had gathered for Jeannie to tell them what had happened. It had been enough to make her want to go and see the man she'd once adored. Right then. Ellie had watched her get to her feet and Fi knew she was feeling that childhood connection just as strongly. When she saw Ellie's gaze shift to the painting over the fireplace she realised that her younger sister's connection might be at an even deeper level. It was obvious to them all that it had been Ellie who'd inherited their father's artistic talent.

Laura had watched them both, her lips so tightly pressed together they were invisible. She had no desire whatsoever to go and see Gordon Gilchrist. He was too sick to see anyone at the moment, anyway. He needed time to get over the shock.

'He's in hospital,' she told Christophe. 'Julien took Mam to the village that turns out to be where my father was born. It was where Julien and Ellie had found the painting.'

Christophe nodded. 'It's an astonishing story. *Incroyable.*'

'We wouldn't know any of it if it hadn't been for Julien. When they took him into the hospital in Nice they were able to find his medical history. It must have been only days after he ran away from us all those years ago that he was found on a street in Calais – almost dead because of the tumour in his brain.'

Christophe whistled silently. 'Brain tumours can be devastating.'

Fi nodded. 'It wasn't drinking too much that made him unable to walk properly sometimes, or even speak properly. Or turned him into a man with a violent temper. Mam knew something was wrong but... maybe it was the tumour stopping him from listening to her. Stopping him from going to see a doctor.' She cleared her throat. 'Anyway... the surgery was successful but removing the tumour created damage as well. He'd totally lost his memory. He couldn't even talk for years after that. He was sent to an institution and, when he did start to talk again, it was in French. And he had no idea who he was or what had happened to him.'

'It makes sense that he spoke French.' Christophe parked the car near the cemetery again but made no move to get out. 'It was the language he was hearing around him and it was already in his head from his first years in France.'

'Maybe those earliest memories were why he eventually found his way back to this part of the country, to where he was born.'

'*Peut-être.* Does he remember English as well?'

'He dreams in English sometimes. But only bad dreams.'

'*Cauchemars,*' Christophe murmured. 'Nightmares.'

'He recognised Mam from them. They must be his memories. Do you know what flashbacks are?'

'*Le flash-back.*' Christophe nodded. 'We use the same word. Or *retour en arrière* but that's only to go back. Flashback is... more violent, yes? Something that you don't want because it's bad. They come from something traumatic and they can damage your life and steal what makes you the person you want to be.'

Fi couldn't meet his gaze. She had to fight back tears, in fact. In any attempt to heal herself, she'd never found anything online or in books that captured that feeling so well.

Aye... The person she had wanted to be had been stolen. She almost wanted to tell Christophe why his definition resonated so deeply with her. She wouldn't, of course. She didn't want him to think about her in that way. It would be excruciating to think he might be imagining what had happened to her to create her own flashbacks.

'They think that he must remember the violence. Perhaps that's all he remembers about his marriage as well as the attack that made him go on the run from the police and probably stow away on a boat to France. The flashbacks terrify him. Seeing Mam terrified him because he thought she was a ghost. She's been going into the hospital and just sitting in the room with him. Talking to him. He's only starting to wake up properly now. It's been...' Fi blew out a breath as she gave her head a small shake. 'Well... intense. I've discovered that being near donkeys is the best thing when you feel so...' She wrapped her arms around herself and could feel her muscles tightening so that she shrank a little. 'It's like being in a plane,' she added. 'When you hit turbulence that nobody was expecting and you have no idea what's going to happen next but there's the possibility that you could actually fall out of the sky.'

Christophe's smile was all the response she needed. '*C'est parti, mon kiki*,' he said. 'Let's go. Let's find Joseph and Mary and look after the rest of their friends.'

* * *

Maybe the donkeys remembered the peppermints and ginger biscuits that Fiona had in the pockets of her dungarees. Or perhaps they remembered her voice reassuring them that they had nothing to fear and the kindness and skill she had shown in making their feet comfortable? Whatever the reason, they crowded around her as she entered the enclosure. They wanted to be near her. To be touched by her. It made Christophe smile.

He knew how they felt.

He, too, was happy to simply be this close.

For the most part, they had worked together in silence that first day. This time, it felt easy to start and stop snatches of conversation.

'Did you bring some stromboli for us to have for lunch today?' Fi asked as she straightened to stretch her back after finishing a set of hooves.

'No. Today I have made a pizza with mushrooms and onions that have been cooked with balsamic vinegar and are on top of goat's cheese and spinach. With a lot of garlic, a little sage and some... *romarin*. I don't know what that herb is in English.'

'Neither do I but it sounds delicious. I wish I'd had a nonna to teach me to cook Italian food.'

'There is no one else in the world like my nonna,' Christophe said with conviction. 'She is the person I love the most. Apart from my mamma, *bien sûr*.' He caught the lift of Fi's eyebrows and smiled as he shrugged. 'What can I say? I'm half-Italian. For us, family is everything.'

'Do you have brothers and sisters? Cousins? Nieces and nephews?'

Christophe sighed deeply. 'Sadly, *non*. My mamma and my nonna were counting on me to grow our family and I wanted that too. I had been an only child and I envied my friends who had big families. I almost got married when I was eighteen but fortunately I realised what a bad idea that was before I made such a big mistake.'

He wasn't about to tell her that he'd been discarded by Marcella in favour of another man – an older, wealthy man. That, in the end, who he was had not been enough for the girl he had loved so passionately. Why would he want Fiona to know that? Or that he'd been so broken, he'd vowed to never risk that kind of pain a second time? She might think less of him.

He didn't want her to think less of him.

'It still seems like a bad idea.' This time his shrug signalled an end to this subject. '*Qué sera sera*.'

When he started another conversation as they put halters on the last two donkeys who needed attention, he made sure it was not going to get too personal.

'Donkeys' feet are very different to horses' feet, yes? I know they are prone to laminitis, like ponies.'

'Yes. The hooves are quite a different shape. They're longer than they are wide and it's very important that they walk on the wall of the hoof and not the sole.'

'Why is that?'

'I can't quite remember. It's a very long time since that particular lecture at university and it was about all sorts of hooves – cows and goats and sheep as well as donkeys and horses.'

'Did you go to university to learn to become a farrier?'

'No. That was by working as an apprentice. University was for vet school.'

Christophe unhooked the stethoscope from around his neck but didn't put the earpieces in place. He was staring at Fi's back as she bent over the hoof she was holding in her hand, using her knife to clean it.

His tone was astonished. 'You went to university to become a vet?'

He saw the way she froze. He heard how strangled her dismissive words were.

'For a while. It didn't work out.'

He could also hear the regret that she had shared the information in the first place and he could almost hear distant doors being slammed shut. He was not welcome in this space. He suspected no one was. Was it because she didn't want anyone to think less of her because she had failed in some way?

Christophe, of all people, could understand that.

He made a sound of what he hoped was acknowledgement with no hint of judgement and they worked in silence again after that. They both seemed to have stepped a little too close to boundaries that were there for a reason.

Perhaps the picnic lunch, which he'd made with such care last night, would make things right again between them?

* * *

She'd let her guard down, hadn't she?

Enough to open a window into a part of her life that she had no intention of sharing with Christophe.

It was a relief to focus on finishing the work they'd come to do. By the time the last physical check, dosage of worm paste and foot trim had been completed the peacefulness of both the forest and the small herd of donkeys had worked its magic.

With Heidi lying under the hunter's table as Christophe unpacked the picnic, any residual fragments of discomfort had evaporated. He was smiling as he offered her a drink and a slice of the pizza he'd made for their lunch.

Maybe the fact that the food was cold somehow enhanced the flavours. Or perhaps it was just astonishingly delicious at any temperature. Fi closed her eyes as she chewed the first mouthful.

Very slowly, so she didn't miss anything. Rosemary, that was the herb that Christophe hadn't known in English. She'd recognised the baked leaves scattered over a cheese layer above the spinach and goat's cheese that had created a golden-brown bed for the mushrooms. She savoured everything, swallowed and made an appreciative murmur. And then she licked her lips in anticipation of the next bite.

She could feel that Christophe was watching her. He was sitting at the head of the table, at right angles to Fi, and he was close enough for her to feel how still he was. She knew he was waiting. That her opinion of his food was important to him. She opened her eyes, lifted her gaze, a smile already beginning to emerge, as she tried to think of an appropriate superlative for his amazingly good cooking, but then it died on her lips.

Oh, *my*…

The way he was looking at her mouth in the heartbeat of time when she'd just finished licking her lips.

The look in his eyes the moment they met hers as he lifted *his* gaze.

Was it her imagination or was he thinking about *kissing* her?

Did she *want* him to think about kissing her?

No.

Absolutely *not!* She hit the notion on the head with a mental sledgehammer but it also killed what she'd intended to say about the food.

In the nanosecond before it could all become incredibly awkward, salvation came in the form of a ringtone and Christophe pulled his phone from his pocket and swiped the screen to answer a call.

'Ciao, Mamma. Ça va?'

Fi could see the screen of his phone. A woman with dark, shoulder-length wavy hair was staring back – at *her*.

'Christophe?' A stream of what sounded like rapid-fire questions followed in Italian and Fi heard her name more than once
as they were answered.

Christophe switched to English. 'This is my mamma,' he told
Fi. 'She wanted to know who you are and what we are doing in
the middle of a forest. She wants to say hullo. And to see whether
I'm feeding you properly.'

'Hi,' Fi said, shrinking a little under the intense gaze she was
receiving. She lifted the slice of pizza she still had in her hand so
that Christophe's mother could see it. 'Your son is an amazing
cook,' she said. 'This is *so* good.'

There was a moment's silence as the older woman smiled
back at her but then there was a new flow of words that held a
note of urgency. Christophe's responses – between what sounded
like distressed exclamations – were clearly questions and he got
to his feet, walking away from the table as if he needed to move
more than just his hands as he spoke.

Something was wrong.

Fi's appetite deserted her. She reached down to find the
comfort of Heidi's soft coat and warmth and she gently
fondled the dog's ears as they both watched Christophe. He
was on the far side of the clearing now but, when he
lowered his hand, the phone call clearly ended, he didn't
move. He was standing very still, his head bowed and his
shoulders curved as if he'd just taken on the weight of the
world.

Fi had no idea whether she would be welcome to step past
what felt like another personal boundary, but she couldn't simply
sit there and watch someone so caring and kind suffering like
this. Heidi seemed to approve of her decision to walk to where he
was standing and came with her, close enough for her shoulder
to be brushing Fi's leg.

'What is it?' She was horrified to see tears on his cheeks. 'What's wrong, Christophe?'

'It's my nonna.' He rubbed his face with his hand. 'She's in hospital. There's something wrong with her heart. Mamma thinks she will die.'

'Oh... no...' Fi touched his arm. 'You must go to her.'

'*Si*...' Christophe's ragged snatch of a new breath was audible. He turned and started walking back towards the table. 'I must. I'm sorry, Fiona. We will have to abandon our lunch.'

Fi shook off the apology. 'It doesn't matter. How far away is your nonna?'

'Menton. It's only about an hour's drive.'

Fi helped him wrap up the pizza and stuff it back into the bag, along with everything else he had unpacked for their picnic, but she was watching Christophe as well. She could see the pain in his face and her heart was breaking for him. His grandmother was the person he loved most in the world and this was tearing him apart. She spoke without thinking.

'Let me come with you,' she said. 'I can drive. I don't think it's safe for you to drive when you're this upset.'

A huff of something like laughter escaped Christophe. 'You don't want to do that, *amore*.'

'Why wouldn't I? I have nothing else I need to do right now.'

'Because my mamma will... she...' Christophe shook his head. Then he let his breath out in a long sigh. 'My mamma thinks you're my girlfriend,' he said. 'I'm sorry – I told her it wasn't true but she said even if it wasn't, the least I could do is to pretend it was because...' His voice caught. '...because it's the one thing that would let my nonna go in peace – to think that I've finally found the woman who will be my wife. *La madre dei miei bambini...*'

Fi blinked. She recognised the Italian word for children. Christophe had been at school with Julien, which made him the same age, mid-thirties. The closest he'd been to getting married had been when he was eighteen, which was a very long time ago. No wonder his family were concerned about his future happiness when there was no sign of him finding the person he wanted to create a family with.

'You should pretend,' she said quietly. 'I don't mind.'

'It would be a lie,' Christophe said. 'I do not tell lies.'

'Only a white lie,' Fi countered. 'And white lies to make someone happy are okay. Especially if it's their last wish.'

She had a sudden image of an elderly, frail Italian woman, lying on a hospital bed, a gnarled hand resting between those of her grandson. And then she could imagine the woman's eyelids fluttering as she opened her eyes and looked up – to where Fi was sitting beside that beloved grandson – and then drifting shut again, as she took her final breath. With a smile on her face?

'I could pretend too.'

The words came from nowhere, startling Fi as much as Christophe.

They stared at each other.

'You'd do that?' Christophe's tone was incredulous when he finally spoke. 'For me? Why?'

'I like you,' Fi said simply. 'You're a very kind man. You're kind to your mamma and your nonna and your dog and...' She tried to smile but it was a bit wobbly. 'And you're kind to donkeys when they're frightened. You deserve someone to be kind to *you* and... maybe that person is me. I'm here. I could do this for you.'

How hard would it be to look at this man in front of his family as if he was the most beautiful, desirable man on earth?

It would be playing with fire but she could do this without putting herself in any real danger. The desire to do it was strangely compelling, in fact.

The real question was whether Christophe could make it

convincing. Or whether he even wanted to try. Fi had no idea what was going through his head as he stared at her in astonishment.

But those questions were answered when his smile lit up his face and crinkled the corners of dark eyes that were sparkling with new tears.

'*Grazie*,' he whispered. '*Grazie mille*, Fiona. It would only need to be one visit to the hospital and I can bring you back home tonight.' He picked up his backpack and the picnic bag. 'But we need to hurry. I don't know how much time we have.'

12

They hurried.

Fiona ran into La Maisonette only a short time later, tore off her work clothes and threw on the only really tidy outfit she had, which was the tiered dress, tights and shoes she'd worn for Lili's birthday party. She stuffed a pair of jeans and a jumper into her shoulder bag in case she was in need of something warmer by the time they were driving home again and was back in the passenger seat of Christophe's sleek black SUV in less than ten minutes.

He didn't bother stopping at his own house in Vence.

'I visit so often I already have anything I might need, like food for Heidi, at my mother's apartment. I have biscuits in the car for her, too.'

It took less than an hour to get to Menton, France's most southern town, which Christophe told her was about the same size as Vence. They bypassed Nice and Monaco using the motorway and only had to slow to get through the kind of bottle-necks at toll gates that Fi had initially found terrifying when she'd made the long drive through France by herself.

The neatly marked lanes that led to the individual machines

and barrier arms vanished on the other side and it was a free-for-all to see which vehicles could make it back to the motorway lanes first. Fi had never tried to compete because she found it so intimidating. Christophe won each time but, surprisingly, it didn't scare her at all. Neither did it seem to annoy any other drivers. Maybe it had something to do with the subtle hand signals and that smile of his – the one she could always feel right down to the tips of her toes.

This skill and speed of his driving was seriously impressive, however – a definitive touch of sheer masculinity in a man who came across as being such a gentle soul. It was, Fi had to admit, something else that was very attractive about Christophe Brabant. Perhaps that was partly because it balanced his softer side.

Or maybe it was simply an alpha-male characteristic that was, undeniably, dead sexy with its notes of confidence, assertiveness and leadership. A kind of bad-boy vibe that she suspected almost every woman would find compelling.

Fi didn't dare let her gaze drift to Christophe's face with that thought, even though it was highly unlikely he would notice anything odd about her expression. From the moment she'd seen how devastating the thought of losing his grandmother was, Christophe's focus had been on getting to his destination as rapidly as possible. Just as clearly, conversation of any kind would be an unwelcome distraction and Fi was happy to sit as quietly as Heidi was being in the back seat.

She was starting to feel more than a little nervous, to be honest. She wasn't going to try and back out of what she'd offered to do for Christophe, but she was going to be much happier when it was all over and done with. It was both a relief and even more nerve-racking when they took the motorway exit and dropped to a lower speed limit as they wound their way downhill towards the coast.

Menton looked like an average French town to Fi. She watched the tall apartment blocks slide past along with supermarkets, pharmacies and hairdressing salons. There were petrol stations and roundabouts and so many signs, helpfully shaped like arrows. Green ones with white writing for major destinations like Nice or Ventimiglia. White ones with black writing for directions to the *Centre Ville*, *Office de Tourisme* and – their destination – the *Hôpital*.

There were glimpses of the beach that hugged this seaside town, and so many palm trees. Perhaps that was why the main hospital was called La Palmosa? They got out of the car, having found a parking space that was in shade for Heidi's sake, and Christophe let his dog out for a minute or two to stretch her legs and have a drink of water.

Fi looked up at the huge building that looked modern and light with so many windows but as daunting as any hospital always looked. It felt warmer here. Not enough to be a problem for Heidi being inside the car but it felt different to the village she'd left behind in the mountains. As if they'd arrived at a holiday destination, but this was anything but a welcome break for Christophe. He was looking so pale it made his eyes look black as he put Heidi back into the car and then turned to Fi.

'*C'est parti...*'

Fi drew in a deep breath and followed Christophe.

She could do this.

* * *

For one horrible, heart-stopping moment as he walked into the small side room of the cardiology ward, Christophe thought he was too late.

That his beloved nonna was dead, despite the machines

parked by her bedside that were emitting flickering lights and numbers and soft beeping sounds. Eighty-eight-year-old Flora Romano was lying so unnaturally still and her face was a ghastly shade of grey. His mother's colour looked almost as bad but she was moving – holding out her arms to him as tears sprang to her eyes.

It wasn't until Maria Brabant broke the fierce embrace and held her arms out again that Christophe remembered that Fiona had come into the room right behind him. His mother was about to welcome the woman who was – to all intents and purposes right now – his *fidanzata*. A step up from merely a girlfriend to being not necessarily a fiancée yet but in a relationship that was being taken seriously. As seriously as it needed to be taken if it could make his nonna happy before she left this earth.

'Call me Maria,' his mother said, as she put her arms around Fiona. '*La ringrazio molto*. Thank you so much for coming.'

Christophe could see the emotion on Fi's face and it was obvious that she was returning the hug with genuine warmth and it made him feel proud of her. Proud of her warmth and her generosity in going along with this pretence for the sake of people she didn't even know. It was enough to make his breath catch in his chest and make him want to take Fiona into his own arms and hold her tightly enough to let her know how special she was.

The sound from the bed made them all jump, despite not being more than a loud sigh – almost a whimper.

Maria went straight to her mother's side and held her hand and Christophe went to the other side of the bed, aware of an overwhelming wash of relief that his nonna was still alive enough to be waking up. Her eyes flickered open but Christophe wasn't sure if she recognised him. Or was she even looking at him?

No. He could see exactly what Nonna Flora was seeing when he turned his head a fraction. Fiona hadn't moved from where she was standing, and the afternoon sunlight coming through the window behind her was creating a halo effect with that extraordinary hair of hers. A halo that was a mix of red and orange and gold, like the luminous glow of the kind of exceptional sunsets this stretch of coastline was famous for.

Christophe could feel the corners of his mouth trying to curl upwards into a smile but being held back by how poignant this was. And how astonishing. With her pale, perfect Scottish skin and her body no more than a shadow in those black clothes, Fiona Gilchrist looked... like an angel? If this was the last thing his grandmother was to ever see, at least it was this. Something so *meravigliosa. Magnifique.*

Stunning, in any language.

The moment only lasted a heartbeat. Flora's eyes drifted shut again as the door to the room opened and the medical staff came in to crowd around the bed. It didn't matter that Christophe could no longer see Fiona. He was watching and listening to the doctors. Looking at the recordings of blood tests and the function of his grandmother's heart shown by the ECG and an echocardiogram. Moving to put his arm around his mother as they asked questions to help them understand what it was they were being asked to give consent to for the next stage of her emergency treatment for a heart attack.

And then there were more people in the room and they barely had time to lean in and place gentle kisses on Flora's forehead before the bed, all the monitoring equipment around it and the old woman lying with her eyes closed on top of it were being moved. Taken away as one unit. Maria kept walking behind the bed until it reached the swing doors at the end of the ward and she wasn't allowed to go any further. Christophe stood at the door and watched.

Then he turned back into the room.

'They are taking her to a laboratory,' he told Fi. 'To do something called an angiography. She has a blockage in an artery in her heart and it has caused a heart attack and is now making her very unwell. If they can't open the artery and let the blood flow again, she will die.'

His voice broke on the word and Christophe squeezed his eyes shut to stave off tears. He felt Fiona coming close to him. Touching his arm but then, a little tentatively maybe, she lifted her arms to offer him a hug. Or maybe she was responding to him moving closer? Had he initiated this gesture of comfort?

'They're doing everything they can,' she said softly, so close to his ear that he could feel the puff of her breath. 'Don't lose hope.'

Christophe swallowed around the lump in his throat. The softness and warmth of Fiona's body offered an unexpectedly powerful solace but something told him not to sink into it too far. To step back a moment later before it became something it wasn't intended to be.

'I don't know how long this will take,' he warned. 'If they can't open the arteries with the... I've forgotten the word – the little metal cages?'

Fi shook her head. She didn't know.

'Well, if they don't work, they will have to do surgery. Open her chest and operate directly on her heart to do a bypass, but even then...' He swallowed hard. 'They seem to think she has a good chance to survive.'

Fi nodded this time. 'I couldn't understand what they were saying but I could *feel* that.'

Her smile was so hopeful, the expression in her eyes so sympathetic, that Christophe decided it didn't matter that she might be here under false pretences. He was very glad that she *was* here.

* * *

Waiting was never easy.

Waiting for news that could potentially be devastating for a family she was not connected to in any meaningful way felt awkward.

The windows of this side of the cardiology ward looked down on some of the parking areas outside the hospital, and Fi scanned the distinctive shapes of the pine trees that looked like umbrellas until she found where Christophe had parked his car.

'Would Heidi like to go for a walk, do you think?' she asked, turning back from the window to where Christophe was sitting on a chair beside his mother, holding tightly to her hand.

He looked so disconcerted Fi kicked herself mentally. It made her feel like giving him another hug by way of apology. 'I can take her,' she added swiftly. 'You need to stay here with your mum.'

Already, it felt like the tension in this small room had eased a fraction.

'She'd love that,' Christophe said. 'Her harness and lead are in the back of the car.' He pulled out his keys. 'Don't go too far, though. I don't want you to get lost.'

'I've got a map of the entire world on my phone,' Fi said. 'I won't get lost.' She smiled. 'I'm sure Heidi would find her way back to you from wherever she was, anyway. I would only need to follow her.'

Heidi was, indeed, delighted at being let out of the car. When Fi opened the map on her phone she found it was only a ten-minute walk to the beach. Then she did a search and discovered a dog-friendly section of the coast that was half an hour's walk away. Finding that Heidi was very well-mannered on her leash, it was a pleasure to walk through a park with a children's play-ground at the end, down some narrow one-way streets and onto the wide footpath that stretched along the coast. She stood for a moment to breathe in the sea air and admire the view of a very calm Mediterranean Sea with only tiny waves lapping the pebbles of the beach and several small boats moored near a breakwater of massive flat blocks of stone.

She felt guilty being a tourist, however. Should she even be here supporting a family that wasn't her own when the Gilchrists were dealing with the fallout from their own crisis?

Was this another possible case of jumping from a frying pan into a fire, in fact?

Had Maria Brabant believed her son when he'd told her that Fi wasn't his girlfriend and they were not on some romantic picnic in the forest? The way she'd hugged her at the hospital had felt more like a welcome into Christophe's family and, for just a heartbeat, it had also felt like that moment when Ellie had found her in the olive grove with the donkeys.

As if she'd found what she had been missing for what felt like forever.

Family.

And home.

But was that wishful thinking on her part? Was it a form of justification for what she'd been doing for too many years – running away from the difficult things in life instead of trying to deal with them?

She'd given up on her university degree.

She'd put more and more distance between herself and her family.

She'd gone to help Christophe with the donkeys today to escape the escalating tension in her own family, but she hadn't even stayed in that hospital room with him when the whole reason for coming here had been to support him with his own family crisis.

Heidi was sitting quietly beside Fi as she stood there. The dog's head was at the perfect height to rest her hand on the silky hair and scratch behind her ears. Fi glanced down to find Heidi looking up at her and, when eye contact was made, the dog's impressive plume of a tail swept the footpath and her flattened ears and narrowed eyes were an obvious canine smile.

It felt like approval. Maybe Fi didn't need to stand here and grapple with a growing disquiet that she was still running through life like a headless chicken, too afraid to face her demons. Maybe she could take a leaf out of Heidi's book and simply enjoy the moment.

'Come on. Let's see if you want to get your feet wet.'

The beach where dogs were allowed was deserted apart from a small white dog that looked a bit like Pascal at the far end by another rocky breakwater. Heidi didn't want to brave the waves but she was fascinated by the smells to be found amongst the stones and sticks and shells. Fi bent down at a glint of colour to pick up a piece of pale green sea glass, well-worn and dulled by being tumbled amongst pebbles. She turned it over in her hand to find it was an almost perfect heart shape.

And that felt like a sign of approval as well, so she slipped it into her pocket. She pulled her phone out at the same time. She called her mother's number but it went to voicemail so Fi left a message.

'I hope everything's going okay,' she said. 'I'm with Christophe at the moment because his grandmother's in hospital, but I'll call you again as soon as I'm back at the cottage. Probably tomorrow, because it might be quite late by the time I get home.'

She expected to feel a pang of guilt, as she ended the call, because she wasn't close at hand to support her mother, but it didn't happen.

Fi knew she was where she was supposed to be at this precise moment in her life.

Almost...

It was time she went back to being exactly where she was supposed to be.

With Christophe. And his family.

* * *

Flora Romano's procedure was finished and she was back in the ward by the time Fi found her way through the maze of corridors, stairwells and signs in a language she couldn't read. Fortunately a lot of words were close enough to be helpful, like *cardiologie*.

She was also awake, propped up on her pillows, with Maria sitting on one side of the bed and Christophe on the other. Six dark eyes were fixed on Fi as she entered the room and they were all smiling a moment later. Even Nonna.

Especially Nonna?

She took her hand away from where it was being held by Christophe and held it out. Fi could see it shaking. She could hear the waver in Flora's voice as well, but her words were clear.

'Fiona...' she pronounced it just like Christophe did. '*Ciao, mia cara...*'

'She's happy to meet you,' Christophe translated.

Fi could see that. The eyes under the thick, silver waves of her hair were bright and her smile was deepening the crinkles of her entire face. She looked like a woman who smiled often and always with complete sincerity, and it was impossible not to respond to the invitation. Fi couldn't remember a grandmother on either side of her family and this, apparently unconditional, welcome from Nonna Flora made her realise that this was some-thing else she'd missed out on in life. She moved close enough to take Flora's hand and hold it, but that wasn't what happened. Instead, Flora reached up to pat her cheek as she leaned past Christophe, and when Fi saw what looked like tears of joy in the old woman's eyes, she leaned down and kissed the soft skin of her cheek.

'*Ciao*, Nonna...' she murmured.

'Oh...' Flora sighed. '*Bellissimo. Perfetto*, Christophe.'

'She likes you,' Christophe said.

Fi straightened and caught his gaze. She knew that was not an accurate translation but, when her gaze met his, it didn't matter a jot.

He was looking at her – and smiling – as if she *was* as beautiful as Flora clearly thought she was.

As if she was the most beautiful woman in the world.

The only woman in the world he wanted to be with.

And, as if he wanted everyone to know how he felt, he lifted his hand and touched her hair, letting his hand drift down to a soft stroke on her cheek with his fingers that ended with just one of them tracing the line of her jaw. It was an echo of the way his grandmother had welcomed her but so much more intimate, and along with the way he was looking at her it felt absolutely like the caress of a lover.

Fi could feel it in her whole body. A spear of sensation in her belly. A tingle as far as her toes.

She knew this was only a pretence but... *ohh*... imagine if this man *was* actually looking at her as if she was the love of his life. She shouldn't have worried about not being able to play a convincing role of being in love with Christophe Brabant, because, in this instant with that gentle touch on her skin and the far more intense touch of his gaze, it felt ridiculously real.

But there was a safety net of knowing it wasn't real.

And...

Dear Lord... it felt so *good*...

Utterly compelling.

It was touching a place in her heart, or possibly her soul, that she didn't even know she had and she could feel herself falling into that feeling.

Wanting more.

Wanting something she had believed she could never dream of – having someone who wanted her. More than anyone else on earth. For that person to be someone like Christophe Brabant was beyond her wildest imagination and Fi knew she was staring up at him as if she was experiencing some kind of miracle.

Because she was?

Was *this* what it would feel like to be in love and not simply be caught in the riptide of a crush?

It would certainly look like that for anyone who saw them looking at each other like this.

And someone was.

It was the sound that Flora made that broke the moment. Not quite laughter, more a sound of contentment. Fi realised she had been staring at them as intently as she had been gazing at Christophe and, as Flora started speaking with far more animation than she had up to now, Fi could guess that she was telling her daughter exactly what she thought of Christophe's choice for his future wife and the mother of his children.

They were all talking around her and nobody was translating the conversation, but Fi couldn't miss the glances in her direction, including one from Maria that was a mix of curiosity and satisfaction – as if she'd received confirmation that she'd been right all along and that her son, for whatever reason, had been hiding the fact that he was in a serious relationship for the first time since he'd had his heart broken so badly.

She listened to them talking over each other. She watched the smiles and gestures. And Christophe's increasingly embarrassed expression.

'Enough,' he finally said, in English. 'It's rude to be speaking in Italian in front of Fiona.'

'It is,' his mother agreed. 'I'm so sorry. And Mamma...'

'She's telling Nonna she needs to rest,' Christophe whispered to Fi as Maria switched back to Italian. 'That she's going to get something to eat from the cafeteria in the hospital and then come back to stay the night with her.' He joined in the conversation briefly and then nodded. 'We will stay here to keep Nonna company until Mamma comes back, and then she says I have to take you somewhere to eat. Somewhere nicer than the cafeteria.'

He was smiling at her again. With *that* smile. And *that* look. He must have had so much practice to be so good at this, Fi thought. How many women had he had in his life, and his bed, since he'd decided to join the elite 'library' that was readily available to charismatic, gorgeous men? Perhaps he could even fall in – and out – of love as easily as clicking his fingers and be charming enough about moving on to leave those women feeling privileged instead of heartbroken?

Not that his past mattered at all given the way Nonna was also smiling. And nodding, even though her eyes were drifting shut. She looked from Christophe to Fi and back again, and he clearly received an unspoken message because he leaned close to Fi. Close enough that his lips were tickling her ear and his voice was no more than a hum.

'Thank you,' he murmured. 'She thinks you are perfect for me and she is *so* happy...'

13

They had succeeded.

This whole plan had been to make Nonna happy in case these were the last hours of her life.

Christophe had never seen her looking as happy as she was, but just as he was breathing a sigh of relief, it suddenly began to look as if these really *were* going to be her last hours.

As he and Fiona were keeping watch over a sleeping Nonna Flora so that his mother could get something to eat, his grandmother suddenly woke up, groaning and clutching her chest. The trace on the monitor beside her bed was showing a very rapid heartbeat and then an alarm sounded that brought a doctor running.

It wasn't unusual, he told Christophe, for someone to feel chest pain and have some irregular beats after the invasive procedure she'd undergone but they would make sure nothing serious was happening, like one of the stents they had inserted into an artery moving. Doing this involved a cardiac CT scan and an ECG, blood tests and medication. By the time the event was declared nothing to worry about and pain relief had been enough to get Flora peacefully asleep again a couple of hours later, Maria told her son that it was high time he looked after Fiona. And Heidi.

It wasn't only the reminder that his dog had been patiently waiting in the car for too long now that broke his reluctance to leave. While Fi had been quietly present as they waited for tests to be done and the verdict given and had shown no sign of impatience to leave, Christophe knew she had to be tired and hungry. She deserved to be treated a lot better than this and not simply for the support her presence had given him.

'Thank goodness you took Heidi for a walk earlier,' he told her as they walked out to the parking lot. 'You are an angel.'

'I gave her some water and some of her biscuits, too, so she shouldn't be too hungry yet.'

'I'm sure *you* are. We didn't even get to finish our lunch today.'

'It's still in the car, isn't it? That delicious pizza with the mushrooms and the goat's cheese?'

Had that only been a matter of hours ago? It felt far longer. Long enough for his life to have undergone what felt like a significant change. A rollercoaster of fear, potential grief and relief. A reminder of how short life was and how every moment should be treasured.

An even more powerful reminder that family was everything?

And friends were chosen family, weren't they? He needed to let Fiona know how much he appreciated what she'd done for him today, and the best way to start doing that was to provide a delicious meal. He could take her to one of the local restaurants that he knew she would enjoy. Or he could take that pizza home to his mother's apartment and heat it up and it would taste even better than it had when it was cold, but Christophe looked at his watch. 'I promised I would get you home tonight,' he said. 'Will it be too late if we have a meal first?'

Fi shook her head. 'You can't take me home,' she said. 'You're exhausted. It wouldn't be safe to be driving there and back again and I know you don't want to be that far away from your family. *I* don't want you to be that far away.'

She didn't need to remind him how distressing it would be if he was an hour away and received a call to say that time really was running out and his grandmother needed him to be by her side.

'You don't mind staying here?' This was perfect. He could get back to the hospital within minutes if necessary. 'There's plenty of room at my mother's house. You can sleep in my bed.'

Oh... the sudden beat of silence made Christophe aware of the potential misinterpretation. He should add that Nonna's bedroom had two single beds, one of which he could use on the rare occasions he didn't make the drive back to Vence after a visit. He could have excused himself by the fact that it was harder to grasp the nuances of a language that wasn't his from birth, but reassuring her was more important than any explanation or excuse. He thought she was attractive – of course he did, who wouldn't? – but he'd never considered hitting on her. Not for a second!

Okay... maybe he had, for a heartbeat, when he'd first met her, but that had evaporated the instant he'd sensed that aura she had of something dark, like fear. They had become closer by working together but this was nothing more than a friendship developing between himself and his best friend's sister-in-law. A friendship that was now solid enough to have allowed them to pretend it was something more, for the sake of his family, and that meant that he would always be grateful to her. That if she ever needed a friend, he would be there for *her* and that he would always protect her from anything she was afraid of.

'*I* will sleep in my mother's bed,' he added firmly. 'In *her* room. You are absolutely safe with me, Fiona.'

Oddly, the silence still felt the same. Loaded. Full of something that could shatter if you didn't tread very carefully. Not that her tone, when she spoke, gave him any clue as to why that might be.

Just quietly, she said, 'I knew that.'

* * *

Christophe inched his big car into a small parking space that had been hard to find and was, apparently, as close to the apartment as they were likely to get this late in the day.

The streets in this central part of Menton were narrow and steep and Fi's first impression was that of endless stairs. Stairs for pedestrians on the sides of streets that were crammed with tall apartment buildings, and alleyways between the buildings that were simply stone staircases with treads wide enough for a step or two. Heidi knew where she was going and led the way uphill until they reached their destination. The main entrance to the building that led into a beautifully tiled foyer was open but Heidi ignored the staircase to the upper levels and went beneath it to wait beside a dark wooden door that looked rather forbidding.

Inside, the space was anything but. The apartment was small – only two bedrooms, Christophe said, as he flicked on some lights – but it didn't feel either cramped or dark. It was, in fact, one of the most homely spaces Fi had ever stepped into.

The floor reminded her of the *tomettes* that tiled the living areas of La Maisonette, but these were big terracotta squares with a charming quirkiness to levels that almost made the floor look like the slow, subtle waves of a very calm sea. The front door opened straight into a lounge area that had two sofas draped with throws of coloured fabric with the rich colours of Persian rugs. Further in was a small dining table to one side but it was the kitchen space on the other side that dominated this whole apartment. A row of shining copper pans hung above a surprisingly modern-looking cooktop and oven. Shelves were crowded with racks of plates, stacks of bowls and jugs full of cutlery and cooking utensils. There were jars of ingredients neatly lined up along the back of the bench space, baskets full of vegetables, like potatoes and onions and braids of garlic, and a fridge that was big enough to hold supplies for a family of six.

This was the heart of a home that was all about cooking and baking. Feeding people and making them welcome, or a family gathering to spend time together. Fi could imagine huge pots of pasta on the boil and pans of sauce splashing droplets of tomatoey lava. She could actually catch a whiff of oregano and garlic and basil. Or maybe it was the rosemary from their picnic pizza that Christophe was unwrapping on the bench after turning on the oven.

'If you open the doors there' – Christophe gestured towards the end of the L-shaped bench – 'Heidi can go outside. Being at the back on the ground floor is one of the best things about this apartment. Go and see Nonna's garden. She grows every herb we could possibly need. And tomatoes.'

* * *

The small courtyard garden was exactly where Fi needed to be right now.

If it hadn't been so obviously the worst thing she could have even thought of doing, she would have let Christophe drive an hour away from his adored nonna to take her back to Tourrettes-sur-Loup where she could have slipped quietly into the little stone cottage and had the peace of complete solitude to lick what felt like an uncomfortably deep wound.

'You are absolutely safe with me, Fiona.'

Funny how it sounded like an echo of the most haunting thing that had ever been said to her.

'Look at yourself in the mirror, Fiona... Who'd want you...?'

It was her own fault that it had stung so much.

When she'd first met Christophe at Lili's birthday party, being told how safe she was with him would have been precisely what she would have very much wanted to hear. It would have also helped when she'd been wondering if she was brave enough to spend a day alone in the forest with him. He'd told her she was safe then, too – from any *sanglier* they might encounter – but that hadn't felt like this.

If anything, the idea of Christophe physically protecting her nudged her closer to what had happened in that room in the cardiology ward this evening. When she'd found herself buying into what she knew perfectly well was no more than a fantasy. She'd offered to pretend to be Christophe's lover, that was all.

The last thing she'd expected to happen was that the idea could plant tendrils that might prove hard to control. That they might even start to wind themselves around discarded thoughts somewhere in the back of her mind. Around her heart, even. That their movement created seductive whispers that could make her want to believe that fantasy could be real.

That dreams could come true.

Christophe had said it so well, when they'd been talking about her father on the way to the forest, and he'd said that some-thing traumatic could damage your life. That it could steal what makes you the person you want to be.

Good grief... Had that been only this morning?

Surely that wasn't enough time for it to feel as if she'd taken a huge step forward in her life? Not only that, but to feel as if she might be brave enough to take another step?

That she could actually see the person that had been stolen from herself? The person she desperately wanted to be?

A lover.

A wife.

A mother.

Part of a family that wouldn't exist without her.

In a home with a kitchen like the one behind her with light glinting from the copper pans and, already, an aroma of hot food that had persuaded Heidi to go back inside. Fi wasn't quite ready to follow her. She needed just another moment or two, hidden in the darkness out here in a small garden that was fragrant with delicious herbs.

* * *

What was she doing?

Oddio... was she crying?

She hadn't seen him come out of the kitchen to tell her that her dinner was ready. The way she was standing so still in the dark, with her head bowed and her hands covering her face, certainly made it look as if she was deeply upset about something.

Christophe didn't hesitate to go towards her and he wasn't thinking of anything other than offering comfort when he put his arm around her shoulders.

'What is it, *amore*?' he asked. 'What is wrong?'

Her gaze was startled as she looked up. The light from behind him caught her eyes and it reminded him of when he'd seen them lit up by a shaft of sunlight filtered through the shifting mass of leaves above them in the forest. He'd noticed the flecks of gold in her hair then, but he hadn't registered that they were in the depths of her eyes as well. They weren't simply brown, they were an intriguing shade that made him think of burnt caramel.

'Nothing's wrong,' Fi said. 'I was smelling the basil. See?' She opened her hands to show him the sprig of green leaves, crushed a little between her palms. She turned beneath his arm at the same time, which made it an invitation for him to dip his head and inhale the peppery, slightly minty perfume of the herb.

Without thinking, he put his hand beneath hers to bring the leaves closer to his nose. He took a deep breath and, as he lifted his head, he let it out in an appreciative sigh that was almost a hum.

He was also looking straight into Fiona's eyes.

And she was looking back. And it felt... different.

So different to that first time they'd met and she'd barely been able to let her gaze touch his for the space of time it took a heart to beat once.

He couldn't sense the fear that he'd been aware of then, either.

There was something else there.

Something utterly compelling.

And, in that moment, Christophe knew he hadn't been honest with himself. He *was* attracted to Fiona Gilchrist and it was an attraction with a power he'd never experienced before. The only sensation he could compare it to was how he'd felt when he'd been so insanely in love with Marcella – when he'd been a teenage male with raging hormones and no life experience whatsoever.

That wasn't who he was now. He'd had more experience in the realm of romance and sex than he'd ever expected or, to be honest, had really wanted.

Perhaps he'd been aware of that undercurrent of power when

he'd first laid eyes on this woman, and maybe he'd not only sensed the fear in her but had felt an echo of it within himself and had been more than happy to back off.

To keep them both safe...

And that's exactly he should be doing again, right now, but somehow the message wasn't getting from his brain to the rest of his body. Even the tiny muscles around his eyes were refusing to move and this intimate, almost physical, feeling of their gazes touching was getting completely out of control.

A spell was being cast and, for the life of him, Christophe couldn't summon the desire to break it.

* * *

Kiss me...

It was the only thought in Fi's head and it felt like every cell in her body was contributing to the force of it.

That she actually wanted this so much took her completely by surprise. She'd never wanted any kind of sexual touch from any man since that night. She had nightmares about it. She'd flinch if someone got too close to her in a shop or brushed past in a crowd.

But this was different.

New.

And, okay, maybe it was simply part of the fantasy she'd allowed herself to drift into the edges of, but...

...but what if that was making the difference?

What if that miracle, of feeling what it might be like to fall in love with someone, had given her the clarity to see the person she wanted to be? That the first step towards believing that it might actually be possible could be finding out whether she could get past that fear of being touched?

Maybe that was why this felt important enough to be feeling as if she might die if Christophe didn't kiss her?

Because the dream would die?

The path that she'd taken the first huge step on today would vanish from sight and render it impossible to take another step.

He was still holding her gaze and it felt as if he was looking right into her soul. Or hearing her thoughts, anyway, because his gaze finally shifted from her eyes to her lips. And then it lifted again, for just the tiniest fraction of time.

Enough time for Fi's body to try sending another message.

Yes…

And then, oh… *God…* it was happening. Fi closed her eyes as she felt Christophe's lips on hers.

Moving over her lips like the softest imaginable caress. Her lips were moving too. Responding to the infinitely small changes in pressure and direction. Feeling the warmth of his mouth – the *taste* of him – and it was… it was the most delicious thing she could have ever imagined.

Her mouth was open beneath his. She expected the touch of his tongue. She *wanted* it.

Until it happened.

Just the tip of his tongue against her lip. Touching the tip of *her* tongue.

She still wanted it but something in her brain and then her body decided differently and she could feel herself stiffening. Bracing herself.

Freezing.

Noo… Fi didn't want this to stop but that was happening.

Just as softly as the kiss had started, it was finishing. Christophe was looking at her again, but if he was disappointed by that kiss she couldn't see it in his eyes. He was looking at her like he had by Nonna's bedside – as if she was the most beautiful woman in the world – and it wasn't for the benefit of anyone who might be watching them, so what did *that* mean?

He must have felt the way she'd frozen, but she couldn't see that in his face either. There was a hint of a smile on the lips she could still feel the imprint of on her own. As if this was no big deal. Because, for him, a kiss probably wasn't a big deal?

'Come inside, *amore*,' Christophe said. 'Dinner's ready.'

* * *

Much later, Christophe opened the door in the kitchen again and let Heidi out into the garden.

'Be very quiet,' he whispered. 'We don't want to wake up Fiona.'

He was assuming she was asleep, given that it was 3 a.m., but the escape into much-needed rest was so elusive for him that he'd got up to get another glass of wine in the hope that it might work some magic and slow a spiral of thoughts that was so relentless it was making him feel dizzy.

Sick, even.

If he hadn't been so emotionally exhausted after those hours at the hospital with Nonna yesterday, he would never have been able to step back far enough to pretend that nothing had changed between himself and Fiona with that kiss. It was one of the hardest things he'd ever done, but something told him that, if she could see how shocked he was, it would only make it worse. Pushing closer could hurt her.

And hurting her was the very last thing Christophe wanted to do.

Because he now knew, instinctively, that someone else had already done that to her. Someone had hurt her physically. Emotionally. *Sexually...*

He'd seen the scars that first day they'd met – that hint of darkness in her eyes that told him she knew about fear. And pain. But it was that kiss that had let him feel how big that darkness was. And what it was that she was so afraid of.

He could actually *taste* it in the moment she froze when his tongue touched hers.

That, as much as the concern he had for Nonna, was what was keeping him awake and making him feel heartsick.

It had been like the flip of a coin with a perfect kiss on one side and a *cauchemar* on the other. It had, in fact, been a kiss like nothing Christophe had ever experienced before, and perhaps that was partly due to what he hadn't known.

He'd earned Fiona's trust – enough for her not to have run from his touch. If only he'd known how huge that had been for her. If he hadn't let the fire of an unexpectedly powerful desire flicker into that kiss to see if she would like it to go further – as much as he did.

And she had. For just the tiniest fragment of time, as his tongue met hers, he'd sensed a passion that was coiled – as if it had been waiting for a chance to be unleashed. It had thrown an astonishing amount of spice into the taste of that kiss until it was instantly obliterated by the bitterness of fear.

This was his fault.

It could have been the perfect kiss if only he'd stopped it in time. He'd known he was on the cliff edge of losing all the trust he had earned from this extraordinary woman, and the only way he could think of trying to fix it was to pretend he hadn't noticed her reaction.

That nothing had changed.

And now he was remembering other moments with her. Tiny hesitations that, in retrospect, were there because she'd needed courage to choose to be in his company. Like the shy way she'd greeted him when they were introduced and when he'd asked her to help with the donkeys. He remembered the first smile she'd given him that had reached all the way to her eyes, and hearing her laugh for the first time. The way she'd looked at him yesterday, as if she really was as madly in love with him as he wanted his nonna to believe.

He'd felt a depth of emotion like that in the first touch of their lips last night and, if there was any truth in that impression, it would be heartbreaking, because Christophe could never give her that kind of love. He couldn't give it to any woman and he would never give them reason to believe that it was possible, so that no one would get hurt.

He wondered now if he'd simply imagined a depth that wasn't actually there, because Fiona seemed to have been as happy as he was to brush the kiss aside and simply ignore the fact that it had happened.

Trust was very like love, wasn't it? That was more likely to have been what he'd seen in Fiona's eyes and felt from her lips.

Like love, if trust was broken badly enough, you could only sweep up the pieces and either try to stick them together again eventually or take the easier option and throw them away and get on with your life.

Christophe had thrown away the pieces of a lifelong love. He had made a considered decision not to keep them or to try to stick them back together, only to have it nearly destroy his life all over again.

But what if Fiona had kept the pieces of her broken trust? It he could help *her* stick those pieces back together, it could change the rest of her life.

She deserved to believe in trust again. And in love.

To find someone who would love her the way she deserved to be loved.

It was his fault the kiss had been ruined, but perhaps that was actually a good thing. Because now he knew.

He didn't know whether he was the first man to have earned this level of trust from Fiona.

He did know how fragile it was, however.

It had cracks in it but he also knew, beyond a shadow of doubt, that he was going to do his best to make sure he didn't break it completely.

She *could* still trust him.

14

Fi woke to the aroma of freshly brewed coffee the next morning.

She dressed in the jeans and top she'd thrown into her bag yesterday and went into the apartment's living area.

Heidi was by her side in an instant, her tail waving. Christophe's smile was just as welcoming but, my goodness, he looked as if he hadn't slept at all. He was also wearing jeans, with sneakers and a black tee shirt, but his hair was rumpled and the lines around his eyes were far deeper than usual.

He looked absolutely gorgeous and that disconcerting flash of sensation that happened deep in her belly reminded Fi all too clearly of what it had been like to have Christophe looking at her as if he was her lover. And of what had happened in the garden last night.

That... *kiss*...

She could feel colour beginning to creep into her cheeks as she had to fight the urge to touch her lips with a fingertip, as she'd done when she'd been alone in her bed, as if she wanted to do more than remember that kiss. As if she wanted to *feel* it again.

The start of it, anyway. Not the end. That had kept her awake for too long, afraid of the nightmares that could well be circling, like vultures just waiting for the opportunity to swoop. Finally, when she couldn't fight her exhaustion any longer, she'd understood what that look that Christophe had given her straight after that kiss was all about.

He knew she'd been afraid.

He'd known exactly how to back off.

How to protect her.

Had she slept so surprisingly well because she still felt safe?

Fi hid her red cheeks by leaning down to cuddle Heidi, letting her hair screen her face. It gave her a chance to take a breath as well and try and stop the endless questions that had been popping into her head from the moment she'd woken up.

Would it be awkward between them this morning?

Had it ruined the bond that had been forming?

Were they going to talk about it?

Or were they going to keep pretending that that kiss had not happened, like they had during dinner last night?

That last option felt like the best one and it seemed like Christophe had already chosen to tick that box from any list he might have devised.

'Coffee?' he offered, his tone cheerful. 'I'm onto my second already.'

'Please. It smells wonderful.'

'I have pastries too.' He waved at paper bags on the dining table. 'And bread. I took Heidi for an early walk and we went past a boulangerie that is also a patisserie, so I got some favourite treats to take in for Mamma and Nonna. Sweet things, like aragostine and cannoli.'

'I only need coffee,' Fi said. 'With milk, please.' She took the mug he handed her and took a sip. 'What is Nonna's favourite treat?' she asked.

'A chocolate and hazelnut aragostine. But she also loves a cannolo siciliani.'

'I don't know what either of those things are. They sound very Italian.'

'They are. But so is Menton. You can walk along the coast to the Italian border from here in about thirty minutes. Menton is a perfect blend of France and Italy.' Christophe's smile was cheeky. 'Like me.'

Aye... this was how it was going to be.

And, if Fi had been given the choice of exactly how she *wanted* it to be between them now, this would be it.

Playful – which implied both understanding of the significance and a promise of trust. Nothing bad was going to happen. Perhaps something even better was waiting in the wings.

The reset button had been pushed but the growing friendship had a totally new dimension. Yesterday, Fi had learned just how much Christophe loved his family as she'd shared the fear he'd faced of losing his grandmother. She knew that he had learned she had a fear of intimacy. That was enough to have deepened their friendship, but there was so much more to it than that.

The notes of that kiss were still hanging in the air, like dust motes caught in a sunbeam. Maybe they were the opening notes of a symphony that might have ended in a discordant jangle, but they'd been enough, in those first seconds, to cast a spell strong enough to stop time.

Something magic.

Fi might never hear – or feel – them again but she was never going to forget them.

They were the sound of hope. That, one day, Fi would be able to get past the walls she had built around herself.

That she would be able to stop running because she would find the courage to face what was hiding behind those walls.

That the path was still there and she hadn't lost the first big step she had taken.

So it was perfect that Christophe was still smiling at her as if he, too, was aware of the change but was not going to let it break anything. Making a joke was all the reassurance she needed that nothing had been broken. That she was still safe with him, although it felt like a completely different kind of safety now.

It was enough to make her laugh but she still needed to hide her face again – this time, by peeping into the bags.

'The long tubes are cannoli, which is a fried pastry that is stuffed with sweet ricotta cheese and flavours like pistachio or lemon. The ones that look like lobsters' tails are aragostine – that is a baked pastry filled with cream.' He shook his head. 'I'm quite sure that Nonna's cardiologist will not be happy with her eating them but... just a taste wouldn't hurt, would it? They are her favourites.' He shrugged. 'And I want to make her happy because I love her.'

* * *

Seeing Christophe was quite clearly more than enough to make Flora Romano happy.

Propped up against her pillows, she was beaming as she held out her arms to enfold her grandson as he sat on the edge of her bed. Then it was Fi who had to be hugged, by both Flora and Maria, as the babble of Italian words flowed around her.

When the smile suddenly vanished from Flora's face, Christophe patted her hand and said something more.

'She's disappointed that I'm going to take you home after this visit,' he explained. 'But I've said that you'll come back soon.'

'You must,' Maria put in. 'You haven't seen anything of our lovely city yet, have you?'

'Not yet,' Fi agreed. 'But what I saw this morning on the way here is so beautiful. The colours of the buildings are gorgeous. All the shades of pink and orange and yellow, like a pastel rainbow – I've never seen anything like it.'

Maria nodded. 'We are famous for the beautiful colours of our old buildings. And lemons, of course. You've missed our festival of lemons this year but you'll have to come back next year. In February.'

Fi just smiled and nodded. Who knew where in the world she would be by the beginning of next year?

'We are the world capital for lemons,' Christophe added. 'You can forget California or India. There's a legend that when Eve fled from the Garden of Eden, she took a lemon with her and she planted it here, in Menton. Or threw it away, because Adam was afraid of God's wrath. Whatever...' His smile matched his shrug. 'Our *Fête du Citron* is famous. We will have to go to the next one.'

'I'd love to,' Fi said. It didn't matter if this was still part of the pretence for Nonna. It was true. She *would* love to go to that festival.

Flora's eyes lit up as she saw what was inside the paper bags and she spoke with great animation to Maria, who shook her head but then smiled fondly at her mother.

'Mamma wants coffee to go with her cake,' Maria translated for Fi. 'Coffee for all of us. Could you come with me to the cafeteria and help me carry everything?' She lowered her voice. 'I think Christophe would like a moment alone with his nonna.'

'Of course.'

Fi was happy to follow Maria through the hospital corridors, bustling with staff members and visitors at this time of day having to dodge trolleys and wheelchairs and beds. There was a queue in the café as well, and it was when they were standing still, side by side, that Maria caught Fi's gaze.

'Christophe has made his nonna so happy,' she said. 'We are blessed that you came with him.'

'He loves his nonna.' Fi had to swallow a sudden lump in her throat. 'And you.'

Maria's gaze was warm but something in her face changed in a very subtle way that made that lump in Fi's throat feel sharper.

'He was such a sad little boy after his papa died. He had no brothers or sisters – only our adored little dog, Biscotti. He was just as sad when Biscotti got too old and *he* died.'

Fi's heart broke for a young Christophe who'd had to say goodbye to a beloved companion. 'How old was he then?'

'About fifteen. Too old to let anyone see how sad he was but... a mother knows, you know?' Maria's gaze was unwavering. 'He tried to tell me that it is not something special between you, but...'

Had Christophe's mother learned to do that eloquent shrug from her French husband or was it an ability that Italians were also born with? She didn't need to say anything else. As far as she was concerned, the truth of that statement had been roundly dismissed. And a mother knew.

Fi should have been getting more used to that curl of sensation that was like a fuse being lit in her body and sending sparks in all directions, but she wasn't. It took her completely by surprise every time. Even more so, this time. Because it was getting stronger?

Could Christophe's mother see something that neither she nor Christophe was consciously aware of? Fi thought about that as Maria gave the order for their coffees. She collected a ticket and they moved to one side to wait.

'We thought it would never happen,' Maria said quietly. 'Me and my mamma. We thought that his heart had been so badly broken by Marcella that he would never find the woman he could trust enough to finally get his dream of a big family.'

A big family? Babies? The reminder of his love for children and babies was enough to douse any internal sparks. Fi was not going to be creating a big family with Christophe Brabant. Or anyone else, for that matter. It might be a dream of her own to become a mother but... she'd had that chance already, hadn't she? And she'd destroyed it.

She wanted to change the subject. But she was also curious.

'Marcella? Is she the girl he nearly married when he was eighteen?'

'*Sì... Pfft!*' There was disgust in that sound. 'Until she met someone older with a job and a better car and a lot more money. Then Christophe was gone.' She clicked her fingers. 'Just like that. He thought his life was over. We thought he would never be happy again.'

'Ohh...' Fi's breath came out in a sympathetic sigh. 'He must have loved Marcella very much.'

'He made a bad choice,' Maria said. 'So bad, I think he believed that he could never trust himself to make a better choice. Or perhaps he decided he would never repeat the disaster of letting himself fall in love. The girls came along again but never for long. His nonna would tell him he needed to hurry up and find a wife, but he would always say there was plenty of time. Maybe one day...'

Maria's words faded and she caught Fi's gaze again.

'I hope this is one day,' she said softly. 'But I think he's still afraid. Deep down, where nobody is allowed to see. Be patient with him, *cara*, won't you?'

Fi smiled. She nodded. She didn't want Maria to know that she'd got this one wrong. That if anything had been going to happen between her and Christophe it would have to be him who would need the patience. Maria nodded back and then hugged her – an embrace that was swift but sincere. It was warm and tight and motherly but so incredibly soft at the same time.

Hugs from her own mother had never felt like this, but Jeannie Gilchrist was a tough, wiry Scotswoman. Jeannie was self-disciplined and kept her life as tidy as her garden and her kitchen. She kept secrets. She loved her children with all her heart but there had always been rules to follow. Standards to be met.

There was nothing wiry about Maria Brabant and her kitchen was ample evidence of her enjoyment of life, and food. She adored her son and she seemed to truly believe that Fi was the person he should be spending the rest of his life with. If secrets needed to be shared or rules broken to achieve that, it was no problem.

Their number was called and they went to pick up the paper coffee cups. And then they were back in the busy corridors with the noise of people and crying babies and announcements happening over the overhead paging system, so the private conversation was over.

Enough had been said already, however.

More than enough to give Fi something to think about.

She wasn't the only one hiding behind walls, was she?

In the end, Maria and Flora were going to be disappointed that Christophe hadn't found his bride and the mother of the big family he dreamed of, but... maybe she could help him rebuild the trust he'd lost in women and that could open up the possibility of finding the one who would be that wife and mother.

Friends were the people who could help build that kind of confidence. Perhaps Julien hadn't been able to persuade Christophe that he could get past his walls, but maybe she could – because she was a woman?

And he trusted her, Fi was sure of that.

As sure as she was that nothing was broken between herself and Christophe in the wake of that kiss. That whatever it was that made it so easy to be in each other's company was, in fact, stronger than ever.

* * *

Nonna had no more than a tiny bite of each of the treats that Christophe had brought.

Fi ate one of lobster-tail pastries and it was delicious. Maria ate a cannolo but then folded the tops of the bags and put them out of sight in the bedside cabinet.

'She's hiding them,' Christophe whispered to Fi. 'Until after the doctor has been for his ward round.' He raised his voice. 'Let me know everything the doctor says after the tests this morning, Mamma. And when Nonna will be allowed home. I will come and stay for the first night.'

'You could talk to the doctor yourself later today.'

'I need to take Fiona home. I need to go into work and make sure there are arrangements in place for me to take some more time off.'

'Right now? Can't you take a little time and show her Menton? Then you can talk to the doctor yourself and you'll know how much time you need to arrange for.'

Christophe glanced at Fi. 'I would like to talk to the doctors later. Are you in a hurry to get back?'

Fi knew she should be. She couldn't avoid the minefield of what was going to happen when her father was released from hospital, and that could be happening today for all she knew. If nothing else, coming here with Christophe had been a reminder of how important family was, and she'd failed to support her own family for too long now.

But Maria and Flora had made her feel like an honorary member of *their* family and she'd felt as if she belonged. Nonna was adorable and Maria had treated her like an equal. A friend. The hope that she would genuinely become a part of the family had been totally sincere and Fi admired how open Maria had been with her. Christophe was lucky that he hadn't grown up in a family that kept things hidden or ran away from them. The love in this small family was unconditional. There was nothing that could be said or done that could dent it.

Christophe had asked for Fi's support to help his family and she was very glad she'd provided it. They had made Nonna happy and that... well, that had made Christophe happy and that kind of joy was contagious.

Could she be selfish now? For just a few hours? She really did want to see more of the pretty old part of this city.

And... aye... she wanted to spend more time in Christophe's company and see if her instinct might be based on something real.

That feeling that she had something she could give him – as his friend. A gift that nobody else would be able to provide or even know how to find.

A gift that you couldn't possibly purchase, not only because it couldn't be wrapped up but because it would be beyond priceless.

15

They collected Heidi, parked near the old port and walked through a green space dotted with tall palm trees. The sun was shining against a clear blue sky, the smell of salt flavoured the air and it was easy to imagine that people coming towards them were seeing a couple out walking their dog.

It didn't feel like they were a couple but it didn't feel as if they were simply friends, either.

It felt different.

New.

Like nothing Fi had ever experienced before. She thought about it for a minute or two and then decided that she liked it. It felt safe. Real. A solid enough base to let that feeling of being able to help Christophe stay there and put down some roots.

They were heading for what looked like a miniature castle with tiny turrets on each corner of the roof.

'Cute,' Fi said. 'What is it?'

'It's a museum now, for the artwork of Jean Cocteau, but it was originally a military fort built for the defence of Menton from the Barbary pirates in the seventeenth century.'

'Really?' Fi blinked. 'Pirates attacked cities then and not just other boats?'

'They were the Barbarians,' Christophe said. 'They captured and enslaved about a million people. Both the sea and the coastlands of this part of the Mediterranean were dangerous places in those days. It's a complex history. I'll tell you more about it one day.' He quirked an eyebrow in her direction. 'I think there are happier things to see and talk about today.'

'Okay.'

One day...

Fi liked that as much as she liked how it felt to be in Christophe's company. It made it feel as if this was the start of something big enough that she didn't even need to think about its ending yet. The kind of feeling you got from loving the first page of a book or the initial notes of a song – it wasn't quite a promise but it held the same seduction as hope.

They crossed a road just past the fort and went onto a walkway with gardens on either side, Heidi walking between them. This was the closest Fi had been to the old apartment blocks that were painted such pretty shades of ochre – a dark terracotta building with tall, pale blue shutters on its windows, a dark gold with sage green shutters and then a pale orange. Some had balconies with wrought-iron balustrades, some had a scramble of vines climbing their walls and others had bright flowers in window boxes.

Oban was also a coastal town with wonderful old buildings just across the road from the sea, but it didn't have these colours. This softness. Even the ocean was more likely to be a moody grey than this extraordinary deep blue with a twist of turquoise. This place was enchanting. It felt summery and light-hearted and... happy. Fi was falling in love with Menton and her breath came out in a contented sigh before she broke the silence.

'You were born here, yes?'

'Yes.' Christophe sounded surprised. 'How did you know that?'

'Ellie told me. She said you were born here but you moved to Vence and that was how you met Julien and became such good friends.'

Christophe nodded. 'I lived here until I was about eight years old and then my father got sick and died quite suddenly. My mother was offered a job as a housekeeper in Vence and it came with a small apartment and she was allowed to bring me, so that's where we went. I met Julien on the first day of school. I think he knew how scared I was, and he was standing beside me when we went to lunch and he said that I could sit with him. He was my first friend and he's the brother I never had.'

'When did your mother come back here?'

'When I went to university in England for a year before I started my training as a vet. Nonna wanted her to go down south to where she'd been born but, in the end, she moved to Menton to be with Mamma. Maybe she knew that it made Mamma happier to be living again in a place that had memories of my father for her.'

'So she's never met anyone else?'

'I think she's chosen not to ever look for anyone else. I think that sometimes love is so big it cannot be replaced and it's better to live with happy memories than to live with something... less? Is that the best word?'

'It's a good word. Something less means that you've taken something away. Good when it's something bad but not if it's something that makes you happy.'

They were walking past a marina now that was crowded with all shapes and sizes of boats, from yachts with their tall masts, sleek modern catamarans built for speed, and the charm of vintage wooden boats. Fi could see the curve of a white sandy beach further ahead against the backdrop of craggy hills.

'I think it was the same for my mother,' Fi said. 'But she would never have admitted that. It would have been too shameful.'

Heidi took advantage of Christophe's steps slowing to sniff at the base of a palm tree. The look Fi was receiving from Christophe was almost bewildered.

'The ability to love is the greatest gift people have,' he said. 'It's what makes life worth living. It should never be something to be ashamed of.'

Fi stood still. 'But what if the person you love is not worthy of being loved?'

Christophe was frowning as he caught her gaze but then his whole face seemed to soften. 'Everyone is worthy of being loved,' he said quietly.

His eyes were saying even more.

That *she* was worthy of being loved?

She dragged her gaze away before it could form anything more than a wisp of sensation, because this was unsettling. Her heart had skipped a beat and it was hard to catch her next breath. She tried to shake it off by starting to walk again.

'What about bad people?' she countered. 'Like murderers?'

'Nobody is born bad,' Christophe said. 'It could be that they end up doing bad things because they grew up without the love they needed. They simply had... less.'

That silenced her. The compassion of this man made him fit right in with the softness of the colours and joyful vibe of this small city. So did the man playing classic French music on a piano accordion near the market as they entered the commercial centre of the old town a short time later.

Christophe led her down narrow, busy streets with shops that looked more Italian than French, with crammed window displays of pasta and salami and... lemons! The glow of yellow shone from every direction, in the shops and market stalls. There were tall, golden bottles of limoncello, lemon-shaped soap and scented candles, tea-towels and aprons printed with lemons, baskets and boxes overflowing with the actual fruit in front of greengrocers, and it had to be lemon-flavoured gelato filling the giant fibreglass cone outside the door of the ice cream shop.

Both Fi and Heidi were staying close to Christophe as he led the way. They wove through the crowds and then he took them under archways that led uphill, through shady tunnels and up *so* many stairs. They went through cobbled squares with leafy trees and ancient fountains and, as they walked, Christophe told her what it had been like to live here and about the famous *Fête du Citron* that had been held every February for coming up to a hundred years.

'Queen Victoria herself came once,' Christophe said proudly. 'But that was a long time before the parade became all about the lemons and oranges. It was my favourite thing when I was little – maybe because I remember being on my father's shoulders so I could see everything above the crowds of people. The last one I went to was the year he died. Tintin was the hero of the show that year. My papa used to read the Tintin books with me and we thought it was very funny that our little dog, Biscotti, looked just like Snowy.'

Ohh... Fi could almost see him as a child. How adorable would he have been with those fine features and big brown eyes and curly hair and that *smile*...? How devastated and lost must he have been trying to understand that his papa would never read him stories again or take him to the lemon festival? She wanted to reach back through time and give that little Christophe a hug.

Maybe he could feel the direction of her thoughts as he stopped to let Heidi have a long drink from a pool beneath the trickling water that was coming from the mouth of a bull's head carved out of stone.

'I haven't been to another *Fête du Citron* since then,' he added quietly. 'Not even when Julien asked me because he was taking Theo this year by himself – Ellie thought it was too cold to take Bonnie when she was only a couple of weeks old. But when Mamma talked about it this morning, I meant what I said. We will go next year, if you are still here.'

'And I meant what I said.' She knew he would hear the empathy beneath her words. And at least some understanding of what it was like to have a father ripped from your life at such a young age, even if her father had chosen to leave her and her grief had been tainted with shame. 'I'd love to go. If I'm still here.'

'Do you think you'll want to go back to Scotland?'

Fi shook her head. 'I drove all the way here,' she told him. 'By myself. It took days and days and some of it was scary, especially driving into the train and staying in your car to watch the land disappear as you go deeper and deeper under the sea.' She pulled in a new breath. 'But it only takes about thirty minutes and then you're coming out the other side, and from the moment I realised I was in France it felt like everything was new. Different. And deep down I thought that maybe this could be a new life for me. That *I* could be different.' She closed her eyes for a moment. 'I *never* want to go back to Scotland. Not to live.'

She opened her eyes to find Christophe's gaze resting on her face but it felt as if they were resting on her soul. As if he could see the person she might dream of being in this new life and all the shiny promises of what it might deliver.

Like feeling worthy of being loved.

Of kisses that never ended.

Feeling *safe*...

It could never happen, not with this man, anyway. Maybe that was why there was a poignant note to his smile as he responded to the tug Heidi gave on the lead and turned away.

Just for that tiny moment, however, Fi had imagined what it would be like to be walking into exactly that future, hand in hand with Christophe Brabant and...

...and it squeezed her heart so hard that it hurt.

* * *

They set off downhill in a slightly subdued silence. Fi was ready to suggest it was time to stop their tour and find somewhere to have a bite to eat, despite knowing that the plan was to drive her back to La Maisonette after lunch, so this time with Christophe would be over. Perhaps he didn't want it to be over quite yet, either, because, when they got back to the road beside the sea and it seemed as if they were about to choose where to eat, he turned instead through a row of yellow archways between two restaurants and there was a mountain of stone steps zigzagging their way uphill in front of her.

He didn't miss the beat of consternation on Fi's face.

'This is the way to the basilica of Saint-Michel-Archange,' he told her. 'Menton's not-to-be-missed tourist attraction.' He gave her an encouraging smile and held out his hand. 'It's worth it, I promise.'

It would have been rude to refuse his hand but it was easier than Fi expected to keep holding it as they went uphill again. His grip was firm and strong and confident. Did Heidi feel something like this with the contact she had with Christophe's other hand through her leash? If so, it was no wonder that she followed him so willingly.

He let her go as they reached the top of the zigzag and they stopped to catch their breath. Behind her was a view of the sea and beach, framed by a terracotta-coloured apartment block on one side and a soft orange one on the other. In front, past a square that was a mosaic of black and white tiles and up yet another set of stairs, was a church with statues set into the walls and even on the roofline and a tall bell tower. To her left was another impressive building with towers and statues and pillars, and this was the basilica.

'I can wait here, if you want to go inside,' Christophe said. 'I can't take Heidi inside but the artwork in the chapels is amazing.'

Fi didn't want to move yet.

'Maybe next time,' she found herself saying.

As if she knew there would be a next time. Or as if she *wanted* there to be a next time. It was like his 'one day' in that it held both an invitation and a promise.

Christophe turned his head to meet her gaze and Fi found herself holding her breath. She didn't let it out until after he'd given a single nod and she caught a glimpse of a smile.

'Next time,' he echoed.

* * *

They sat in the sun to eat a margherita pizza, with tangy crushed tomatoes, melty mozzarella cheese and pops of fresh basil, drinking a Provençal rosé that had been poured into wine glasses filled with ice cubes.

Heidi was lying beside them but she took up a lot of the space between their table and the next and, when a young couple went to sit there, their small child screamed with fright when he saw the enormous dog lifting her head to look at him. He burst into tears and clung to his mother's legs as Christophe apologised and made Heidi move closer to his chair.

'It's no problem,' the mother said. Her French had a Spanish accent. 'He needs to get past his fear of dogs.' She sat down and let her son climb onto her knee. He stopped crying but he was clinging to his mother's neck, his face buried against her chest as she read the menu over his head and discussed it with her partner.

Christophe shared a glance with Fi as they both reached for another slice of the delicious pizza.

'It's common for small children to be afraid of dogs, isn't it? Especially large ones.'

'And yet they can be more gentle than small ones. I got bitten by a little terrier when I was young and I can still remember being scared of walking past where it lived.' She was smiling, 'Didn't stop me falling in love with an Irish wolfhound I met a year or two later, though.'

She took a big bite off the pointy end of her pizza slice and Christophe watched her face as it softened into lines of pure pleasure. He was still watching as she used the tip of her tongue to catch a drop of tomato sauce on the corner of her mouth, and the unexpected shaft of desire made him shift his gaze swiftly.

Kissing Fiona had not only unlocked a door in his head, it seemed to be swinging ajar without being pushed. Or maybe it wasn't simply the kiss. Perhaps it was the thought that he might be able to help her get past her fear of an intimate touch. It was interesting that she'd managed to get past her fear of dogs after she'd been bitten as a young child – and that it had been gentleness that had been what was needed to get her past that fear.

He could be gentle...

And, *oh là là*, he was realising just how much he would like the chance to demonstrate that skill, but patience was possibly an even more valuable trait. The initiation of anything physical had to be Fiona's decision. *Her* choice.

The waiter was delivering meals to the table next to them. A bowl of pasta, another filled with steaming mussels, a basket of bread and a platter of *frites*. The mother offered one to the little boy, still on her lap, but he wasn't looking. He was staring at Heidi.

Christophe dropped his hand to Heidi's head. Just a touch and then an ear scratch, to tell her that she was behaving very well, just lying there so quietly, right against the legs of his chair. She looked up at him, pulling her ears down and crinkling her eyes and her tail thumped the ground. Christophe looked up swiftly – had this scared the little boy again?

He was still staring at Heidi, his eyes huge and his mouth open. And then he lifted his gaze to Christophe's and the seesaw between fear and curiosity was palpable.

'She's very kind,' he said, in Spanish. 'Would you like to come and say "hullo"?'

The boy shook his head very firmly. He turned to accept the *frite* from his mother and stuffed it into his mouth. Christophe went back to his pizza but, from the corner of his eye, he could see the repeated glances going in Heidi's direction. As he saved a piece of his crust for Heidi, he caught the movement from the next table. The boy had slithered down from his mother's lap and was standing between the tables.

Heidi thumped her tail on the cobbles.

'That means she likes you,' he told the boy. 'Her name's Heidi. What's yours?'

'Arlo.'

'Would you like to pat Heidi? She won't hurt you, I promise.'

For a long moment, Arlo stood completely still. Christophe stroked Heidi's head.

'It's *so* soft,' he said. 'Come and feel it. Just with one finger? Like this...'

Arlo's parents were watching. Fi was watching. It felt like they were all holding their breath, and Arlo took a step closer, stretched out his hand and touched Heidi's head. He pulled away instantly, his head turning to look at his parents to see if they'd seen how brave he'd been. They were smiling. His father picked up his phone.

'Do it again,' he urged. 'I will take a picture for you.'

By the time Christophe and Fi were ready to leave and Heidi was standing up, Arlo was ready to give her a farewell hug, his arms around the neck of the dog who was as tall as he was. His mother looked like she was on the verge of tears.

'*Gracias*,' she said. '*Merci beaucoup, monsieur.*'

'*De rien*,' Christophe responded. 'It was nothing.'

* * *

Fi was quiet until they were on the other side of the road from the restaurant, walking back towards the marina and the fort and the car park beyond, but she had to say something then.

'You love kids, don't you?'

'I do.' He grinned at her. 'I was one myself once.'

'You're very good with them. You'll be a wonderful father one day.'

His smile faded fast enough to let her know she'd said too much. 'No. Not going to happen. I gave up on that idea a long time ago.' He shrugged. 'But I'm happy to enjoy other people's children.' He looked down at Heidi. 'And animals. They're very like children in many ways.'

Fi's heart broke a little for Christophe. How had one woman done this much damage by rejecting his first love? Was it possible that he could get past such a deep-seated fear of commitment?

Perhaps her thoughts were visible on her face and that could explain the sharp glance Christophe gave her.

'Did you know,' he asked, 'that Theo is not Julien's biological son?'

'Erm... *no*.' Fi was shocked. 'But Bonnie is his daughter, isn't she?'

'Yes. It wasn't that he wasn't able to have children, it was because his wife was cheating on him.'

'Oh, my God... Ellie's never said anything about that.' Not that Fi had been around enough to give her the chance.

'No. Ellie, the beautiful soul that she is, considers Julien to be Theo's father in every way that matters, which is entirely true. Just as much as she is his mother. Julien believes that himself, now, but it nearly broke him when he found out. It was not that long ago – when he and Ellie were first together.'

A time when Fi was well hidden in a different town and a career she'd never planned to have and a lonely bedroom above a stables. Cut off from her family. Cut off from life, really, behind those walls she had constructed so solidly.

'I tried to help,' Christophe continued. 'I thought I would be able to because I knew, only too well, what it was like to live through that kind of betrayal, but no...' He shook his head. 'It was even harder than when his wife was killed in the accident and he discovered that she hadn't been alone in that car. She was not only leaving him, she was abandoning her child to run away with her lover.'

'Theo's father?'

'Probably. But who knows with a woman like that?' Christophe's snort was a sound of disgust.

The silence that fell was full of dark things like betrayal and deceit and death.

'But... he did get through it,' Fi said quietly. 'And he found Ellie. They adore each other.'

Christophe nodded slowly. 'Ellie is perfect for him but I was amazed that he had been that brave. That he could trust enough to let that kind of love back into his life.' His breath sounded like a sigh of defeat. 'I don't even want to *try* being that brave. My life is just fine the way it is.'

Wow...

Had Fi really thought that her friendship with Christophe could develop to a point where he might believe that at least *some* women could be trusted to be more than just a friend or a fleeting liaison? She'd had no idea of how big this challenge really was or if she was capable of helping him towards a future where the love of his life might have only two legs instead of four.

She could, at least, try to lighten the atmosphere before they needed to spend an hour in the close confines of a car, however. Her cheeks puffed with the breath she blew out as she shook her head sadly.

'Poor Nonna.'

'What?' Christophe looked startled at the change of subject, as well he might. 'Why?'

'She wants those *bambinos* so much.' The children he never wanted to have. 'No... what's grandchildren in Italian?'

'*Nipoti.*' Christophe shrugged. 'Nonna will be okay. She will live in hope as long as she thinks we are together.'

Ah...

It was a lightbulb moment for Fi that swiftly grew into an idea. A way to distract him from the sins of the past. Maybe even a new direction to a goal that had become even more important since she'd seen the way Christophe had been with that little boy at the restaurant. He would love to have his own children and they might be the luckiest kids on earth to grow up with this man as their father. She could hear an echo of something Ellie had said about him.

'*He might not even realise it himself, but he needs a family of his own.*'

Fi's tone was crisp. A decision was being made. A plan of distraction was forming. If nothing else, this would give them something to talk about on the drive back to La Maisonette.

'We'll have to make sure she does think that, then, won't we?'

Christophe's glance was bemused. 'How?'

'We can visit sometimes, but what would be even better is to let her know that we are together at other times. We can go places or do things.'

'Like what?'

'What do couples do in France in the summer? Go to beaches? Swim? Eat at lovely outdoor restaurants? We can take pictures and send them to her. Has she got a phone?'

'Of course. She forgets to charge it sometimes but Mamma could share the pictures.'

Christophe was definitely distracted from memories of past emotional traumas. His eyes were brighter. He liked this idea. 'She would love that,' he said. 'And she would know that you were being a good influence on me. I can be bad at keeping in touch often enough.'

Fi nodded. 'That's what we'll do then. We'll make it look like we're together. We can help her hold onto the hope of some *nipoti* for as long as possible.'

They'd reached the car. Christophe opened all the doors and gave Heidi a bowl of water to give the car time to cool down.

He was beside the passenger door as Fi climbed in.

'What about you, *cara*?' he asked quietly. 'I've seen you with your family and the babies. You love children, too, don't you?'

Fi reached for her safety belt. 'I do.'

She felt the car rock as Heidi jumped in. Christophe closed

the back door but didn't move to the driver's side. He was standing there, looking at her.

'You'd make a wonderful mother,' he said, returning the compliment she'd given him.

Fi could feel herself freezing again. They were only words but they could feel like a physical touch. Like a tongue touching hers. She reached to pull her door shut, fighting the horrible current that was trying to drag her down into the clutches of a flashback.

'Not going to happen,' she said. She knew she was running again but this one was too big to face right now. It might always be. 'I'll never have my own babies.' She shrugged to indicate there was nothing more that needed to be said. 'I can't.'

The door shut with more of a slam than she'd intended but it did the trick.

That particular conversation was over.

16

'He wants to see you.' Jeannie let her gaze rest for a beat on each of her three daughters in turn. 'All of you.'

'Nope.' Laura's voice was as pinched as her face. 'Not going to happen.'

Jeannie could feel the force field of whatever protection her firstborn daughter was pulling around herself. She could understand why but, over the last few days, with the time she'd spent with Gordon Gilchrist in the hospital, she truly believed that this was the way forward. A chance to heal something that had been pushed out of sight and allowed to fester for far too long.

'Just to let him say hullo,' Jeannie added. 'It doesn't need to be more than a minute or two. Seeing him... being in the same room with him...' She had to pause and swallow past an odd wee lump in her throat. 'I know it won't be easy but you might find it makes things... I don't know, clearer perhaps?'

It had for her. She'd known she still loved the man she'd married. That she still missed him. But those feelings had been like faded sepia photographs compared to the ones that were beginning to show signs of life again now. True love never dies, it seemed. Even if you tried to shut it away in a suffocating space so it couldn't continue to hurt.

They might be more like strangers than husband and wife now, and it was impossible to know if they could ever be more than that again, but one thing was becoming very clear to Jeannie: she still cared very deeply about Gordon. And she could forgive him. Maybe the real question was whether he could forgive himself. He was still grappling with the fact that the nightmares that had haunted him for the entire life he could remember were actually memories of something real that he hadn't been able to remember. She could see how bewildering it was for him. That it was frightening. And very, very shameful. She was treading carefully so that it didn't become too much for either of them to cope with.

Laura wasn't about to tread carefully. 'Things are clear enough already,' she snapped. 'He ruined our lives.'

Jeannie kept a steady gaze on her. Neither Laura nor her sisters would exist if it hadn't been for the good fortune of her meeting and falling in love with Gordon. And aye, things had become agonisingly difficult, but from where she was standing now, Laura's life was far from ruined. She had the love of a wonderful man and the blessing of a gorgeous baby girl. She was living in a stunning house in one of the most beautiful places on earth and she was part of a family that was united again. Becoming steadily closer. Stronger.

Laura was clearly aware of her mother's gaze. The way she dipped her head was almost an apology, but there was defiance in the flick of eye contact.

You needed protection back then, the look said. *And you need it now, even if you don't realise it. It was what I was supposed to do when I was the only one of us old enough to know what was happening. I failed back then. I'm not going to fail this time.*

Ellie was frowning. She didn't want to be in conflict with her oldest sister but she didn't want to upset her mother, either. She'd been the first to go looking for a connection with the French side of their family when she'd found the old photos that had taken her to the village of Saint-Martin-Vésubie, where she'd found the painting she'd fallen in love with. She hadn't told Jeannie about any of that because she hadn't wanted to upset her. The girls had all known how shocked she'd been when news of the inheritance of this little house – such a tangible link to a part of her life that had been destroyed – had come out of the blue like that.

Was Ellie curious about her father?

Aye. The way she let her gaze slide towards the painting hanging over the fireplace was a dead giveaway. She'd had no idea that the artist she'd seen in the market when she'd first laid eyes on that painting was her father, and she might not recognise him as the same man when she saw him again. Just yesterday, Gordon had been deemed well enough to pay a visit to the hairdressing salon in the hospital. He'd had his long hair cut, his beard shaved off, even his eyebrows trimmed. It had made him look so much younger.

As young as that photograph of him she still had on her bedside table at home.

As good-looking as he'd ever been in that rugged Highlander way. The kind of man that could make a kilt a completely masculine, and very sexy, item of clothing.

So familiar that Jeannie knew, in that first glance, that her heart had actually stopped, because she'd felt the violent thump as it kickstarted itself again. It didn't hurt but, oddly, she'd been sure she could feel a trickle of blood deep in her chest. It felt as though she'd opened the door of a time machine and she was meeting the older version of the person whose image she'd kept in her mind, and her heart, for so many years.

The man who had been the absolute love of her life.

But, for whatever reason – her age, perhaps? – the last thing she'd expected to feel was any kind of physical attraction to him again. It was more than a wee bit shocking, to be honest. This journey was supposed to be about finding peace, not stirring up new emotional challenges.

And the emotions could be wrenching.

Showing Gordon photographs of his daughters that she had on her phone had not helped in retrieving memories. These were adult women and strangers to him. The picture of Lili, however – who looked exactly like Laura had at that age – had made him cry.

Jeannie had cried with him. She had touched him for the first time, for no reason other than a need for that physical connection. Holding his gaze, for the moment he'd accepted the eye contact, and then holding his hand, even after the screen of her phone had gone dark.

And yesterday he'd had tears in his eyes when he said he wanted to see his daughters. His words had been in English, which he was, haltingly, beginning to use again, but it wasn't just finding his way back to an almost forgotten language that made what he said so tentative. He didn't believe that they would want to see *him*.

One of them definitely didn't.

One was torn.

And Fiona? The child who'd always been the most like her father? The child who had been so afraid that she *was* the most like her father? She was very still, as if she – like Jeannie – was absorbing how her sisters were reacting to the information.

There was something different about Fiona in the last few days. Ever since she'd come back from Menton, where she'd gone with Julien's friend, Christophe, after he'd heard that his grand-mother was gravely ill.

'I just wanted to help,' she'd said, on her return. 'And I could. I looked after Heidi while he was with his family in the hospital.'

She'd stayed the night, though, hadn't she?

Jeannie hadn't missed the glance that passed between Laura and Ellie when they'd heard that.

Fiona had shaken her head and said that was only because it had been late by then. And there'd been a crisis. She would never have forgiven herself if something else had gone wrong and it was her fault that Christophe was too far away to be there for his grandmother's final moments. His nonna was lovely, she'd said. Like the grandmother that none of them had ever had. Nothing had happened between herself and Christophe, she'd added, with a finality that precluded any further interrogation. *Nothing*.

It could well be that she was protesting too much, but Jeannie wasn't going to pry and the warning look she'd given the others seemed to have hit its mark. Whatever had – or hadn't – happened, Fiona seemed...

...more at peace.

Aye... she was happier.

She wasn't planning to go back to Scotland, she'd announced. She was going to apply for a long-stay visa on the grounds of having family here, to get past the ninety-day limit for a visit, and Laura said she'd help her with an application for citizenship, which was possible when you had a French grandparent. Fi said that, if it was okay with Ellie, she'd like to stay on in La Maisonette for a while. She could pay rent. With her share of the inheritance that had come from this house being sold to Julien, she had enough money to live on while she decided what to do next with her life. She might travel, she'd said. Or get a job somewhere.

Ellie's eyes had lit up. She'd told Fiona that she didn't need to pay rent; caring for the house and the donkeys would be enough, especially if she was interested in working for Ellie.

'I've got an idea for a business,' she'd said. 'I was on the point of starting it when I got pregnant with Bonnie and it got shelved. I've even got a name for it. Two names, I haven't quite decided. It's either "Stone Flowers" or "A Touch of France". They're going to be paving stones with mosaic flowers set into them, like small pieces of the old pathways in St Paul de Vence.'

My goodness, how excited had Ellie sounded, and looked, as her words tumbled out. 'I've got bags of concrete and mortar in the cellar and buckets of beach stones I've already collected but I desperately need another pair of hands. Ones that aren't going to be required by a small human at inconvenient moments, like when a batch of concrete needs to be used before it sets.'

Laura had approved of the idea.

'I've got contacts,' she'd said. 'With interior and exterior designers – here and in Scotland. I could help, too.'

Jeannie let the flash of what had been going on with her daughters in the last few days fade from her thoughts.

Laura certainly wasn't about to approve the idea of visiting her father. She was opening her mouth to say something else but Jeannie beat her to it.

'They're going to send him home soon,' she said. 'In a day or two, perhaps. It might make it easier to meet him somewhere that's... neutral ground? Where there are no ghosts of the past and no connection to the future if you decide that you don't want to see him again? Because you don't *have* to see him again, any of you, if you don't want to. But you won't really know what you want unless you do see him at least once.'

Fiona was the first to speak. 'I'll go,' she said. 'I want to see him.'

Laura glared at her. '*Why*?'

'Because he's our father. Because what happened wasn't his fault. He was sick and that was something he couldn't control. And... and I think that people deserve a second chance. A new beginning.'

It looked as if she might be about to cry, Jeannie thought.

'Everyone is worthy of being loved,' she added, her words ending with a shaky intake of breath. 'And that starts with your family, doesn't it? And your friends.'

Ellie was crying. She sniffed and then hugged her sister. 'You're right, Fi. And I want to come with you. I want to see him, too.'

Laura was looking at the old beams in the ceiling, as though she was halfway through rolling her eyes.

'*Grand*,' she muttered. It sounded as if the word came out from between gritted teeth. 'I'll suppose I'll have to come as well, then.'

* * *

Maybe this had been a mistake.

You could cut the atmosphere in this small hospital room with a knife.

Laura, Fiona and Eleanor were standing against the wall. If they'd stretched an arm out, they could have touched the end of the bed that Gordon Gilchrist was sitting up in. Final tests were being done today so that he could be discharged, and he'd just come back from having an MRI scan of his brain. He looked tired and he was wearing a hospital gown that made him look so vulnerable. Facing the jury of his daughters was making him look...

...unbearably sad.

Jeannie had ushered the sisters into the room and introduced them. They were all staring at their father but nobody was saying anything.

In the end, it was Gordon who broke that horrible silence. His gaze was fixed on Laura, and Jeannie could see the moment he recognised her. She could feel him reaching towards his firstborn child even though he hadn't moved a muscle.

'Lulu,' he said. His lips trembled and then began to form a smile. 'Lulu,' he said again.

Laura's face crumpled as she struggled not to burst into tears. The sisters leaned closer to each other.

'Fiona.' Gordon let his gaze rest on her face for the longest moment. 'I'd forgotten,' he said quietly, 'how beautiful your mother was when I first met her. But now I remember because you look so much like her.'

He was speaking in English. His voice was soft but his Scottish accent was as strong as it had always been.

'Eleanor,' he said, as he shifted his gaze. 'Wee Ellie... Your mam tells me that you're the one who has my painting.'

Ellie nodded. 'It's in the cottage,' she said. 'La Maisonette. The house your brother owned.'

'I've never been there,' Gordon said. 'Did I have a brother?'

'Jeremy,' Jeannie put in. 'He was a little older than you. You hadn't seen him for years before you lost your memory, so it will be hard to remember him. He's dead now. His house went to our girls because they couldn't find any other living relatives.'

Our girls...

Jeannie didn't dare look at her daughters.

'It was the painting that led us to you,' she said. 'I knew there was something that felt familiar about it and then I found some sketches you'd done before... before you got sick.'

'I wanted to tell you how much I loved that painting,' Ellie said softly. 'That night in the market. But I couldn't speak French well enough then. Julien told me how to say I really liked it but what I really wanted to say was that it was pulling me in. I wanted to walk into it and touch the stones of that ruined building and feel the sunshine on my skin.'

'So did I,' Fi said. 'When I just arrived in France and I was tired and sad and I wanted to be in that place so much. I wanted to be walking in the grass with bare feet and picking flowers and... and it made me feel happy.'

'Thank you.' Gordon's voice was a whisper. 'That's how I felt when I painted it.'

'Ellie's an artist, too,' Laura said, her tone even sharper by contrast to her father's. 'She's very talented.'

Gordon closed his eyes in long blink but he had a faint smile on his lips. In some part of him, did he remember that Laura could become prickly when she was overwhelmed or afraid of something? Or had this simply become too much for him to cope with now?

'I think that might be enough for a first visit,' Jeannie said. 'Your dad's very tired after all the tests.'

Ellie was the last to say goodbye and then she turned back before she slipped through the door.

'I'd like to see some more of your work,' she said. 'Can I come and visit your studio one day?'

'Yes.'

Gordon's response was no more than that single word, but Jeannie found herself close to tears as she followed Ellie from the room.

It had begun.

A way forward.

She walked with her daughters until they reached the main doors to the hospital.

'Are you coming with us?' Ellie asked.

'Not just yet,' Jeannie said. 'There's something I need to talk to Gordon about before I come home. We don't know if he'll be allowed to go home even if the test results are all okay.'

'Why not?' Fi looked anxious.

'Because he has no one to care for him.'

They were all silent. All looking at her. Ellie's eyes were soft, as if she knew what Jeannie was going to say next.

'I need to tell him that he does,' Jeannie said. 'He has a family again and... and I'm going to take care of him if he will let me. I can go and see him every day – it's not that far to drive.' She smiled. 'And I'm here if you want to talk to me about anything, but I think you girls need some time without me watching you to get used to this. Believe me, I know how big this is. I'm still trying to get used to it myself.'

As she had when she'd first suggested taking this step of seeing their father again, she looked at each one of her daughters in turn. 'Are you okay?' she asked. 'Did it help to see him?'

This time the response was far less divided.

Aye. They were okay. Or would be. They needed some time to process what had been such an intensely emotional occasion and to absorb its implications. Tears would, no doubt, be shed and Jeannie suspected that Laura had more bottled up than either of her sisters.

In the meantime, what they all needed was a family hug.

17

'Ready, Fi?'

'I'm ready.' Fi was feeding long blades of grass to Marguerite and Coquelicot, but it was probably wise to head for the shade of the lemon trees closer to the cottage. She could feel the heat of the sun softly scorching her fair skin. 'Have you got some sunscreen on, Ellie?'

'I'll stay in the shade as soon as we've got everything we need out of the cellar.' Ellie was draping a muslin wrap over the Moses basket that was tucked in beside the trunk of a lemon tree to get maximum shade. 'Julien thinks my freckles are *très mignon*, but I've got more than enough already.'

Pascal was lying beside the basket, his nose on his paws, one ear up as he stayed alert for any protection that might be needed from a fly or a bee.

'How long will Bonnie sleep?' Fi asked.

'Long enough, I hope. This is just a trial run for the first design, so we'll use the smallest frame. It shouldn't take too long.'

Mike the builder, who had helped with the renovation of La Maisonette, had apparently been delighted to help make the frames Ellie had requested for paving-stone moulds. She showed them to Fi when they went into the cellar.

'Look... they've got screws in these two corners. When the concrete is set, I undo those and it'll be easy to lift the frame off.'

'What about the bottom?'

'That's what that sheet of plywood over there is for. Could you bring that out, please? And the bucket of sand beside it with a plastic sheet on top. I'll get the pebbles and tools.'

They took everything outside into the fragrant shade of the lemon orchard. Ellie tipped the bucket of flat, round and oval stones out onto the ground beneath the tree next to where Bonnie was sleeping.

'We need to sort the coloured ones into similar shapes and sizes. Different piles for the grey ones.'

It felt like a game. As though they'd stepped back in time to when they were little girls and playing together on a summer's afternoon. One sister was missing, but Laura wouldn't have wanted to do something as frivolous as play with a pile of pebbles in those days. She wasn't doing something this enjoyable today, either.

'I wonder how Laura's getting on,' Fi said aloud.

Ellie was starting a pile of the smallest grey stones. 'She *was* nervous, wasn't she?'

'I'm glad she's taking Noah and Lili with her. Mam said that Dad cried when he saw a photo of Lili because it looked so like how he could remember Laura when she was little.'

'Is Mam up there today, too?'

'Of course.' Fi smiled. 'She hasn't missed a day since he came out of hospital, has she? And that's what... two weeks ago now?'

'Closer to three. It's been a week since *we* went up to see his studio.'

They were both silent for a moment. That had been another

emotional meeting with their father and they'd both been crying on the drive home, but a new connection was being formed for the children who'd been too young to really remember their father and an old one rediscovered for a father who'd forgotten he had children. There was a long journey ahead for them all but the door was slowly being opened to allow Gordon Gilchrist to be part of his family again, if that was what he wanted in his life. None of it could be rushed. They were going to have to take this one step at a time – a bit like how she and Ellie were tackling their first attempt at making a mosaic pebble paving stone today.

Ellie put a frame onto the plywood that she'd covered with the plastic sheet and tipped sand into it. She handed a plastering trowel to Fi.

'Have a go at smoothing it out,' she instructed. 'It needs to be a thin layer because we don't want the stones to poke out far enough for people to stub their toes.'

'Sometimes I don't know where the time's going,' she said, as she watched what Fi was doing. 'Bonnie's four months old all of a sudden and she thinks being able to roll over is the funniest game ever, which is adorable and I want to enjoy every moment of it but it feels like I'm going to turn around and she'll be ready for school.'

'Time flies when you're having fun.' Fi smiled. 'And slows down when you're not. One of life's meaner tricks. Take lots of photos.'

'I am. And that reminds me...' Ellie dusted sand off her hands and pulled her phone from the pocket of the pinafore-style apron she was wearing. 'I need to find the photo of the pattern I thought we could use today.'

She glanced up from scrolling photos a moment later, however, her eyebrows raised. 'You seem to be enjoying yourself at the moment. Did I see you going off with Christophe again yesterday afternoon?'

'We just took Heidi for a walk.'

'Hmm... and didn't you "just go for dinner" in Menton again a few days ago?'

'I did.' Fi let her breath out in a sigh that was a groan of pleasure. 'You wouldn't believe how good a cook Nonna is. She made a mushroom lasagne that was *the* most delicious thing I've ever tasted. I'm going to ask her to teach me how to make it.'

'Sounds like she's recovering well. She not about to drop dead any time soon, is she?'

'She could,' Fi countered. 'She's got a dodgy ticker now. Christophe and his mum are still really worried about her.'

'And that's what all this time with Christophe is all about, aye? Keeping Nonna happy by pretending you're more than friends?'

'That's the plan.' Fi had told her sisters about the fake dating idea. What she hadn't told them was that she wanted to try and help Christophe regain at least some trust in women. She certainly hadn't admitted that playing her part in the fantasy was irresistible because it wasn't real and that made it feel safe. Safe enough that she could even let another hope simmer quietly in the back of her mind – that Christophe might kiss her again one day and she wouldn't freak out.

'What if Nonna bounces back and lives for years?'

'We've talked about that. If my visa doesn't come through, I'll have to leave France for a few months and we can work something out to let her down gently. That I've got a job somewhere else or I got homesick. In the meantime, I'm getting to go to lovely places so we can take the photos that are, apparently, the best part of Nonna's day.'

Ellie shook her head. 'I hope you both know what you're doing, that's all. Ah... this is the photo I want.' She turned the screen towards Fi. 'I thought we could start with just a single flower and plain grey around it. A coloured roundish flat stone in the middle and the petals will be oval shapes on their sides. I've got a rubber hammer to tap them in. Let's find a nice one for the centre.'

They both turned back to play with the stones again.

'Where did you go to collect all these?' Fi asked.

'The garden centre,' Ellie said. 'Sadly, you can't just go and take buckets of decorative stones off the beaches. You have to buy them.'

'How 'bout this one for the centre?' Fi held it up. 'It's kind of round and it's almost red, like the darkest tiles of La Maisonette's floor.'

'Nice.' Ellie nestled the large flat stone into the centre of the frame. 'Let's find some pale ones for the petals.'

Ellie showed Fi how to settle them gently into place in the sand so that they made contact with the sheet of wood beneath. It took time to choose the right shape for each stone and position them to her satisfaction.

'So...' Ellie asked, as she sat back on her heels a short time later to examine progress. 'Where was it that you went yesterday? Back to that riding school in the forest that you discovered last week?'

'No...' But Fi was distracted for a moment. What a discovery that had been. A house and a riding school, with one group of small children on ponies trotting around a ring and an adult on a horse getting ready to take a group of older children on a trek along one of the forest paths.

'*That would be my ultimate dream*,' she'd told Christophe. '*To have a riding school of my own.*'

'*In a forest?*'

'*Or near a river. Or in the mountains. Anywhere. But a forest would be perfect.'*

'*Because you love trees?'*

'*Oui. Because I love trees.'*

It had become a private joke, hadn't it? Because that had been how Christophe had persuaded her to go and help him with the donkeys in the forest. The day it had all begun. Or had that really been at Lili's birthday party – when she'd seen him smile for the first time? When, so disturbingly, she'd been aware of wanting to be closer to a man, instead of running away?

'Hullo!' Ellie's tone was amused. 'Earth to Fi...?'

She had to shake off the memory of the way Christophe's smile made his eyes crinkle at the corners.

'It was a lovely park near the coast yesterday,' she told Ellie. 'It had cork trees. Have you ever seen one? They're extraordinary.'

Fi had been fascinated – as much by the enthusiasm Christophe had for explaining so many different things as for the actual trees themselves. She loved the way his eyes would light up. She loved listening to his voice with that unique accent and the ability to sprinkle words from all sorts of other languages into what he was saying. He could probably tell her about something as ordinary as, say, the sand or small stones she was working with today, and she would be more than happy to listen.

'Never seen one.' Ellie was starting to place different sizes of plain grey stones around the flower they'd created, filling all the empty space. 'They're a kind of oak tree, aren't they?'

'Yes. They can get the bark stripped off every ten years or so and it doesn't kill the tree. You can get fifty thousand corks for wine bottles from the bark of a single tree.'

'Is that right...?'

Ellie's interest seemed to be merely polite but Fi was back in that park in her head. Watching Christophe's face come alive because he was so interested in something. Feeling his hand reach for hers to put it on the extraordinary bark of the tree so that she could feel it.

'They feel kind of bouncy,' she told Ellie. 'Christophe said that's because it's full of millions of air cells and when they get cut they act like tiny suction cups and stick to the glass inside a bottle's neck. How amazing is that? And the bark is all up and down like ripples in water or rocky hills. You can almost *feel* it growing. It's weirdly warm, too.'

Or had that been Christophe's hand resting, ever so lightly, on top of hers as she explored the texture? Was that why the curious warmth from the tree seemed to filter right into the centre of her body through that touch? Why it was impossible not to close her eyes, just for a heartbeat, and remember the feeling of his lips resting on hers? To let that delicious ripple of sensation deep inside briefly blur the distinction between fantasy and reality.

'I'll show you the photos later.'

'Okay... cool...' But Ellie was focussed on filling tiny gaps now, turning stones so that just an edge or a corner could fit the space.

Fi's thoughts drifted to the photos she was collecting on her phone. She might just show Ellie the ones of the unusual bark. Not the string of selfies that she and Christophe had taken, their heads almost touching as they leaned against one of the trees and smiled happily for the camera until they'd captured one they both agreed would make Nonna smile. It was taking longer every time because it had become another shared joke to make silly faces before they got serious about trying to look like a couple spending meaningful time together on a date.

Or just together? Christophe had taken Fi to a tack shop in Nice when he wasn't spending all his free time in Menton in the first few days of his grandmother being back at home. Did shopping count as a pretend date? It had certainly been a lot of fun. Fi had purchased a child's saddle with a handle on the pommel and cage stirrups so that a small foot couldn't go too far through and get stuck. She'd bought lead reins and new leather halters for the donkeys and spent even more time wandering around what had always been her most favourite type of shop. They'd taken their first selfie to send to Nonna, that day, standing in front of a life-sized plastic horse who was modelling the latest in saddlery.

Marguerite had given Theo his first ride after some lead training by Fi. Christophe had been there and Fi was quite sure he'd loved it as much as Theo had. Nonna had received a photo that Julien had taken that day, when Christophe was lifting Theo down from the saddle and the tall man and small boy were both grinning at each other in pure joy, with Fi beaming at them both as she held the donkey's halter. It looked like an advertisement for a picture-perfect little family, and it might be pure fantasy but it was a photo that she was going to treasure as much as Nonna probably would.

A squeak from Bonnie made them both turn their heads but the baby settled again in seconds. Fi's glance shifted to the donkeys at the end of the lemon orchard, dozing in the shade of an olive tree, but she was still thinking about that photo.

'Theo loved his riding lesson, didn't he?'

'He's begging for another one. It's the first thing on his mind every day. Don't tell Laura but you are officially his favourite auntie. Christophe will always be his favourite uncle but he's now got the status of a superhero. I think Julien might be a bit jealous.'

'He *is* brilliant with kids,' Fi agreed. 'There was a wee boy in Menton that was terrified of Heidi but he handled that so well.' She hesitated for a moment. 'I hope you don't mind, but he told me about Julien's first wife. About her cheating on him.'

'Oh...' Ellie sounded disconcerted but then she nodded. 'I'm glad you know,' she said. 'I never said anything because it doesn't feel like my story to tell and, really, it makes no difference to our lives now.'

'I think it still makes a difference to Christophe's,' Fi said. 'On top of the disaster of his first love, I don't think he's ever going to trust a woman again – not enough to have a real relationship, anyway.'

Ellie had filled the final gap. The swift glance she gave Fi was a silent question.

Do you want him to trust you that much?

Fi got to her feet to avoid responding. How could she have answered that? Yes, she wanted him to trust her that much, but only so that he could then find the woman who could give him the family he didn't know he wanted? Someone who would be the luckiest woman in the world but it could never be Fi? The obvious question then would be 'why not?' And it wouldn't be silent. Or as easy to fend off as she could by simply dismissing it and starting to walk back to the cellar.

'Want me to get the bag of concrete? Are we going to use that next?'

'We are. We need a bucket of water too.'

Ellie got the message. She backed away from any further discussion of Fi's friendship with Christophe as they mixed up sand and cement into a consistency that reminded Fi of the porridge their mother used to give them on cold winter mornings that was intended to 'stick to their ribs'.

'How's Mam doing, do you think?' she asked as she watched Ellie pour some of the concrete gently around the stones and poke it into gaps with a knife. 'You see more of her than Laura or I do. Do you think she's happy that she found Dad?'

Ellie turned to get another scoop of concrete from the bucket. 'I think that sometimes she's happier than she's ever been, but there's also a sadness there that's so deep you can't see the bottom. I found her crying the other day but she said she was happy – she was just grieving all the years that had been lost.'

Fi's breath caught somewhere deep in her throat for a heart-beat. She knew that feeling. She had filled her life with more animals than people for so long, she hadn't realised how lonely she had actually been. It wasn't just her family that had been missing from her life. She needed friends. And the dream of one day finding someone special, like her sisters had. Someone who could share her life. Someone to whom she would be the most special person in *their* life. A relationship that could be enough even without the children that would make it a whole family?

The more time she spent with Christophe, the clearer that truth seemed to become, but Fi knew it was better not to allow hope free rein because that was the only way to temper the disap-pointment of failure. An occasional daydream was fine as long as it didn't begin to feel too real. She wanted horses and ponies in her future, too, and they would probably be far easier to find.

'What's going to happen?' she wondered aloud. 'Mam can't get much more time off work, can she?'

'Julien had one of his wine club evenings with Noah and Christophe last night. They were talking about that and Noah said that Laura wants to give Mam her share of our inheritance. He said she wouldn't let him contribute although Julien said he's very wealthy. In any case, it would mean Mam might be able to retire earlier, if she wants to.'

'To stay here? With Dad? Would they get married again?'

'They've never been divorced. I suppose Dad could have been declared dead, but Mam never took that to court. Technically, I'd say they're still married but... could they live together? Would they *want* to...?'

Would they? Fi wondered if her mother was having

daydreams of her own. Maybe they had more in common than either of them realised.

The pebbles of the mosaic were hidden now as Ellie carefully smoothed more concrete into the frame and then levelled it.

'That's it,' she declared. 'We leave it to dry for a day or two and then turn it over, take the frame off and brush away the sand. I can't wait to see what it looks like.'

With commendable timing, Bonnie decided that was the moment to wake up and let her mother know how hungry she was.

'I can clean up here while you feed her,' Fi offered. 'I'll put everything away in the cellar and wash the tools.'

Ellie was lifting Bonnie from the basket. 'I knew it was my best idea ever to employ you,' she said. 'I'd better go back to the house. This baby has a very soggy bottom and I didn't bring any nappies out with me.'

Fi called out as she began to walk away, Pascal at her heels. 'Doesn't being employed mean I get paid?'

Ellie laughed. 'Aye... we'd better sort that out, hadn't we? I don't want you to get headhunted by someone else. Like Didier, who's probably desperate to find a farrier. Or Christophe deciding he could open a donkey riding school as a side hustle.'

Oh... imagine that. Working – maybe *living* – with Christophe and a whole herd of donkeys. That might make a new irresistible daydream all on its own. Fi started scooping up all the leftover pebbles and letting them trickle through her fingers back into the bucket but it wasn't that she was playing with stones again like a kid that was making her smile.

Ellie hadn't been wrong. Fi *was* enjoying herself. Life had, in fact, never felt quite this good. Ever.

18

The days were growing longer and warmer as summer officially grew closer.

The amount of time each day that Jeannie Gilchrist was spending with Gordon was also growing longer. At first she'd stayed in the old barn with him, talking to him or simply sitting in the sunshine outside in silence. Patchy memories, or at least parts of them, were slowly returning.

'Do you remember working on the fishing boats? How cold it could be? Your hands would feel like blocks of ice when you got home.'

'I remember a fire in a house and how much my hands would hurt as they warmed up. Is that why I feel the way I do when I walk past the *poissonnerie*? Seeing – and smelling – all those fish makes my head spin so much I can't think. I try to not go near them.'

She cooked him meals. The kind of meals she'd made for him when they were first married.

'Remember stovies? And your favourite leftover meat to go in them?'

Jeannie had made the corned beef herself, at Ellie's house, cooking the meat in a brine of vinegar and pepper, brown sugar, bay leaves and mustard. She'd served the favourite family meal of corned beef with hot mustard sauce, cabbage and roasted potatoes and carrots to Ellie and Julien, Laura and Noah, making sure she had enough leftovers to chop up and use to make the classic Scottish dish of stovies. She'd made oatcakes, as well, to go with it.

Oh... the look on Gordon's face when he tasted it! He remembered. Of course he did. Taste would have to be able to evoke memories in the same way a scent could. What else could she make him? Her famous cottage pie? The special Sunday dinner of roast beef and Yorkshire pudding with cauliflower cheese and the garlic potatoes that you could make so crispy by parboiling and then rolling them in semolina before putting them in the roasting pan?

Perhaps she wanted to cook everything for him. Because feeding someone was the first and easiest way to nurture them.

She took the sketches she'd found in the attic in her Oban cottage and he traced that ruined building with his finger and then closed his eyes and was silent for so long she thought he'd fallen asleep. She jumped when he started speaking.

'It was a grey day but that only made the moors more beautiful. I wanted to fix that little stone cottage and live in it in the hills forever. With you...'

She watched him work on a large painting as he began to feel better. And then sketching on tiny cards with a touch of colour from water paints, a simple bunch of daisies on one, poppies on another and lavender on a third. There was a carefully written message inside each card, for each one of his daughters. Jeannie had been carrying them in her handbag ever since, waiting for the right moment to give her girls something she knew would be heart wrenching.

Sometimes, now, she and Gordon went out somewhere, into nearby villages and up into the mountains to walk in the forests. She took him to the hospital, too, for his outpatient appointments that were monitoring his general health and his reaction to the anti-seizure drugs he was now taking. There were appointments with therapists who had been provided to help him through the traumatic process of trying to sort the tangle of what he knew to be reality and what he had assumed to be nightmares. He was learning to catch wisps of confusion and, with Jeannie's help, to find out if they, too, were parts of his missing life.

He had a passport now. A birth date. He knew the names of his parents and that he'd spent his earliest years in the town he'd instinctively gone back to. He'd recognised the brother he'd forgotten he had from the old photograph Ellie had found hidden in the book.

'I'm starting to feel like a real person,' he told Jeannie. 'When I've always only felt like a ghost. This would never have happened without you, darlin'.'

Ohh…

It had taken a long time for Gordon to start smiling much at all but *this* smile – this was the one that had woken something that had been very deeply buried to try and protect it from pain. Perhaps it was the endearment it came with. Or the look in the dark brown eyes of the quintessential Scottish Highland warrior who had been her first true love.

Her only true love.

That was the place that this smile had touched.

Her soul.

She could see the man she'd married so clearly again now.

Her Gordie.

She'd wanted, so much, to kiss him. More than that. She'd wanted to see if his body would recognise hers and remember the familiar rituals they'd created in their lovemaking. That would happen, she realised in that moment.

But not yet.

She could see him coming closer but he still wasn't within that kind of touching distance – because he wasn't ready? Rejection could only damage what was happening between them, so Jeannie wasn't going to be the one to make the first move or to try and encourage Gordon to make it. This was a journey that couldn't be rushed, and it was well past time that Jeannie went back home to Oban and back to her work as a practice nurse in the local medical centre.

* * *

'I can't afford to lose my job,' she told Ellie and Fi, a day or two later. She was sitting on the low stone wall that was part of the terracing of La Maisonette's sloping garden, with Bonnie in her arms. 'They've been very accommodating, giving me extra, unpaid, leave but I've got to get back. Goodness knows the kind of mess my garden is in after nearly two months of total neglect.'

Ellie was knocking the caked sand off the surface of one of the mosaic paving stones she and Fi had made this week.

'You don't really want to go back though, do you, Mam?'

Jeannie sighed. 'I do and I don't. I miss my wee house. I miss my job. But... if I go back...' She paused for a long moment. 'I'll miss Gordon,' she admitted. 'It was so strange at first and I was all over the place but...'

Fi stopped the job she was doing, using a scrubbing brush and water to clean a stone that had already had the sand knocked off onto the plastic sheet so it could be used again.

'You still love him, don't you?'

'Aye... I don't think I ever stopped.' Jeannie blinked away tears, focussing on the pattern on the stone Fi was cleaning as she tried to keep control. There was a flowerpot outlined with the thin edges of dark stones and filled with the round surfaces of paler stones. Three stalks were coming out of the pot and there were five small daisy-like flowers over the top of the stalks.

It was pretty enough to distract her and dry up any tears.

'That's *so* bonny,' she said. 'I'll buy it myself, if you'll let me, and take it home to my wee garden. Except it would be far too heavy for my luggage. And aren't you working to get enough ready for the markets?'

'I'm still thinking about whether I want to commit to going to markets,' Ellie said. 'If I did, it would just be for the evening summer markets in Vence, I think – like the one where I first saw Dad.'

'When do they start?' Fi asked.

'Next month sometime. And they finish towards the end of August, so it's only a few weeks.'

'Maybe you could share Dad's stall,' Fi suggested.

It made Jeannie smile, how natural it sounded to hear them talking about their father when, for so much of their childhood, any reference to him was carefully avoided. It made her proud how willing they seemed to be to forgive him and let him back into their lives. It was harder for Laura, she knew that. She'd seen more during the bad times. Heard more and, more importantly, felt more. Her oldest girl had tried to help mother her younger sisters. She'd even tried to mother Jeannie at times. She'd lost too much of her own childhood, so she had a lot more to forgive, but she was trying. The love was still there, Jeannie was sure of it, but it needed more time for trust to allow it to resurface.

Bonnie was falling asleep in her arms, which made her feel

heavier, somehow. Jeannie shifted her slightly, letting her knees take some of the weight.

'I'm sure he'd be delighted to share his market stall,' she said, '...if he's still here.'

Ellie looked startled. 'What do you mean? Where's he going?'

'Nowhere,' Jeannie added hurriedly. 'Unless he wants to. It's just that I have to go home and it occurred to me that he might like to come and visit for a wee while. Being in Scotland again, where he could see the places in Glasgow where he grew up and went to school and our house in Oban where we were together as a family... well, it might help to bring back memories. The good memories instead of all those terrible nightmares.' She swallowed hard. 'He told me he was sure he'd killed me in one of those dreams. He knew he'd tried to hurt me and that there was blood and that he had to run – as far and as fast as he could – because he couldn't bear to look at me, and he's been fighting that fear and the panic ever since. That's why he thought I was a ghost when he saw me. Why it was such a shock that he ended up having that terrible seizure.'

Ellie and Fi were staring at her.

'You're going to take him home?' Fi whispered. 'To live with you? You'd like to go back to your marriage?'

If Jeannie didn't have the baby in her arms she would have reached to hug Fiona. She could see that this daughter of hers was still struggling. Oh, God... was she still blaming herself for being subjected to that horrific sexual assault? Or for defending herself physically when she was afraid it might happen again? That she'd tried to hurt someone, like her father had?

'Aye,' she said quietly, holding Fi's gaze. 'Everyone deserves a second chance, don't they, hinny? And everyone is worthy of being loved, but I think it's hard to accept that love when you can't forgive yourself. To not forgive yourself for something that's not even your fault would be too sad, so if there's something I can do to stop that happening to someone I love, I have to try and do it. Don't I?'

'Oh, Mam... of course you do.'

Both Fi and Ellie scrambled to their feet. They sat on either side of Jeannie, putting their arms around her and their heads on her shoulders, the way they'd done when they were just wee bairns.

'We love you,' Ellie said.

'*So* much,' Fi added.

Jeannie could feel that love. So strong, and it was going in both directions. Not just between herself and her grown-up daughters but with the granddaughter she was holding in her arms.

'It's going to be okay,' Fi whispered. 'We'll get there. All of us.'

Jeannie looked down at Bonnie's face, with that delicious expression of peacefulness that babies had when they were asleep. The kind of peace that could only come from absolute trust and unconditional love.

'Aye,' she said quietly. 'I think we will.'

* * *

She gave Fi her card from Gordon in a private moment as Ellie wound Bonnie into her wrap to carry her home. She gave Ellie hers as soon as she was back in her own home, and then she went to give Laura hers because she wanted all her girls to have them at the same time.

She knew what they said on the back.

Laura – my first bairn. Today, I remembered you waiting at the door to give me a kiss when I came home from work. I love you so much, Lulu.

    Dada

My Fiona – you look so much like your mam did when I fell in love with her, but she tells me you're the most like me on the inside. You're the quiet one. The thinker. The peacemaker. I know how deeply you will feel things. I love you.

    Dada

Ellie – you see things in a way no one else can, but you can show them what you see through your art. It's a gift. Treasure it. I am so proud of you. How can I thank you enough for what you saw in my art, because that has led to this. I have a family again. I owe you my heart and all the love inside that I can give you.

    Dada

'Where's Heidi?'

'She can't come with us today. Didier's looking after her.'

It felt different being in Christophe's car without the back seat being filled with the huge, gentle dog. It felt oddly a little more intimate, as if a chaperone had taken the day off.

Fi stole a peek at Christophe. She rather liked this new feeling. 'Where are we going?'

'To a village called Puget-Théniers. It's about an hour's drive up into the mountains.'

'Why couldn't Heidi come?'

'Because she would have had to stay in the car and it's far too hot for that.'

'Why would she have to stay in the car? What's in Puget-Théniers?'

Asking one 'why' question after another made Fi feel like a small child. But it wasn't the only feeling that was childlike this morning. Being with Christophe like this – completely alone, with no hint of a chaperone – heading towards an unknown adventure was creating a sparkle of excitement that reminded her of her earliest memories of waking up on Christmas morning knowing that something amazingly wonderful was about to happen.

'A train station,' Christophe told her. 'We are taking a special train from Puget-Théniers to another village called Annot. It is *le Train des Pignes à Vapeur*. A...' He seemed to be focussing on the traffic around them. Or maybe searching for a word. 'A vintage train,' he said.

Vapeur... Almost an English word. 'Steam?' Fi offered.

'Oui. *C'est ça*. I've been wanting to do this train trip for a very long time. It's a good thing that we're collecting photos for Nonna. I was trying to think of something different for us to do and it made me remember the train and it will be perfect. It's exactly the sort of thing lovers would do for a day together.' Christophe threw one of his gorgeous smiles over his shoulder. 'It will be fun, I promise.'

But Fi was still hearing the echoes of his earlier words. Or one in particular.

Lovers...

Just the sound of the word, let alone its implications, made Fi's breath catch in her throat. She had to press her fingers against her lips and finish breathing in through her nose to stop it turning into a gasp. A door had opened, letting in flashes of daydreams – ones that had somehow been absorbed into the fantasy game of being a couple – and allowing them to wrap themselves around her. And how could she stop them? Here she was, on a glorious summer's day, wearing a pretty long, layered sundress she'd purchased at the market last week, with a soft straw hat ready to protect her from the sun, in the company of the most beautiful man in the world, who'd invited her to go to lunch with him.

A man who was completely at ease. Maybe as excited as she was about the adventure to come.

'The train only runs over summer. It's a tourist attraction but many French people love it also. It's famous. So is the railway line. I believe this is the only original part left of *les Chemins de Fer de Provence* – the old railway.'

'*Chemins de fer*,' Fi repeated, adding the words to her increasing vocabulary. 'Isn't *chemin* a path?'

'*Ouais*. Literally, an iron path.'

'Ah... *fer* is iron.'

'And you are a *maréchale-ferrante*. A farrier. Or there's another English word with iron in it. I forget.'

'An ironsmith?'

Christophe nodded.

'Blacksmith is another word for my job. Did you know there is a brownsmith as well?'

'*Non*...' Christophe's eyes were wide as he glanced sideways. 'Tell me all about him.'

Oh, he loved knowledge, this man. His curiosity was as childlike as Fi's 'why' questions and those tendrils of excitement, and it was one of Christophe's most endearing traits. He was genuinely interested in the world – and the people – around him. He had an intelligence that was fast and hungry and he cared. About people. The world. Life. And, above all, his family. Fi could imagine him sitting with his nonna one day soon, entertaining her by talking about the new things he had learned about smithing. It was important that she dredged up every bit of knowledge she'd gathered over the years.

'A smith is someone who works with metal. Goldsmiths and silversmiths explain themselves. A brownsmith works with metals like brass and copper. A blacksmith is an expert in making shoes for horses and there's a whitesmith as well, also called a tinsmith, who makes the pretty polished things like bits and buckles and stirrups. Some smiths are incredible artists, who make sculptures and furniture and oh... so many things. I'd love to do that one day. I could make artwork for gardens. Maybe Ellie could expand her new business. We could call it *Les Chemins de Fer et*... what's the word for stone? Pebbles?'

'Stone is *pierre*. Pebbles is *cailloux*. Could it be *Les Chemins de Pierre et Fer?*'

It sounded even better when Christophe said it. He was nodding with approval at the idea, as well.

'Do you want to do that one day more than having a riding school in a forest or in the mountains or beside a river?'

Goodness... did Christophe remember every single thing she said to him? Fi thought about the question for a moment and then narrowed her eyes as she pursed her lips. This whole day was a fantasy, so why not throw her future into the dream?

'I want *both*,' she declared.

Christophe's laughter filled the car. 'And you shall have it, *amore*, I'm sure of it.'

* * *

There was something about trains and small boys. Christophe Brabant's father had adored them enough to keep his immaculate Hornby train set with its shiny black engine, beautifully detailed carriages, the clip-together rails and the waiting room in the hope of having a son to share the joy with all over again.

Le Train des Pignes à Vapeur was that train set, which Christophe and his father had spent so many happy hours playing with, come to life and he needed a moment to swallow the prickly lump that suddenly formed in his throat. Like going to the *Fête du*

Citron, playing with the train had ended when his father died, but Christophe was quite sure that his mother had the set packed away in a box somewhere. Maybe she and Nonna both dreamed of seeing him sharing the toy with his own son. Or daughter.

Part of that lump was a knot of grief for his father. Another part was grief for the children he would never have himself. How could he even contemplate having a family when he was incapable of giving the mother of his children the kind of love that held a family together through thick and thin?

The moment was broken decisively when the engine puffed an enormous plume of smoke from its chimney and a piercing whistle sounded. Fi squeaked and clutched his arm but her eyes held a gleam of absolute glee. Christophe's laughter swept the ghosts of his grief far enough away to vanish into the cloudless blue sky like the mix of smoke and steam coming from the chimney of a train due to depart any second.

'*Allons-y*! Let's go!'

Christophe led Fi to their carriage as the whistle sounded again, jumped on board and then leaned down to offer his hand to help her climb up the narrow steps. They found their seats and he insisted that she sat beside the window. The train jerked and then slowly began moving and the small boy inside Christophe wanted to squeak with excitement the way Fi had when the whistle had first sounded.

The train conductor came to check their tickets and Fi nudged Christophe.

'Why has he got those little pine cones stuck to his cap?'

'Because this is *le train de pignes* – the train of pine cones.'

'Why is that its name?'

It was obviously not the first time the conductor had answered this question. Christophe listened to a well-rehearsed response in French and then translated for Fi as the conductor moved on.

'There are apparently two reasons. The first is that we are going through country that is covered with pine tree forests.'

Fi glanced out of the window as he gestured towards it but turned instantly back to watch his face. Her expression made him feel as if every word he was saying was important.

That *he* was important.

'The train used to go so slowly that people could get off and collect the pine cones,' he continued. 'The other reason could be that the pine cones were used for fuel if they started to run low on coal to keep the engine going.'

It was going steadily now, the rocking motion and the sound of the train a delight. Windows got hastily shut when they went through tunnels and the smoke was trapped around them but then opened to let some air into carriages that were already hot enough to be stifling. It was a relief when they stopped for a break at a station along the way, giving everyone a chance to stretch their legs and admire the train from the outside again.

Christophe and Fi went straight to the engine. They watched a man with a soot-streaked face shovelling coal into the furnace and sympathised with what the job would be like on a hot summer's day. They admired the shine of the brass rim around the headlights and agreed that the restoration of this train had been a labour of love. And then it was time to get a photograph.

For Nonna.

Christophe took out his phone and took some pictures of the train and of Fi with the side of the engine behind her. Another passenger smiled at him, speaking with an American accent.

'Would you like me to take a photo of you and your lovely girlfriend?'

'Yes. Thank you.'

This was *perfetto*. Christophe handed over his phone, positioned himself beside Fi and put his arm over her shoulders. It wasn't hard to smile, especially when she leaned into him so that her head was on his shoulder. When he looked down he found that she was looking up at him as if... as if...

As if she *was* his girlfriend. His *copine*.

As if they were head over heels in love.

The kind of love that led to marriage and babies and... forever...

He knew it was only a pretence. That she knew this was a photo for Nonna and this was just a game.

But... *oddio*... it felt *real*.

As real as what he was feeling for Fiona in this moment and that was a mirror-image of what he was seeing in her eyes.

He'd always known how easy it would be to fall in love with her. He had also always known that her falling in love with him could only hurt her and she'd been hurt enough already. Had this game for Nonna's sake gone on for too long already? Did he need to make sure she understood that he was not capable of offering anything more than friendship? Was it, perhaps, time to pull the plug out gently and let the game drain away?

Maybe.

But not today.

Not when they had a lunch to enjoy at their destination and time to explore the village of Annot before the train ride back.

And not when being looked at like that made him feel *this* good. It wouldn't hurt to have a day of imagining what it could be like if it *was* real, would it? To imagine what it would be like to be able to reach the part of his heart that had been hidden so long it was irretrievably lost. Not only to find it but then have the courage to offer it to Fiona?

* * *

The shade of the plane trees in Annot's main square was very welcome in the midday heat. So was being able to eat outside. The waiter brought them menus, glasses filled with ice cubes and a jug of Provençal rosé.

'How do you say "no anchovies"?' Fi asked Christophe as she saw the waiter coming back. She wanted to try ordering in French.

'*Pas d'anchois.*'

'*Je voudrais une salade niçoise, s'il vous plaît,*' Fi told the waiter. '*Pas d'anchois.*'

Christophe ordered moules-frites and then raised an eyebrow at Fi. 'You don't like anchovies?'

Fi made a face. 'They're hairy little fish bombs and I hate them.'

His burst of laughter made other people in the café turn to look at them. It also made them smile. The American tourist who'd taken their picture beside the train engine was also eating here and he came over to their table.

'Would you like another picture?' he said. 'You guys look like an advertisement for eating in a cute little French café.'

Fi grinned and handed him her phone. The ice cubes in her glass tinkled as she picked up her wine and held it towards Christophe. He picked up his glass and touched it to hers.

'*Cin cin.*'

'*Cin cin,*' Fi echoed.

'And one looking at me,' the American said, with a laugh. 'If you can take your eyes off of each other for long enough.'

Was that what made it suddenly feel as if the wine glasses had evaporated and it was Christophe's hand touching hers?

Whatever it was, Fi could feel the colour wash into her face.

She took her phone back and put it down without checking the photos. 'We can look at them later,' she said, 'and you can choose the best one for Nonna.' The waiter was coming back already with their meals and she leaned back so that her plate could be placed in front of her. 'This salad looks amazing.'

It was. Crunchy lettuce, green beans and tomato wedges, hard-boiled eggs and chunks of tuna. The olives and vinaigrette dressing made it the perfect Mediterranean summer lunch. She stole a few of the hot chips from Christophe's bowl as well, though.

Then they went walking into a labyrinth of narrow, cobbled streets between tall stone buildings. There were heavy wooden doors with ancient iron handles, which hinted at centuries of secrets hidden behind them, and worn cobbles in alleyways that could conjure up images of the feet or wheels and maybe hooves that must have gone over them millions of times to create those hollows and dips in solid stone – evidence of so many lives that had been lived in this village for hundreds of years.

An old galvanised-iron tub was full of cheerful red pelargo-niums but it was easy to imagine a baby being bathed in it. A lush grapevine smothering a stone wall was full of the bursts of white flowers that were nowhere near becoming fruit but Fi could imagine glasses of wine being raised in a toast like the one she had shared with Christophe. A cat was dozing on an overhead windowsill but from the corner of her eye, Fi could almost see the tail of a small donkey with baskets on its back disappearing through one of the archways to deliver groceries or carry a work-man's tools.

These streets had seen all facets of human existence. Children playing, a funeral procession, women gossiping, lovers meeting each other in secluded corners. They had been the backdrop for births, deaths, marriages, drama, misery and joy and, like every other medieval village Fi had visited, this one had that unique peacefulness engrained in its stones.

A silent whisper that time did, indeed, heal all things.

That the world would continue turning.

They found the remains of medieval ramparts, fountains, ancient chapels and the site of water-driven mills used to make flour and nut oils in the fifteenth century.

'It reminds me of Menton,' Fi said. 'With the alleyways and arches, steps and flower baskets. Without the pretty colours, of course. Or the sea.'

'Which do you prefer?' Christophe asked. 'The mountains or the sea?'

'I love them both,' Fi said. 'And the forests. I love this part of France, because it has everything, doesn't it? Even trains that look like they came out of a giant's toybox.' Impulsively, Fi stood on tiptoes to plant a kiss on Christophe's cheek. 'Thank you so much for arranging this. It's been the *best* day.' She let her breath out in a happy sigh.

She wanted to have fairy tale days like this forever, but they could only continue if Christophe felt like he could trust her. That he wasn't at any risk of getting entangled in the last thing in the world he wanted. Not that Fi was a risk, because she couldn't give him what he needed in a long-term relationship, like marriage and babies, but if that wasn't stopping the fantasy for her, maybe there was also the possibility that it was enough to make Christophe nervous and want to stop spending time like this with her.

So she gave him her brightest, lightest smile. 'Getting photos for Nonna is the most fun I think I've ever had,' she said.

She couldn't interpret the look on his face as she stepped far enough away to see it. Was he about to smile and agree about how much fun it was to be out together? Or frown because that kiss had somehow changed the mood of their day?

Or was he thinking about kissing her back, but not on her cheek?

Fi was holding her breath when they heard it a heartbeat later. The whistle from the train. The signal that all passengers needed to head back to the station for their return journey.

The moment was gone.

Maybe that was just as well, given the way the butterflies had started dancing in her belly at the thought that Christophe might want to kiss her again. Had he been waiting all this time for her to make the first move?

That would make sense if he'd been aware of how and why she had frozen the first time. But what if she had that same reaction again? What if she was never, ever going to experience even a kiss without becoming paralysed with fear? That she would never be able to replace the nightmare with something joyous that other people – like her sisters – were lucky enough to have in their lives. Could she live without even trying to experience that for the rest of her life?

Fi found herself walking a little faster as they headed back to the station. A determined sort of walk.

She wasn't quite sure what to do about it but, no, she didn't want to live with that for the rest of her life.

* * *

Fi was a little ahead of Christophe as they walked back to the station, which was a good thing, he decided. Because she wouldn't be able to see what he was thinking about.

How close he'd come to kissing her again, and it wouldn't have been a mere *bise* on her cheek. He would have kissed her on her lips. Just softly. For just long enough to let her know she could trust him not to go any further than she was ready for.

At least he had the reassurance that she didn't know how he was feeling about her. That her trust was being built on this being nothing deeper than the game of keeping Nonna happy. She would have no idea at all of his more meaningful agenda of making *her* happy and giving her the chance of a new future. Perhaps he didn't need to worry that she was hoping for anything more from him, and he didn't need to rush into giving up the pleasure of times like this in her company. Maybe he was the only one in danger of being hurt because he'd made the mistake of letting himself daydream about things being different. He could deal with that. Starting by shaking off what he'd imagined he'd seen in Fi's eyes. It was trust, not love, and that was exactly what they both needed to take the next step.

The bustle of getting everyone back on the train and being in a crowded carriage helped him step back into reality. Along with others, he leaned as far as he could from the window to get photographs of the train as it chugged around a curve in the track.

It was when he was looking at the images he'd captured, as the train was slowing as it came to the end of the journey, that he found a text message from Didier. His chest tightened painfully at the thought that something had happened to Heidi, but his friend was passing on a message from his brother.

'We need to get to the forest as soon as we can,' he told Fi as they hurried to get back to the car. 'Something terrible has happened to one of the donkeys.'

20

The forest didn't feel peaceful today.

There were horrors lurking in the quiet stillness and blood-stains on the churned-up carpet of dry leaves and acorns.

Didier's brother Alain was there. He had shifted all the donkeys to another area in the forest.

Apart from one.

Mary lay on the ground, barely alive, with a hideous, deep gash in her neck that still had a slow trickle of blood escaping.

Fi knelt by her head, so horrified she was barely able to breathe. She smoothed the hair away from the donkey's eyes that were half open but had an ominous milky glaze to them.

'Oh, my God...' she whispered. 'What's happened?'

'A *sanglier* has attacked her.' Christophe's tone was grim. He took his stethoscope out of the kit he'd brought from his vehicle and he bent his head but hesitated for a moment before putting the ear pieces in to listen to Mary's heart and breathing. 'Alain thinks she was defending her foal. She's just given birth.'

Fi gasped. She looked sideways at Alain, who was standing

close to Mary's back feet but he hadn't been following the conversation in English.

'*Le bébé*?' she asked, her voice cracking.

Alain's face folded into deeper lines and he turned his head to look down at what Fi had thought was a sack he'd packed the electric fencing into. It became even harder to drag in a new breath as she saw a tiny hoof resting on a fold in the sack.

'See if it's alive,' Christophe said quietly. 'I'll stay with Mary. I don't think there's anything we can do for her. She's lost too much blood.'

Fi knelt beside the sack and peeled back the folds. The newborn donkey was lying on its side, completely limp. Its coat was still damp and so dark it was almost black, but it had a white belly and chest. It was automatic for Fi to reach out her hands to touch this beautiful little creature who had a muzzle that was also white except for a black smudge around the nostrils and... oh... there was white fluff inside ears that were also limp, flat against its neck. The baby's eyes were half shut, like its mother's.

But it was warm.

And when Fi moved her hands to the foal's ribs and pressed gently, she could feel a heartbeat.

'It's alive,' she told Christophe. 'What should I do?'

'Keep her warm,' he said. 'I'll be there in a minute.'

The sack wasn't enough. Instinct drove Fi to scoop the baby into her arms so that she could share the warmth of her own body. She curled her back to wrap it even more securely into her arms, and it was only when she could feel the chill of the damp beginning to recede that she lifted her head to see what Christophe was doing.

He was very close. He was also kneeling on the ground and he was also bent over. He had Mary's head on his lap and he was stroking her face. She could hear the comforting murmur of his voice but couldn't tell which of his languages he was using, and she could also hear the awful sound of the last breaths before Mary's struggles were over.

Then there was only silence.

It felt as if the forest around them was absorbing the death with a serenity that simply gathered it into the circles of life that had been repeated endlessly for thousands upon thousands of years.

Nobody moved for a long, long moment.

Alain had turned his back, his hand over his eyes.

Christophe had Mary's head in his arms, his own head bent so far over it they were touching.

Fi had tears streaming down her cheeks as she watched Christophe.

As if he felt that gaze, he looked up and his eyes held hers. The moment they were sharing was bigger than the tragedy that had taken place here. The bond of friendship and trust between them was experiencing a fire that was forging it into something so much deeper that Fi could feel it in every cell of her body. It was in this precise moment that she knew, beyond any shadow of doubt, that she would never feel like this about any other human on the planet.

She loved him more than she had believed it was possible to love anyone.

She was *in* love with him.

She had no choice but to silently, privately, gift her heart and soul to this man.

* * *

It was Christophe that broke that intense eye contact.

But the private moment of communication had given him not

only the strength to think and move swiftly but the resolve to try and make this somehow less distressing for Fi.

The depth of emotion in her eyes had stolen his breath. And his heart. If they'd been alone, he would have taken her in his arms and held her the way she was holding that foal, but what she had in *her* arms was also the clear direction to take them out of this nightmare.

'We have to help the baby,' he said.

He examined the foal briefly, listened to its heart that sounded unexpectedly strong, ran his hands over the small body to make sure it hadn't also been injured by the *sanglier* and dipped the stump of the umbilical cord in some iodine.

'It's a girl,' he told Fi. 'And the best thing we can do for her now is to make sure she gets some colostrum.'

He found a small basin in a sterile package in his kit. He splashed disinfectant on his hands and then on Mary's udder and teats. He knelt beside her, totally focussed on milking as much as possible of the valuable first milk. It was a horribly grim task to have to do – he could already feel her body cooling beneath his hands – but he clenched his jaw and kept going. This colostrum contained all the nutrients, extra calories and, most importantly, the antibodies that were vital to give a newborn mammal the best chance of survival.

Alain emptied an unopened water bottle he had so that Christophe had a container to transport the milk, but he left a little in the basin and filled the syringe again. Fi held the baby's head up as he slowly trickled some liquid into its mouth, but it was too weak to swallow and it dribbled out to drip onto Fi's arm. Christophe got some sterile tubing and, as gently as he could, he fed a soft tube in through the foal's nostrils to get it as far as the stomach.

'Can you hold her with one arm as if she was standing up?' he asked Fi. 'And keep her head higher than her body with your other arm?'

He needed both hands to hold the tubing and put the nozzle of the syringe inside to push in the fluid that could mean the difference between life and death.

Alain stood behind him, watching. They had a conversation in French that Christophe didn't translate for Fi.

Alain told him that he would take care of Mary and bury her, here, in the forest. He said that the rest of the herd was safe and that he thought they'd helped fend off the attack but none of them were injured. He shook his head as he watched the care with which Christophe was feeding the foal and wondered aloud how he would be able to look after this orphan on his own.

Christophe told him he couldn't. That, being a vet, he was better placed to look after it and that Fiona would help him.

She glanced up, hearing her name, so he switched back to English. 'I've told Alain I will care for the foal. I said you'll be able to help me. Is that okay?'

'I want to take care of her,' she whispered. 'I want to take her back to La Maisonette so I can look after her myself.'

'We will take her back there,' Christophe agreed. 'It's a better environment than the veterinary clinic, but I will need to help you. As you can see, the feeding is more than one person can do alone and she will need feeding a little bit but often. Every hour or so for the next few days. And nights.'

Fi nodded. 'I can do that,' she said. 'If you can show me what to do.'

Her gaze hadn't moved from his. 'I need to save this baby,' she added, so softly he almost couldn't catch her words. Not that it mattered. He could see exactly how important this was to her and he loved the fierceness he could see in her eyes right now. The determination to protect – and love – this helpless orphan.

She was the person anyone, human or animal, would want by their side in whatever battle life could face you with.

Christophe was going to be by *her* side for as long as it took.

End of story.

* * *

Fi sat in the back of Christophe's car with the foal in her arms, its nose tucked under her chin. She could feel every breath the baby took and breathed in the scent of its fluffy hair. She could feel the soft muzzle pressed against her skin and, at one point, she was sure she felt the lick of a tongue.

The foal must be breathing in her smell too, she realised, and feeling the security and warmth of being held. A bond was forming and it was remarkably similar to the kind of bond she felt when she was near Ellie's baby, Bonnie. It was an emotional ocean that, for her own protection, she'd barely dipped her toe into so far, but this was different and she had willingly thrown herself into it. Oddly, she didn't feel as if she was going to drown.

The baby donkey could smell her and see her and feel her. She may have even tasted her and she could definitely hear the sound of her voice.

'It's going to be okay, hinny...' she told her softly, again and again. 'We're going to look after you. You're safe, wee one... I'll keep you safe...'

Fi was quite sure about that. She desperately wanted this baby to live and she knew she had the power to make it true, because she'd had the power to make the opposite happen, hadn't she? For her own baby. A wish that had come true so fast she hadn't had the time to change her mind.

If only she'd known that she would never, ever be able to take it back.

That it would haunt her forever.

Saving this baby might be as close as she would ever get to something she didn't actually deserve to get a second chance at – being a mother.

'I've got some things we'll need in my clinic,' Christophe said. 'Like clean straw and medications. But for the specialist milk replacement for equines, we'll go to another clinic where a friend of mine works. Martine has a passion for horses and works in a clinic that specialises in work with big animals.'

Martine was a tall, blonde woman who had blue eyes and a gorgeous smile that blossomed the moment she opened the door and saw Christophe. She was more than happy to supply everything he needed – bottles, teats, a big sack of replace-ment milk powder. She came out to the car to greet Fi and coo over the tiny foal before they left, and then she hugged Christophe after he opened the driver's door. A hug that was tight enough and long enough to make Fi's heart sink like a stone.

She didn't want to ask the question but it wouldn't budge when she tried to push it off her tongue. 'Martine's a good friend?'

Christophe's gaze met hers via the rear-view mirror so swiftly she knew that he'd picked up on what she was thinking. Had it been the tight note in her voice, despite her best effort to keep it casual?

'We've known each other for many years,' he said. 'And we... went out a couple of times. A very long time ago.'

'She seems very nice,' Fi said, relieved that the need to watch the road meant that the eye contact had been broken. They were past the jumble of ancient buildings of the old walled city of St Paul de Vence and heading up the hill with forest on either side of them, on their way home now.

'She thought the baby donkey was *tellement mignonne* – super cute,' Christophe added. 'She offered to help care for her.'

Fi swallowed hard. 'What did you say back?'

His gaze met hers again in the mirror. 'I said that I had everything I need,' he said. She couldn't see his mouth but she could hear the smile in his voice. 'Including you.'

Fi ducked her head, letting her nose brush the foal's muzzle, hiding her own smile.

* * *

Back at La Maisonette, Fi put the foal, wrapped in a blanket, onto the couch while they made a nest of clean straw in the corner of the living room, after shifting the confit pots.

Christophe checked his watch. 'It's time to feed her again. Martine said we need to get all the colostrum into her within the first twelve hours. That's when the most antibodies are absorbed.'

Fi nodded. 'I'll get some hot water to put a bottle in and warm it up to body temperature.'

'I'll check the instructions that Martine said are easy to find online, but she said she needs to be fed in a ratio of one hundred mils per kilogram. She's about ten kilos now, so that means a litre a day, divided into at least ten feeds. If she can't take that much at a time we need to feed more often.' He held out the water bottle full of Mary's milk. 'We've got more than half a litre of colostrum here.'

Fi took the bottle. 'I've helped bottle raise a foal once, after its mother rejected him. I remember a lot of things.'

Like how to try and persuade the foal to drink from a bottle. After several futile attempts, she put her index finger in and rubbed the roof of its mouth and waited patiently to feel the foal sucking. Then, very slowly, she removed her finger, replacing it with the teat. Christophe was holding the foal in a standing position, one arm supporting her body and his other hand cupping her head, because that was the most natural way for any foal to be feeding.

They'd put just fifty mils into the bottle for this first attempt, partly because they didn't know how successful they would be and didn't want to waste a drop of the precious colostrum. They exchanged a look of what felt like almost triumph when the bottle was empty. Christophe settled the baby onto the straw.

'I'll check her over again,' he said, 'in case I missed anything in the forest.'

Fi took the bottle into the kitchen to sterilise it ready for the next feed. By the time she came back, Christophe was draping his stethoscope around his neck.

'She seems healthy,' he said. 'A little weak but her heart sounds strong and her breathing is clear. I don't think she's premature, which is a good thing. It gives her a much better chance to survive.'

Fi let her breath out in a sigh of relief and covered the fact that she had to blink back tears by touching a tiny hoof with the odd rubbery growths that she'd seen before on newborn horse foals. They were there to protect the mother during pregnancy and the birth.

'Fairy fingers, we call these,' she told Christophe. 'Or horse feathers.'

His huff of breath was amused. 'They will fall off very soon, yes?'

'As soon as she's standing up. Within a day or two. They look creepy, don't they?'

'Creepy?' Christophe was frowning. He didn't know the word.

'Strange. Weird. What is that in French?'

'*Bizarre.*' Christophe nodded. '*Oui. C'est ça.*'

'And the rest of her is so... *perfect*. Look at those ears...'

The foal was curled up in the straw with her legs tucked in like a cat. She was looking back at them, her head up, although it was wobbling. Her ears weren't as limp now, either. They were only at half-mast but that just made her look even more adorable.

Fi touched the foal's face with gentle fingers. 'She needs a name.'

'What would you like to call her?'

'Will she be able to go out in the olive grove with Marguerite and Coquelicot when she's older? She'll need role models so that she can learn she's a donkey. Or will Alain want her back in his herd?'

Christophe's lips tilted. 'She's your donkey now, Fiona, if you want her.'

Fi nodded. She had to clear the sudden lump that had formed in her throat. 'Then she needs a flower name,' she said. 'A French flower name.'

'I agree.'

Christophe reached to stroke the tiny donkey's neck. Fi was rubbing the gorgeous ear with its black hair on the outside and long white fluff on the inside. Their hands brushed and Fi felt the electric current of the touch run up her arm and become a warmth that filled her chest.

'Daisies and poppies are wildflowers, aren't they?' she asked.

'Yes.'

'So we need a wildflower name. Which ones do you know?'

'Ah... *Bluet*? I don't know the name in English.'

Fi looked it up online on her phone. 'It's a cornflower.' She tilted her head. 'What else?'

'*Pissenlit*?'

It was a dandelion, Fi discovered. She read more and then her jaw dropped. 'It translates as pissing in the bed? It's a diuretic?'

Christophe laughed. 'Yes. A *diurétique*. It makes you lose water.'

Fi was laughing too and the aftermath of the horrific scene in the forest was fading. 'We're so *not* going to call her *Pissenlit*.'

'What about *Bouton d'or*? *Bouton* is a button and *or* is the word for gold.'

Fi didn't need to look for a translation. 'That must be a buttercup. Oh... I love that. And a button is exactly what she is at the moment because she's so little and cute.'

* * *

Despite the warmth of the late afternoon, they could see a shiver ripple Bouton's body. Fi was coming back downstairs with a blanket when she saw Ellie out on the terrace. She opened the French doors for her.

'*Cou cou*, Christophe.' If Ellie thought there was any significance in finding him alone in La Maisonette with Fi, she hid it well. Or perhaps she was totally distracted by what else she could see.

'Aww... is that a baby *donkey*?'

'Her name is Bouton,' Fi said. 'Short for Buttercup.'

'How old is she?'

'Just a few hours, I think,' Christophe said. 'Her mother was killed by a *sanglier*.'

'We're going to bottle-feed her,' Fi added. 'She can live with Marguerite and Coquelicot when she's a little older. If that's okay with you?'

'Of course it is.' Ellie was crouched beside the straw nest, stroking Bouton's head. The baby was lying flat again but her eyes were bright and she didn't seem to mind the amount of attention she was getting.

'Do you want some nappies to put on her while she's inside?'

'That's a great idea. It'll make the straw stay clean for much longer. We'll just need to cut a hole for her tail.'

'Bonnie's size might fit for now but I'll tell Laura to bring some of Lili's over tomorrow. Oh, Lili and Theo are going to *adore* Bouton.'

'It'll be a while before they can play with her. I think she's been confused and frightened enough for her first day in the world.'

'We'll wait. Or they can just have a peep from the door. And Mam will want to see her before she goes. Oh...' Ellie gave her head a small shake. 'That's what I came over to tell you. She's busy packing to go back to Scotland tomorrow and... guess what?'

'What?'

'Dad's going with her.'

'How long for?'

'There's no time limit. Mam says they'll take it one day at a time and if he's not happy or it's too much, she'll come back to make sure he's home safely. Laura's going to drive them both to the airport.'

Fi found herself going very still as she absorbed this news. The love was there for her father. From all of them but especially from the woman he had married. He was being given a second chance. A chance to get past the nightmare that had destroyed life as he'd known it.

This was huge.

And just as emotional as having a newborn to nurture.

It was a heady mix of family and love, forgiveness and healing and... hope. It shone like a star that was almost close enough for Fi to touch.

To believe in for herself?

Ellie must have picked up on how overwhelming it was. She wrapped her sister in a tight hug.

'Is there anything I can do to help?' she asked.

'I'll let you know,' Fi said. 'The next few days are going to be intense, with keeping her warm and feeding her every hour or two round the clock. If Christophe needs to go into work during the day, tomorrow, I might need some help with the feeding but...' She looked past Ellie to see Christophe tucking the blanket around Bouton and her heart melted. 'We'll manage for tonight,' she said.

Ellie followed her gaze and she smiled. 'I'm sure you will,' she murmured.

* * *

It was well past midnight when they managed to get Bouton to drink the last of the colostrum and they both went into the kitchen to clean the bottle and teat.

'This is good,' Christophe said. 'She's had most of it probably within the twelve hours of being born. We'll make up some formula for her next bottle.'

Fi turned her head to look at the only part of the foal that was visible – a face framed by the blanket and straw. 'I think she's asleep. Can I get you something to drink, Christophe? A cup of tea or a glass of wine?'

He considered this. 'I think we both deserve a glass of wine. It's been... what's the expression... "a hell of a day"?'

It had been a total rollercoaster, starting with the shock of suspecting that Fiona's feelings for him were as deep as his were for her and the decision that it was time to kill this game of pretending they were a couple, only to put it off because he simply didn't want it to stop yet, and finishing with the horror of having to milk a dead donkey that became a poignant joy when the little baby managed to drink all the milk in the bottle. Fiona had to be feeling even more emotionally battered – she now had to factor in the news that her mother was leaving, taking her newly found father away with her.

It was a surprise to see the smile that softened her whole face now. And to see in her eyes that the peaks of the rollercoaster were overriding the swoops and low points. He loved that she could choose to see the positive things in life. He loved how strong she was and how she was embracing all the new challenges that life was throwing at her. Christophe felt so proud of her, in fact, he could feel a lump in his throat.

'It *has* been a hell of a day,' Fi said. 'I'd love a wine, too. And there's plenty more of the bread and ham and cheese that Mam and Ellie brought over, if you're hungry.'

They took sandwiches and wine and went to sit on what felt like the most comfortable couch in the world.

For a while they ate in silence. It was Christophe who broke it.

'Are you happy that your mamma is going back to Scotland, with your father?'

Fi nodded slowly. 'I'll miss them both but I am happy. And I really hope it goes well and she doesn't need to bring him back too soon because it's too much for him.'

She took a sip of her wine. 'I love that my mother still loves him. And that she can forgive and forget what was such a hard time for our family when her children were so young. It's astonishing that she's been lucky enough to find the man who is the love of her life again. But...' She bit her lip. 'I do envy the fact that she found him in the first place, to be honest.'

Christophe nodded. 'It would be wonderful to find that person. To know that there was no one else in the entire world that you wanted to be with. And even better, that they felt the same way about you.' He held Fi's gaze. 'You'll find that person,' he added softly. 'One day.'

'So will you,' she said. 'It will be easier for you.'

'Why?' Did she have no idea, Christophe wondered, how impossible it was for him?

'Because you're... kind and clever and...' Colour was flooding Fi's cheeks and she dipped her head to avoid his gaze. '...and... beautiful,' she added in a whisper.

Oh... There was a pain in his chest that was right where his heart was. Christophe put a single finger under Fi's chin and gently lifted it.

'And you think you're *not*?' he asked, making it very clear in his tone how wrong she was.

Time stopped. The way it had in that moment before he'd kissed her the first time. It could happen again, Christophe realised. Fiona was thinking about it too, he was sure of that, and if she came to him it might mean she trusted him enough for the fear to be overcome.

But time hadn't stopped, of course. And the chiming sound that unexpectedly filled the space between them totally shattered the moment.

'That's the alarm on my phone,' he said. 'It's time to feed Bouton again.'

* * *

Fi learned how to mix the milk replacement formula.

She held the bottle and fed Bouton while Christophe held the foal upright but she was doing everything with less than half her mind on it.

She was thinking about what Christophe had said, and it was

another spiral of emotion that was pulling her every which way like everything else that had happened today.

He thought that she was beautiful? His words had been a physical caress that she'd felt skimming her skin and leaving goosebumps in their wake.

But he also thought that she would find someone else who would be that person for her? The one she would want to be with more than any other person on earth? At least she'd managed to hide her feelings as well as she'd hoped to. Christophe had no idea that *he* was that person. That finding someone else remotely like him would be, quite simply, impossible.

By the time they'd finished getting the small amount of milk into Bouton, Fi was so exhausted that, when she curled up on her end of the couch, she drifted into sleep almost instantly. It felt like only seconds when she heard the chimes of Christophe's alarm again. He looked as half asleep as she felt, but they went through the motions of making the formula, feeding the baby foal and then cleaning up again and again that night.

Laura arrived early the next morning, with croissants and pains au chocolat, still warm from the boulangerie in Vence. She had hot, strong coffee in paper cups as well.

'You are an angel,' Fi told her.

Christophe nodded his agreement, his mouth too full to say anything. There were tiny flakes of croissant around his lips. His hair was rumpled and there was even a stalk of straw caught in it. His jaw was shadowed with stubble and his clothes were covered in stains that were a record of the traumatic hours yesterday. He looked as if he'd been living on the streets for weeks but, to Fi, he'd never looked this beautiful.

She probably looked just as bad but Christophe was looking back at her and, if she let herself, she could believe that he was thinking exactly the same about her. She wasn't going to let

herself believe that. She couldn't afford to, not when she was this
tired and could make a mistake and reveal too much. Better to
focus on what was around her and real. Like the tote bag Laura
had brought with her along with breakfast.

'Did you bring some of Lili's nappies?'

'Yes,' Laura said. 'And I wondered if you might want to make a
coat for Bouton, to help keep her warm. There's an old jumper in
there.' She grinned. 'The one I used to hide my pregnancy when I
came here for Ellie's wedding.'

Fi lifted out the oversized soft, black woollen jumper. 'This
will be perfect,' she said. 'I can cut it to fit. The sleeves can cover
her front legs and I can make some more for the back legs. Are
you sure you don't mind if I chop it up?'

'I haven't worn it since I was pregnant,' Laura said. 'And I have
nothing to hide now.' She gave Bouton another gentle stroke,
hugged Fi and smiled at Christophe. 'I'll be back later,' she said.
'I'm going to take Mam to collect Dad and then take them both to
the airport. Ellie will be over soon to help you today. She said
Julien thinks Christophe might need to go to work for a while.'

Christophe was nodding again, this time not nearly as enthu-
siastically. 'I'll help with the next feed,' he said, 'but I do need to
do a surgery today. I have to collect Heidi from Didier's house
and...' He made a face. 'I really need a shower and some clean
clothes.'

His gaze shifted to Fi. 'I'll bring some more clothes tonight.
And my toothbrush. We can try leaving it longer between feeds
soon but it's still going to be a long night.'

21

Bouton's legs might have been a bit wobbly but she managed to stand by herself for the first time to drink a bottle of milk in the early hours of the following morning.

This was a real milestone because it meant that soon it would be possible for just one person to do the feeding and they could take turns and get some real sleep instead of the fitful dozing for what felt like only minutes at a time.

Being this tired was kind of like being rather drunk.

'That was nearly two hundred mils,' Fi said, as she rinsed out the bottle. 'Does that mean we can increase the time between the feeds to two hours?'

'I think so. Why don't we try it this time? I'll stay on the couch and you could go to bed for a couple of hours. I might even be able to manage to do it by myself.'

'That's not fair. You're the one who'll have to go to work later.'

'I'm good at sleeping. Thank you for bringing pillows and blankets down for the couch.'

They both pulled a blanket over themselves as they settled back onto the soft leather cushions of the couch. Being this tired also seemed to make you feel cold. Fi was almost shivering, so she snuggled into the blanket she had taken from her bed upstairs, pulling it over her shoulders to tuck around her neck.

Bouton raised her head to look at them but then let it droop and closed her eyes again. She didn't need a blanket over her tonight. With a little time to spare before the car trip up to the old barn in the mountains, and hearing what Fi was planning to do with Laura's old jumper, Jeannie had dashed over with some wool needles, a ball of yarn and instructions. Ellie had helped her cut the garment up and make it into a soft, warm coat for the foal. She also had the warmth of another animal lying close by. Heidi had taken her time to greet Bouton and let herself be sniffed and then she'd settled on the edge of the straw nest to guard the new baby.

Christophe smiled at his dog. 'I think she's in love,' he said.

'Bouton might start to think Heidi's her mother.'

'Marguerite and Coquelicot will take her place but it's nice that she can have an animal friend inside, yes?'

Fi was smiling too. 'It's always special to see different animals that love being together.'

Christophe put a pillow behind his head. It was close enough to be touching Fi's pillow. For a long moment, they sat there in silence. Fi was beginning to drift into sleep when she heard Christophe's soft query.

'Have you ever been in love, Fiona?'

Oh... She didn't open her eyes. 'Only once,' she said. 'So far.'

With *him*... and it wasn't in the past tense.

Christophe's body was close enough to her own to feel the tension gathering, like the string of a bow being pulled back. 'Was it with *him*?' The word was the arrow being fired. 'The *bastardo* who hurt you?'

'*No.*' Fi shook her head sharply. Her desire for the attention of

Murray McKay had been based on nothing more than a crush. It had never been love. She hadn't known him and she'd found out the hard way that she couldn't trust him. 'I didn't even know what being in love felt like back then.'

'But you do now?'

Fi nodded. She couldn't meet Christophe's gaze and she couldn't even begin to explain what it felt like to be experiencing this for the first time. It was so totally different from the love she had for her mother and sisters. The love that was still there for her father and was being uncovered enough to feel real but not the same as it had been. It was different from the love that she felt for the children in her life now and the animals she loved to be around so much. There were elements of how deep all those kinds of love could be but, if the love she had for all these people and animals were the shining stars of a night sky, *this* kind of love was the sun coming up the next morning.

Christophe's voice broke the spell being cast by her thoughts.

'Did he feel the same way?' Christophe asked.

'No.' The word came out in a whisper.

'That was unfortunate.' Christophe's tone was sympathetic. 'Perhaps he couldn't see how lucky he was.'

Oh, help... this was becoming a dangerous conversation.

'It wasn't his fault. He had his own issues and it didn't help that I can't... that I'm...'

...*frigid*?

No. She couldn't use that word. She had no doubt that the people who'd thought she was weird, like her old boss, might have used it when they were talking about that 'weird Gilchrist girl' behind her back, but maybe it wasn't true. She'd just never had the chance – or the courage – to even try and find out. Not that she could say that to Christophe, of all people. Fi knew she should stop talking. Right now. But the words just formed themselves and fell out of her mouth.

'It's just because no one has ever wanted me,' she said. 'Not like that.'

She'd shocked herself as well as Christophe. The breath she caught a heartbeat later sounded horribly like a stifled sob. It was no surprise that Christophe put his arm around her shoulders, as if he wanted to comfort her.

'That's not true, *amore*,' he said softly. 'You might not have seen it, but I can tell you that there are many people out there who will want you and... the man you choose will be the luckiest man in the world.'

Fi blinked hard. She didn't want to cry. She especially didn't want to cry in front of Christophe. She didn't want to move out of the circle of his arm, either. She turned her head just enough that her cheek could press against his ribs.

'Your trust got broken when you were hurt,' he said quietly. 'It's no wonder that you find it hard to let anyone close enough to... to love you back. But, you know... that kind of touching is simply the way to feel the love, instead of hearing it in words or seeing it on your lover's face. It can be the most beautiful thing.'

Fi swallowed hard. 'Is it like that for you?'

Christophe's breath came out in a heavy sigh. 'Yes and no. My trust got broken too. I can be *in* love, the sex can be *extraordinaire* but only for a short time. I can't stay long enough to get hurt again. I have to escape before there's any chance of that happening.'

'I want that...'

She could feel a rumble of stifled laughter inside his chest. 'To escape?'

'No...' Fi caught her bottom lip between her teeth as she tilted her head to look up at him. 'I want to know what it's like to have sex like that. I...' This time, her new breath in was a tiny gasp. 'I want to know if it's even possible for me...'

'I'm sure it will be,' Christophe said. 'If you are with someone you trust enough.'

This was it. The chance to take a leap of faith like no other.

'I trust *you*...'

She felt the press of Christophe's lips against her hair. It wasn't a kiss, just a soft pressure. The edges of his voice were rough now. 'You *are* safe with me, Fiona. I promise you.'

It was that thought that undid her.

The thought that Christophe could care enough for her to promise what she needed more than anything else. The reassurance that she *could* trust him.

She felt safe.

More than that, she felt cared for.

Loved, even.

'I do want to kiss you,' Christophe said then. 'I want to show you that it's possible for you, *cara*. If you'll let me? You can tell me to stop at any time and I promise you I will.'

Fi's heart missed a beat and then started racing. She had never trusted anyone as much as she trusted this man but a part of her was still terrified. The pain and shock of losing her virginity to rape was a big part of that, but there was something even deeper that was always there and that had come from the chant of shame in her childhood that she didn't look like her sisters.

'The chubby one – with the hair like a wire pot scourer, poor bairn.'

And the worst one?

'...look at yourself in the mirror, Fiona Gilchrist. Who'd want you...?'

Christophe did.

He'd grown up with women who looked very much like her

and he adored them, so maybe she didn't need to feel ashamed of her body. And maybe he was doing this simply out of the kindness of his heart because he could see the walls she'd built around herself, but did that matter?

Even if it could only ever happen this once, Fi wanted it.

This could be the only chance she'd ever have of finding out what it was about sex that could be so amazing. She would understand, then, the undercurrents of a physical bond that Ellie and Julien had with each other. And Laura and Noah. Maybe it was even being found again between her parents. A facet of love that might be a key ingredient she still hadn't discovered in the magic of being in love.

Aye... she wanted this. More than she had ever wanted anything. And she wanted it beyond anything her head was telling her. This was a need rather than merely a want, and it was coming from her heart and soul, not her head.

Fi could feel the beat of her blood pulsing in her neck as she finally looked up to meet his gaze. His face was so close to hers she could feel the warmth of his skin and the puff of his breath. She felt his forehead touch hers for a steady beat and then the tip of his nose against hers, giving it a tiny rub.

'I want you to kiss me,' she whispered.

She didn't close her lips after the last word left them and his lips were so close to hers she could feel them tingling with the touch that was like a butterfly's wing as he moved his lips across hers. The way he let the air out of his chest was a sigh that sounded like pure pleasure. He was savouring this. He wanted it to last. He was enjoying being so patient.

Fi could feel the sigh reverberating in her own body. She was relaxing. Sinking into this space that had just become their own private world. Okay, there might be a large dog and a tiny donkey in the corner of the room but they were both sound asleep. It was just her and Christophe.

And she was safe.

Fi pressed her mouth closer to his and let her tongue emerge far enough to taste his bottom lip. Could he feel the ripple of sensation that made a tiny shudder skate down her spine?

He must have, because one of his hands slid onto the skin of her neck, softly rubbing each bump of her spine down to her shoulders. He was still kissing her but his tongue hadn't come to meet hers. He wasn't going to go any faster than she wanted him to. Or do anything that would scare her.

And, suddenly, that made her brave.

She knew she wanted this.

And now she wanted *more*.

Her tongue found his and it took this kiss into a realm that was completely new to Fi. How was it that she could feel the slide of his tongue against hers echoing in the most secret part of her body? The place that she'd thought she would never want any man to touch again.

Amazingly, she wanted that now too, and it was an ache of need that she'd never felt before. Strong enough to break a kiss that was more than capable of drugging her senseless.

'Touch me,' she murmured. '*Please...*'

With a soft groan, he moved his mouth so that his lips were against her neck and she knew he could feel that pulse beating against his lips. He traced his fingers along her collarbone and then flicked open a couple of buttons on her shirt, and he was touching the soft skin of her breast and finding the hard pebble of her nipple to send a streak of sensation fanning out like flames erupting.

It was her turn to make a sound – one of astonished pleasure

– and his hand stilled instantly. He pulled his head back and Fi stared up at him.

'Don't stop,' she begged, her words urgent. 'I want you. *All* of you...'

* * *

Christophe hadn't intended to rush this in any way.

He'd been waiting for this moment and he wanted it to be the best it could possibly be.

This was the lesson in lovemaking he had imagined more than once – the one that would show Fiona how beautiful it could be to communicate by touch. To stroke and kiss and taste the body of someone you could absolutely trust not to hurt you. This was exactly the gift he'd hoped to give her. A healing experience that could quite possibly change the rest of her life.

He hadn't expected it to be the best sex of his own life.

He could feel her responses as sharply as his own when they had helped each other undress and were skin to skin on this wonderful old couch. He soothed goosebumps on her skin with his tongue and lips. He guided her tentative hand to show her how he liked to be touched but he let her decide if, when and how she wanted him inside her. It felt as if she knew she was in control and she was safe – right until the moment the ripples of her climax made her fall apart in his arms with a cry of ecstasy that was somehow in the shape of his name, and it only took one more thrust for him to join her in falling over the edge of bliss.

Christophe wasn't at all surprised that Fiona was crying in his arms afterwards. He had no words to tell her that he understood how big this had been for her. Or what a privilege it had been to be the one who had led her past such a barrier in her life. He knew he didn't actually need to say anything.

He just needed to hold her.
And let her cry.

22

So...

This was what being in love was *really* like.

When it was hard to think about anything else. Any*one* else.

When just a glance could melt something deep inside your body and create sparkles that filled the air. It made colours brighter and the scent of flowers – like the rose-smothered archway outside the front door of La Maisonette, and the lavender hedge that lined the path leading to the gate – smell so amazing. It made food taste so much more delicious, especially when Christophe took over the small kitchen and created something mouth-wateringly Italian.

Fi knew that, for the rest of her life, she would never be able to breathe in the aroma from a sprig of lavender or a slice of pizza without thinking of Christophe Brabant.

And feeling this... *yearning* for more.

Because, as perfect as it was, it was never quite enough.

She also knew that showing her how good sex could actually be had only been intended as a one-off. For both of them, despite it lifting their bond to a level Fi hadn't even known two people could share in real life and not in the pages of a fairy tale where everyone got to live happily ever after. That intention had lasted all of two days, as Bouton continued to thrive and could now drink enough milk to last for three hours between the night feeds.

Fi had been at the kitchen sink, sterilising the bottle with boiling water, but she could feel Christophe's stare on her back as strongly as if it were a physical touch. When she'd turned and locked eyes with him, they were both completely lost – along with any good intentions they might have had.

They made love in the old brass bed upstairs in the cottage that night and, this time, Fi found her fear was far enough in the distance to not be able to see it clearly. There was a lightness in the touching and kissing. A playfulness was dancing amongst the swirls of intensity and expressed in soft ripples of laughter and whispered words in languages Fi didn't need any translation for because the intensity of passion needed nothing more than touch to be understood perfectly well.

Fi was ready to embrace every bit of this lovemaking, and it was surprisingly easy to try and give back as much as she was being given by a man who had to be the most generous, considerate lover any woman could wish for. Was this what both her sisters had been lucky enough to find in the men they had fallen in love with? If so, it was no wonder they wanted to build a family and life around it. That they wanted it to last forever.

* * *

When Bouton was two weeks old, they taught her to drink from a bucket.

Fi explained the process to Christophe.

'Ellie took me to the bricolage and we found this flexible bucket which is perfect because it's wide and shallow and it has handles. We'll put the milk into it and hold it at head height but she won't know what to do at first. We'll have to show her.'

They had been taking the foal out to get some sunshine and exercise for days now after Christophe had finished work. He and Julien had built a pen near the terrace that would keep her safe when they weren't outside to watch her, and it was close enough for her to see Marguerite and Coquelicot and for them to get used to the baby before they were properly introduced. It turned out that the rock wall in the lemon orchard that made up one end of the pen was the perfect height to set the bucket onto and teach Bouton to feed herself.

Christophe sat on the wall and held the bucket steady and Fi sat on the other side of the bucket and put her fingers into Bouton's mouth. When she started sucking, Fi slowly lowered her fingers into the milk. Bouton threw up her head when she found herself sucking on liquid and gave a disgusted sounding snort that splashed milk all over Christophe and Fi's faces. They both dissolved into laughter.

'It might take all of today for her to learn. Why don't you try this time?'

Christophe was looking down at Bouton as he offered his fingers to the foal but, as soon as she started sucking he glanced up and caught Fi's gaze and he knew she'd found the sensation on all the nerve endings in her fingertips had made her mind wander in exactly the same direction. Christophe could feel his entire body responding to what felt like a desperate need to take Fiona into his arms and make love to her again.

Once hadn't been enough.

Neither had twice.

It was so easy to think of a reason for just one more time. Maybe there were other things he could teach her. Maybe it was a process that needed longer to become truly confident in, like most learning situations.

And maybe... just maybe... it didn't even have to end?

Oddio... Where had *that* come from? It should have been a warning but this wasn't the time to worry about the implications of what was no more than a fleeting thought. He managed to focus on his task instead and it seemed as if Bouton had managed to swallow some milk as he dipped his fingers just below the surface.

The rest of this learning session for Bouton went past in a blur that ended with her alone in her pen, under the shade of a lemon tree, with enough milk in her belly to keep her happy for at least an hour or two. She had some hay in the pen to practise nibbling on, as well.

It was the first time they'd made love in daylight. It was also when Christophe realised that he did have more to teach Fiona. He saw a shyness that hadn't been there in the safe cover of a dim light at night, and when she tried to hide herself with the sheet, he gently coaxed her to let it go.

'Why?' he asked, leaning in to kiss her. 'Why would you want to hide something so perfect?'

* * *

When Bouton was four weeks old, they put her into the now dusty, sun-baked olive grove with Marguerite and Coquelicot for parts of the day so she could learn to be a donkey. She adored Fi. And Heidi. But neither of them could explain to her that she was actually a donkey. The older jennies accepted her presence without any fuss and tolerated the baby's antics patiently, but if she had any ideas of them providing the milk instead of her having to go to her bucket, they politely, but firmly walked away.

Heidi loved the antics. The big, gentle dog would play with the foal, sometimes being the one to initiate a game with a play bow and then a very sedate chase that Bouton was always allowed to win. At other times she would find herself being chased or jumped on without warning when Bouton felt the need for a frolic.

The adoration between the little donkey and Fi was mutual. She didn't need any help to care for the foal during the day now but she still brought her inside at night to her straw bed, which now had a guard made out of a child's wooden playpen, and she got up at least once to give her a feed during the night. She could easily have managed that by herself, too, but it was a reason for Christophe to stay and, if Fiona's sisters or his friends were reading any significance into his frequent overnight visits, they weren't saying anything to intrude on their privacy.

His mother had guessed they'd taken another step in their relationship, the last time he and Fiona had gone to Menton to have dinner with her and Nonna. She'd been watching them and perhaps she'd caught a glance they shared, or the way they seemed to find an opportunity to let their hands brush in passing or their legs touch when they were sitting side by side. It was no more than a fleeting smile but Christophe knew that she was thinking of the joy a *bambino* would bring. Maybe she was wondering where it was that she had stored the box with the toy train set inside it.

He couldn't blame her.

Despite his best efforts, he was starting to think about things like that himself.

Somehow, this friendship with Fiona had snuck past the

boundaries that he'd considered unbreachable. This was no longer a means to help her to have the better future she deserved and enjoy all the good things that life could offer – including sex. It wasn't the kind of being 'in love' that Christophe had learned to dip into long enough to enjoy the buzz but to walk away from before he'd got out of his depth.

That errant thought that this might not have to end had taken root in the back of his mind and it kept coming back to whisper more. Okay... Christophe's trust had been broken beyond repair. But it wasn't Fiona who had broken it, was it?

She was nothing like Marcella.

She was nothing like any other woman he'd ever known.

He *could* trust her. How could he not, when she had trusted him with something so huge that was far more than a purely physical act with her body?

He'd put up a wall to prevent this becoming anything serious. Was that wall his declaration that he could never provide the bride his family were so desperate for? Or him telling her how much his mother wanted grandchildren that Fiona would never be able to have?

What if he could get past the fear of the ultimate vulnerability of telling someone that you were in love with them, that you wanted to share your life with them, and be able to face the risk of a rejection that could destroy you?

What if he could find the courage to tell Fiona how he felt about her?

And that it didn't matter if she couldn't have babies herself. There were other ways to create a family, weren't there?

* * *

The days only seemed to get hotter as summer neared its end.

Laura and Noah were talking about putting a swimming pool into their garden.

Julien and Ellie purchased a flash new barbecue for their garden and invited the whole family and Christophe for dinner on their terrace the day it was delivered. They had more to celebrate than the gourmet outdoor kitchen they were creating. Jeannie and Gordon were coming back soon for a visit. Gordon was missing his studio in the old barn and they were both missing France, they said. They were missing their 'girls' – their daughters and granddaughters.

It had been very obvious for some time on video calls that the Gilchrist parents' reunion was entering a new phase and they were closer than ever. *Happier* than ever. They'd had a wonderful summer – they'd even been swimming at the beach – and taking Gordon back to Scotland had been the best idea. Both the environment and the therapies he was receiving were helping good memories to sift slowly back and the bad ones to be modified. The suggestion that they might look for a little house in France to share had been casually thrown into more than one conversation recently. Everyone who knew them on the French side of the channel agreed that they both looked years younger. They really did look like a couple in love.

So here they all were, meeting to talk about the upcoming visit, where Jeannie, and possibly Gordon, would want to stay and whether Noah should line up a few houses for them to look at. They had gathered on the Rousseaus' terrace with its rustic wooden table that had long bench seats on either side, beneath a grapevine so lush it was sending out tendrils long enough for Theo to be able to jump up and catch the lowest leaves.

At the far end of the terrace, Noah and Christophe were admiring the features of the shiny, stainless-steel barbecue, watching Julien turn sausages on the grill with a pair of long tongs. The aroma of the Provençal herbs in the pork sausages was already scenting the air with flavours like thyme, oregano, marjoram and tarragon.

The men had glasses of red wine in their hands and, judging by their gestures, shrugs and animated conversation, they were discussing the order in which to cook the rest of the array of meat, seafood and vegetables on the side wings of the central grill plates and hooded temperature-controlled oven. They had plenty of choice with steaks, chicken kebabs and prawns to add to the sausages. Heidi and Pascal were lying in the shade nearby, clearly hoping that they were going to share whatever it was that smelled so good.

The Gilchrist sisters had all made their favourite salads. *Insalata Caprese* for Ellie, with its sliced mozzarella cheese and tomatoes, fresh basil leaves and olive oil. A *salade niçoise* for Fi – without anchovies, of course – not just because she loved the flavours and freshness but because it was always going to remind her of the romantic lunch she'd shared with Christophe in Annot.

For Laura, it was a classic French *salade verte*, a simple bowl of the freshest green lettuce leaves with a dressing she had perfected, deliciously aromatic with Dijon mustard, fresh garlic and lemon juice.

'I've got a potato gratin in the oven, too,' Ellie said.

'And I've got heaps of bread. French baguettes and Italian ciabatta.' Laura laughed. 'All we'd need is some Scottish plain breid and we'd have covered all cultural bases. I'll go and start slicing it up for the baskets.' She turned to hold out her hand to Lili, who was walking quite confidently now as long as she had a hand to hang onto. 'Coming to help Mammy, poppet?'

Ellie had Bonnie in her arms. 'I should go and check on the potato gratin.'

They both turned as they heard Theo's cry of pain. The small boy was clutching a handful of grape leaves but he'd missed his footing as he'd jumped and was now sitting on the paving stones with a freshly grazed knee and a face that advertised he was about to start crying.

Julien turned, tongs in one hand and his wine in the other but Ellie moved faster.

'Here,' she said to Fi. 'Take Bonnie for me.'

Without waiting for a response, she shoved her baby into Fi's arms and went to Theo. When Julien saw the way his son held up his arms to Ellie he gave a nod and turned back to his task. Ellie carried Theo into the house and Fi was left on the terrace alone.

Holding Bonnie.

The baby she had, so far, managed to avoid holding like this.

She could have followed Ellie into the house and got Laura to rescue her but... she couldn't move. The weight of the baby was so warm and surprisingly solid and Bonnie was awake and looking back at her. For a long, long moment, they simply stared at each other.

And then Bonnie smiled at her. A smile that grew into a wide, gummy grin and looked as though she was using her whole body to produce it. Bonnie was fair beaming at her – as if Fi was the best thing to happen to her all day.

It was impossible not to smile back. Not to feel her heart filling up and overflowing with love for this small human who was part of her family and would be part of her life forever. She would be able to share all her milestones of taking her first steps and saying her first words. She would be there to cuddle her if she was sad and put a plaster on an ouchie like Ellie was doing for Theo at the moment. Maybe she would be there to celebrate this child's graduation from university or watch her walk down an aisle to marry the love of her life.

The things she would never be able to do with the baby she could have had.

It was then that Fi realised she wasn't alone with Bonnie any longer. Christophe had left Julien and Noah to supervise the barbecue and he had a hip perched on the end of the long table, his body very still, his eyes resting on her and a smile that barely tilted his lips but somehow reflected the kind of huge emotions that Fi was suddenly struggling with, like loss. And guilt.

His voice had a note in it she'd never heard before.

'You would be the best mother ever,' he said softly. 'I can feel the love from all the way over here.'

Fi had to blink back tears. 'I told you... I can't...'

Christophe put his wine glass down on the table. He straightened and then took a step closer to her and he still had that smile and a look in his eyes that made her think he could see right into her soul.

'You don't have to give birth to a baby to be the mother,' he said. 'Look at Ellie and Theo.'

'*No*...' The word was desperate. 'You don't understand. It's not that I can't *have* babies. It's...'

Words failed her completely as panic slid out of hidden spaces. She couldn't say anything more. She couldn't bear what Christophe would think of her if he knew. She had sworn she would never tell anyone. It was a terrible secret she had to take to her grave.

The furrows on Christophe's forehead were a clear indication that he still didn't understand. Was he thinking that Fi simply didn't want a baby? That she had no ambition to be a mother? He was Italian and adored his family, so of course he wouldn't understand that.

Behind Christophe, Fi could see Ellie coming out of the house. Theo was beside her, with a tear-streaked face and a plaster on his knee. Ellie came straight to Fi and scooped Bonnie out of her arms.

'Sorry about that,' she said. 'I know you don't really do babies.'

'It's fine,' Fi managed. 'She's the bonniest wee bairn ever. You picked the perfect name.'

'We did, didn't we?' Ellie lifted her baby to kiss her. 'And it's part French as well as Scottish. *Bonne* for good.' She kissed Bonnie again. 'But you're better than good, aren't you, *ma poupée*? You're just *perfect...*'

She looked up at Fi. 'We could see Bouton out of the window when we were upstairs washing Theo's knee. Is she okay?'

'What do you mean?'

Christophe had turned away to pick up his wine glass, the sound of laughter from Julien and Noah clearly pulling him back to his friends, but he turned back swiftly as he heard the concern in Fi's voice.

'She's just lying in the middle of the olive grove. Sound asleep. As flat as a pancake. We saw Marguerite go and sniff her. She might have even nudged her but she still didn't wake up.'

Fi's gaze caught Christophe's, her heart sinking like a stone.

Something didn't feel right.

Ellie must have seen the flash of fear in her eyes as she realised that something might be wrong. She touched Theo's head and said something about his papa that made him run towards the other end of the terrace.

'I'll keep him here,' she said, as Fi turned to go to the fence that separated this garden from the olive grove. 'And Heidi.'

Christophe gave a single nod. He opened the gate for Fi and then clicked it shut behind them.

Fi was frozen, holding her breath for a long moment as she stared at the black shadow on the ground that was Bouton. A very still, lifeless-looking shadow. She felt Christophe take her hand and squeeze it. She could pull in a deep breath, now. And move again.

She could do this.

She could do anything, with Christophe beside her like this.

23

Bouton wasn't dead.

She was, however, very sick.

Noah was left to cope with the barbecue alone. Christophe carried Bouton back into La Maisonette and Julien went to fetch both their medical kits. Ellie and Laura looked after the children next door. And Fi...?

Fi knelt as close as she could to the little donkey foal who had stolen such a large part of her heart over the last few months. When Christophe had finished shining a torch into Bouton's eyes and checking the colour of her gums and had his stethoscope against her ribs, Fi wriggled closer so that she could keep Bouton's head on her lap and stroke her face and scratch her gently under her chin, just behind her muzzle with the smudge on top. It was one of Bouton's favourite ways to be petted but she wasn't about to nibble Fi's arm or clothes with her velvety lips to let her know how much she was enjoying it. The effort of even lifting her head was too much. And then she coughed, a dry sound that was so unusual it made Fi blink.

'How did she get so sick, so quickly?' she asked, in disbelief. 'I know she didn't want much milk this morning but we're well into weaning her, so I wasn't worried. What did I miss?'

Christophe took out the earpieces of his stethoscope. 'She's got crackles in both her lungs,' he told Fi. 'She's breathing too fast and her temperature's high. I think she has pneumonia and that can be hard to spot until it becomes serious.'

'Oh... *God*...' Fi had to squeeze her eyes shut for a heartbeat. 'I know how dangerous that is for foals.'

Bouton was in real danger of dying and Fi could feel her heart trying to break already.

'I'm going to call Martine,' Christophe said. 'And get her advice on the best treatment.' He crouched in front of Fi and waited for her to lift her gaze to his. 'We may still have caught this early enough.'

He had a long conversation with Martine on his phone. A video call so that she could see the foal. It wasn't until the call was ended that he translated any of it for Fi.

'This is the age that foals are most likely to get pneumonia,' he told her. 'The immunity that comes from colostrum is fading and their own immune systems are not strong enough yet. It's also the time of year that it's most likely, because of the summer heat. It could be either viral or bacterial, but it's more likely that it's bacterial because the organism lives in the soil and it's very dusty out in the olive grove. We will take a blood sample to test but we will start her on antibiotics straight away. A combination of antibiotics.'

Julien was nodding. 'A combination of antibiotics is often a lot more effective.'

'There are other things we can do. Martine is getting things ready. We can give her intravenous fluids and treatment with oxygen if it's needed. She's on duty in her clinic, so I'll have to go and get everything, including the drugs.'

He headed for the door, but Julien stopped him.

'I'll go,' he said. 'You stay here with Fi. I think she needs you.'

* * *

Staying with Fiona was exactly what Christophe wanted to do.

What he *needed* to do.

He could feel her distress and, above all, he wanted to take that away. He knew what she wanted and, if it was in his power to give her that, he would do whatever it took to achieve it.

He had to save Bouton.

Fi cradled the foal's head in her lap as Christophe clipped the hair from a patch on the neck and disinfected the skin. He took a deep breath to steady his hand as he slipped a needle into the vein and then slid a cannula into position. He screwed the plug into place and filled a syringe with saline.

'What's that?'

'Just salty water. To help keep the line open. I've got enough antibiotics to give her the first doses now and one needs to be injected into the vein. The others we'll give her by mouth. She needs fluids too, but she's too weak to drink, so we'll put that into her veins as well. Her blood pressure is dropping because the level of oxygen in her blood is too low.'

Oh... the fear in Fiona's eyes squeezed his heart so hard that it hurt but he held her gaze.

'We're going to fight for her, *tesoro*, I promise.'

Tears spilled from her eyes as she nodded.

'Help me put this bandage over her head. We don't want the IV line to get accidentally pulled out.'

Being able to do something to help was what Fi needed. She helped ease the stretchy, tubular bandage over Bouton's ears onto her neck to cover the cannula plug and loop of tubing and they found a way to secure the bag of IV fluids from a hook on the wall to keep it high enough for the fluid to maintain a steady drip. Christophe got a blanket from the cot in the upstairs bedroom to cover Bouton and some pillows and blankets for the couch so they could take turns to get some rest, perhaps.

When Julien returned, he helped set up the oxygen tank Martine had provided. Christophe attached tubing from the cylinder to the cup-shaped mask designed for foals. Fi had another job now, to hold the mask in place, and she looked as though her own life depended on this supply of oxygen, the way she was curled over Bouton, watching the mask mist up with every rapid breath. She barely looked up when Ellie arrived to put food from the barbecue on the table for them.

'Is there anything I can do to help?' she asked.

Christophe smiled his thanks but shook his head. 'We've done everything we can for now. We can only watch. And wait.'

Ellie lowered her voice to no more than a whisper. 'Is Fi okay?'

'I'll look after her,' Christophe murmured. 'I'm not going anywhere. Can you keep Heidi with you tonight?'

'Of course.'

Julien went back home with Ellie but told Christophe to call him if he needed any help during the night. He could be back in a matter of minutes.

* * *

The second IV dose of antibiotics was administered in the early hours of the next morning but, if anything, Bouton's condition was worse. Her heart rate and breathing were too rapid and her blood pressure still too low. They could almost smell just how ill she was.

Christophe moved the couch and used pillows to provide some support behind Fi when she refused to move to somewhere more comfortable for a rest. He knew why. If this little donkey that she loved with all her heart was going to die, she wanted to be holding her. Giving her the comfort of knowing that she was loved as she slipped away.

He sat beside her, his body providing support when she leaned sideways and let her head rest on his shoulder. He pressed a soft kiss onto those amazing curls of her hair and then turned, his cheek on her head so that he could watch Bouton but not lose the contact he had with Fi.

He could still feel that love she was pouring into the fight to save a life that meant so much to her but, as he sat there quietly and the minutes ticked past, the feeling was changing. Not the amount of love. No… that was growing. Getting stronger. But it wasn't coming from Fi and flowing over Bouton. It was coming from his own heart and…

…and it was all for Fiona.

Had he really thought he'd lost the ability to care this much for someone? This love was filling his heart so hard and fast it was making it ache. He turned his head just far enough for his lips to touch her hair again but he didn't get a chance to leave a kiss.

A sob broke from Fi.

'This is *my* fault,' she said.

'*Quoi?*' For a moment, Christophe was too startled to remember which language he needed. Then his focus sharpened. 'How could this possibly be *your* fault?'

'Because I killed my own baby. I didn't deserve another one.'

The shock was stunning. Christophe knew that Fiona hadn't let another man touch her since the rape, so was *that* when she got pregnant?

'It was just a baby,' she whispered – as if she was talking aloud to herself. 'It wasn't his fault, the way he came to exist but... I hated that he was there. In my body. It felt like... like I was still being raped by his father.'

'*Oh, mon Dieu...*' Christophe put his arms around Fi. '*Ma pauvre.*'

He couldn't think of the right words in English to tell her that he could feel the suffering she must have gone through all those years ago. That he wanted to reach back in time and be holding her like this. Offering her all the love that was needed to try and help her through something so horrific.

'Who helped you?' he asked.

'You're the only person who even knows about it,' she said.

It was one shock on top of another. 'So you went through it by yourself? Were the doctors kind, at least?'

'No doctors.' Fi shook her head. 'I wished it away. I was its mother and I didn't want it and I made it die. And that's why I can never have another baby. Because I don't deserve to be a mother.'

Christophe could see the way her hand was trembling but still wasn't letting go of Bouton's oxygen mask. He could feel her body shudder with a sob that was trying to escape. He held her tighter.

'It hurt,' Fi said, so softly he could barely hear the words. 'It hurt so much but I deserved that too. I was nearly sixteen weeks pregnant, I think.' The sob was agonised. 'I could see its tiny hands. Fingers, even. I could see it was a boy...'

Christophe's heart felt like it was bleeding. She had gone through all this alone and lived with it alone for all these years. How strong was this woman? How courageous?

'What did you do?' he asked gently.

'I buried him. In some woods. There were bluebells everywhere. I've always loved the smell of bluebells. And they look like a place fairies might live. I thought a baby would like that.'

Fi looked up at Christophe, tears streaming down her face. 'Do you understand now? Why I don't deserve to be a mother? Why it might be my fault that Bouton's going to die?'

He brushed her tears away with his thumbs.

'Listen to me, *tesoro*. I have two things to say, okay?'

Fi gulped in a breath but nodded. 'Okay...'

'The first thing is you did *not* kill your baby. You had a miscarriage. It is not possible to wish a baby away. If it was, nobody would ever need to have a termination, would they?'

Fi's forehead was on his shoulder now, so he couldn't see her face. She was looking down at the sleeping foal and it took so long for her to break the silence that Christophe wondered if he'd said the wrong thing and pushed her away.

'And the other?' she asked.

'The other what?'

'The other thing you had to say.'

'Ah...' Christophe put his thumb under her chin and tilted her head so that he could see her face and she could see his.

'You shouldn't have had to do that alone,' he said. 'You never need to be alone again, Fiona. Not even for one day or one night because... I love you.' He could feel tears gathering somewhere behind his eyes. 'You've opened my heart again and I thought that could never happen. Not only opened it but you've come inside and you'll be in there for the rest of my life, however far apart we might actually be. But I don't want us to be apart. I don't want to live without you, *amore*. I love you. *Je t'aime...*' Christophe tried to swallow the lump in his throat but his voice was still raw. 'I love the person you were and the person you are and I will love the person you will be.'

'*Ohh...*' Fi's eyes were already telling him what he needed so desperately to hear but the words mattered as well. 'I love you, too, Christophe. I knew I was in love with you the day that Bouton was born. I think I really knew a long time before that but I knew I had to hide it.'

'Why?'

'Because you didn't want that. From anyone. And because we were only supposed to be pretending. To make Nonna happy.'

Christophe found himself smiling, albeit with lips that wobbled. He kissed Fi, long and slow, to steady them and then he kissed her again before he lifted his head.

'I think Nonna's going to be even happier now,' he said.

'Even if I can't have another baby?'

'There's no reason that you can't. Miscarriages are common. I think that baby just wasn't meant to be.'

'Because of how he was conceived?'

Christophe shrugged. They didn't need to go there. He had been gifted the privilege of being the only person in the world who knew about the struggle Fi had gone through and how much it had affected her life. He could take as much of the weight of that burden as she would let him carry from now on.

'Maybe it was because it wasn't the right time for you.'

* * *

Fi knew what he meant but she still wanted to hear him say it out loud.

So she asked the question.

'Why not?'

And she got the answer she wanted.

'Because *we* hadn't found each other.'

Fi loved that he made it sound like the obvious answer. She

loved that he kissed her again, just as tenderly as he had a few minutes ago when he'd said how happy Nonna was going to be.

Not that his grandmother's joy could compare with how happy Fi was in this moment. This was real now and not simply a game. This was about being with the man she loved, who, miraculously, loved *her*. It was about the rest of their lives. Those shiny promises that were already coming true. She did feel worthy of being loved. How could she not, when Christophe was looking at her like *this*? There would be kisses. So many that it would feel like they were never going to end. She had never felt this safe before in her life. But aye... it was also about making a family.

'Our babies, if we're lucky enough to be blessed, will be conceived in love and raised with love,' Christophe said softly. 'It feels like you have all the love I have to give, but I know there will be more. An infinite amount of more. Enough for all of us.'

'I have enough, too,' Fi told him. '*Ohh...*' Her breath was released in a sigh of pure joy.

She'd learned what it was like to be in love. But now she was learning, for the very first time, just how happy it was possible to be. 'I love you *so* much, Christophe.'

He didn't say it back straight away. He was looking down, his brow creasing as he focussed on Bouton, and Fi felt her heart miss a beat. She'd been holding Bouton this whole time but she'd been thinking about very different things. She held her breath, watching Christophe's face for a clue, before she summoned the courage to look down.

Christophe's expression was softening. 'Her breathing's not so fast,' he said.

Fi felt his fingers brush hers as he felt for the artery just under the jawbone. 'Her heart rate is down, too,' he said. 'And she doesn't feel too hot.'

Fi could feel Bouton's muscles moving in response to

Christophe's touch. She saw those gorgeous, oversized ears twitch as she dropped her gaze, and then Bouton's eyes opened and she was looking up at them.

Fi caught her bottom lip between her teeth, feeling the rush of hope. 'She looks like she has complete faith in us to look after her.'

'Of course she does. Because we will.' She heard Christophe take in a deep breath and he was smiling at the same time. 'This is where it really begins. I will look after you too, *tesoro*. For every day that I'm alive.'

'We'll look after each other.' Fi lifted her face for another kiss. 'And Bouton.'

'Donkeys can live for a very long time,' Christophe murmured. 'I believe I've heard of one in the UK that lived for more than fifty years.'

She loved that look she could see in his eyes. She could feel it in the spiral of sensation it ignited in her body. He was about to kiss her again.

'I'm not sure if that's quite long enough,' she whispered.

'I agree.' Christophe's lips were close enough to hers to make them tingle. 'We'll just have to make the most of every moment, yes?'

'Aye...' Fi closed her eyes and closed that tiny gap between them. 'I couldn't agree more.'

EPILOGUE
CHRISTMAS EVE, TWO YEARS LATER...

The ancient church in the main square of Tourrettes-sur-Loup – the Église Saint-Grégoire – had not only been the beautiful setting of Ellie Gilchrist's wedding, it was the perfect backdrop for a nativity play that seemed to be including as many children as possible from the local primary school.

It was getting dark on this chilly but dry late afternoon, which made the sparkle of fairy lights more magical. Strings of the tiny lights were draped through the bare branches of the plane trees in the square and outlined the archway over the tall wooden doors that were the main entrance to the church. Spotlights picked out the small statue in the alcove above the doors, the round window above it and the cross on the roof. The spire and belltower were also illuminated but the bell had stopped ringing now.

It was almost time to begin.

Marguerite was looking fabulous, beautifully brushed and not wearing her saddle, so that the dark cross on her back and down her shoulders could stand out and look appropriately biblical for her task of carrying Mary to centre stage. An antique wooden cradle was positioned there, in the middle of a semicircle of haybales, that the youngest children in the school were already sitting in front of, wearing the cutest fluffy lamb onesies.

Fi had one hand on the halter, ready for the signal to move forward when the choir of little angels had finished singing their first Christmas carol. On Marguerite's other side a young boy dressed as Joseph was standing tall and proud, holding the donkey's lead rope – and probably holding his breath as well in anticipation of his starring role. Theo had been beyond thrilled to be chosen to be Joseph. He was wearing a robe with a tasselled belt and a long vest that Ellie had made for him. She had used a tea towel for his head covering and twisted a length of fabric to hold it in place as a headband. He had black face paint smudged on for a beard and Julien had found a shepherd's crook that was taller than Theo even though he was nearly eight years old now.

Fi had a lead rope in her other hand but it was only for show. Bouton had decided as a foal that she would follow Fi anywhere she chose to lead her, and she was the happiest and most well-behaved donkey in the world. Her favourite thing was an outing where she could meet people and get cuddles, and she often visited nursery schools and old people's homes. An appearance at a Christmas market or a nativity play was just as much fun. She didn't live at La Maisonette any longer. Neither did Marguerite or Coquelicot. After the problem with the dust in the summer, and knowing that the olive grove was really too small for two donkeys, let alone three, a family decision had been made to let them go and live with Fi and Christophe on the property they had purchased up in the hills between Tourrettes-sur-Loup and Vence.

Their home was a ranch-style dwelling with stunning views of both mountains and the sea and more than enough room to cater for the small riding school that Fi was running. It had forest on all sides and, along with the ponies for children to ride, Fi was expanding into treks where people could lead a donkey into the forest and enjoy the serenity of both the trees and the company of these animals she adored. Sometimes, if it hadn't been possible to go to work with Papa, there would be a large, gentle dog plodding along behind the line. Heidi was in the back of Christophe's car tonight, however. Theo's teacher had been thrilled at the idea of having a real donkey in the *jeux de la Nativité* but she had shaken her head firmly at the idea of creating a role for a dog.

The angels, all wearing white dresses with wings on their backs and halos on their headbands, had finished singing and the audience of proud family members were clapping.

Fi looked up at Theo's friend, Genevieve, dressed in a beautiful blue dress with a white shawl over her head and shoulders. She was sitting on Marguerite's bare back, using handfuls of the tufty mane to keep her balance.

'*Tu es prête, chérie?*'

'*Oui.*'

'Theo? Are you ready?'

'*Oui.*'

'*C'est parti.*' Fi clicked her tongue and Marguerite obediently started walking. Bouton gave a little skip and nudged Fi's elbow to let her know she wasn't far away.

There were gasps and then audible happy sighs from the crowd as they came around the corner to lead in a large cast of characters. Around another corner of the uniquely shaped church a child dressed all in yellow and holding a huge, cardboard star on a long stick was waiting for their cue to walk on next, leading the three wise men in their robes and golden crowns.

Fi and Theo led the donkeys to centre stage and the narrator began the Christmas story as Joseph and Mary sat on one of the haybales. Christophe, who'd been discreetly to one side, went in to lay a well-wrapped bundle in the cradle in front of them and then lead Marguerite to where she would stand on the edge of the group. Fi took Bouton to stand beside him and they exchanged a look that told her Christophe was loving this Christmas *spectacle* as much as she was.

Not that it would last long. Families needed to get home for their Christmas Eve family feast. That's where Fi and Christophe would be going, too, as soon as they'd taken the donkeys home. All the food, from the smoked salmon and oyster entrée to the Christmas Yule log cake and champagne for dessert, was ready and waiting at Laura and Noah's house and the entire family would be gathering.

Not that Laura would be enjoying the champagne, being heavily pregnant with her second child. Fi could see her now, standing to one side of the audience. Was she trying to relieve her backache or had three-year-old Lili decided she needed to stand on Maman's chair so that she could get a clear view of her cousin Theo in the play? Bonnie was standing on the chair beside Lili but her little feet were on Julien's legs and he was holding her around the waist. Ellie had her head against Julien's arm and, as Theo waited for Mary to sit down first, Fi saw them exchanging the kind of look that parents gave each other to acknowledge that their child thoroughly deserved the amount of pride they had in them.

Shepherds appeared to mingle with the sheep and the Christmas star was carried aloft to lead in the three wise men and their gifts. After that came characters that Fi had never seen in a nativity play before but she'd been in France long enough now to know that the *santons* – the figurines that represented not only the traditional characters in the Christmas story but every person in the village – were a big part of Provençal Christmas traditions.

Children dressed in costumes and carrying accessories crowded in around the edges. There were bakers and butchers, girls wearing the traditional costumes of heavy dresses with white aprons and frilly hats, some carrying bread sticks or bundles of dried lavender.

Everybody had a part and, as the grand finale, they all sang '*Il est Né, le Divin Enfant*'. Fi had to smile as she saw Lili and Bonnie dancing on the edge of the audience now, holding hands as they turned in circles. Laura was sitting down beside Noah but two other family members had got to their feet to watch over the little girls. Jeannie looked just as happy as Lili and Bonnie and, beside her, stood the rock of a grandpapa that Gordon Gilchrist had become. He still couldn't remember everything of his life in Scotland and he would never get back the years he'd lost of his children growing up, but they were all adjusting to something new and, it seemed, better.

Jeannie and Gordon were both living in La Maisonette at the moment, after selling the cottage in Oban they'd been spending a lot of time in over the last couple of years. They hadn't quite found the perfect house in this part of France yet, because it needed to be close to Saint-Martin-Vésubie, within easy driving distance of their growing number of grandchildren and with a big enough space to give Gordon the studio he needed to keep painting. Noah was working on that. He thought that maybe they should think about a gallery space as well – perhaps in Saint Paul de Vence. Ellie and Fi might like to share the space to display their pebble mosaic work and the hand-forged, wrought-iron sculptures that were becoming very sought-after additions to beloved gardens.

The final song was met with clapping and cheers but it wasn't quite the grand finale after all.

The silence that fell to allow the school's headmistress to

deliver a final message and wish everybody a *Joyeux Noël* was broken by a collective gasp from the crowd as they saw a tiny arm emerging from the bundle in the cradle.

It was a *real* baby?

Christophe and Fi exchanged another glance.

'The applause must have woken her up. Do you want to go and get her or shall I?'

'I'll go.' Christophe handed her Marguerite's lead rope and walked to the cradle. He stooped and gathered the bundle into his arms. The little hand was still in the air and now it reached for a handful of Christophe's hair as he bent to kiss the small face that Fi knew would be smiling up at him in pure joy.

Fi also knew that her own smile was just as joyous as Christophe carried their daughter, Isabella, towards her.

'Would you like a baby, Fiona?' Christophe's words were light but the message in his eyes was so full of love that Fi could swear she could feel her heart actually melting.

'Yes, please,' she said. 'I'll swap you for a donkey.'

* * *

MORE FROM ALISON ROBERTS

Another book from Alison Roberts, *From Provence, With Love*, is available to order now here:

https://mybook.to/FromProvenceBackAd

ACKNOWLEDGEMENTS

I started writing this series of stories for the Gilchrist sisters because I wanted to try and capture the magic I discovered, living in the South of France. These are, truly, books of the heart for me.

I wanted to capture the unique light and soft colours, the taste of the food, the music of the language and the personalities – not just of the people but the landscape and the buildings because they're characters in their own right. I wanted to revisit the fountains and the flowers I remember; the market stalls, the scent of lavender and the taste of socca. Most of all, I wanted to capture the sense of peace that I discovered drifting in the air I was breathing – the perfect background for stories of new beginnings, healing and love.

As always, many thanks to my wonderful editor, Megan.

And to my copyeditor on this series, Helen – I hope you realise that flagging a description or phrase that you love, as well as the ones that are in need of a tweak, is so very much appreciated. To everyone else in Team Boldwood, thank you so much for your part in helping me achieve the dream of sharing a part of this astonishing patch of the world that is the home of my soul – along with my perpetual love of romance and happy endings.

Perhaps most of all, I need to acknowledge – and thank – all the people who read my books and take the time to leave reviews that make me feel like my life's work is worthwhile. Like those who vouch for the authenticity of the setting and Joan who said she felt like she was right there with me and could see it all.

Sarah, who said that on finishing *From Provence, With Love,* she released a sigh from the weariest parts of her soul. Calista who put a PS on her review to say that she wanted to eat socca now, and Eileen, who was inspired to go and find a recipe for making it. I hope it was delicious!

These stories are fiction but they are enveloped in reality. Provence *is* this beautiful. There *are* donkeys in the forests.

The magic *is* real.

ABOUT THE AUTHOR

Alison Roberts is the author of over one hundred romance novels with Mills and Boon, and now writes romance and escapist fiction for Boldwood.

Sign up to Alison Robert's mailing list here for news, competitions and updates on future books.

Visit Alison's website: www.alisonrobertsromance.com

Follow Alison on social media:

facebook.com/rosie.richards.75

instagram.com/alison_roberts_author

ALSO BY ALISON ROBERTS

A Year in France Series

Falling for Provence

From Provence, With Love

The Magic of Provence

Medical Romances

The Doctor's Promise

Doctor Off Limits

The Surgeon's Surprise Baby

A Kiss Before Midnight

Resisting the Surgeon

The Doctor's Second Chance

Stranded with the Surgeon

BECOME A MEMBER OF

THE SHELF CARE CLUB

The home of Boldwood's book club reads.

Find uplifting reads, sunny escapes, cosy romances, family dramas and more!

Sign up to the newsletter
https://bit.ly/theshelfcareclub

Boldwood

Boldwood Books is an award-winning fiction publishing company seeking out the best stories from around the world.

Find out more at www.boldwoodbooks.com

Join our reader community for brilliant books, competitions and offers!

Follow us
@BoldwoodBooks
@TheBoldBookClub

Sign up to our weekly deals newsletter

https://bit.ly/BoldwoodBNewsletter

Printed in Dunstable, United Kingdom